Tom closed his eyes as his cheek pressed against the warmth of her sun-dappled hair.

He didn't dare move. The moment was so delicate— like having a butterfly poised on his wrist.

"I thought…" Zena began in a voice barely more than a whisper. "I imagined you needed comfort."

"Comfort?" he murmured against her hair. Women had offered him many things over the years, but comfort wasn't one of them.

"Coming home that way to find your wife and child. I…I imagined your pain." She sighed softly and lifted her face. "But if those were only lies, then there's no need."

The light shifted in his eyes and Zena thought it was as if a cloud had passed over the sun.

A muscle worked along his tight jaw, and when he spoke, his voice was low and rough. "There's need…."

Dear Reader,

Tired of living in seclusion, ex-gunfighter Tom Bolt
becomes the new sheriff of Glory, Kansas, in
The Gunslinger by Mary McBride. But when Tom
finally discovers a woman who sees the man behind the
legend, he can't escape from his dangerous reputation in
this heartwarming love story you won't want to miss.

This month we also have *Sweet Surrender* from
Julie Tetel, the third title in her North Point series.
This delightful story features a half-Iroquois, half-
Welshman hero whose wit and charm win him the
hand of a small-town spinster.

Lord Liar, a medieval tale of secrets and deception by
Laurie Grant—the author of *Beloved Deceiver* and
The Raven and The Swan—and *The Vicar's Daughter*
by Deborah Simmons, a frothy Regency about a
nobleman who meets his match when he agrees to
shepherd a naive vicar's daughter through a London
Season, complete our month.

We hope you will enjoy all four and will keep an eye
out for Harlequin Historicals each month, wherever
they are sold.

Sincerely,

Tracy Farrell
Senior Editor

Please address questions and book requests to:
Harlequin Reader Service
U.S.: 3010 Walden Ave., P.O. Box 1325, Buffalo, NY 14269
Canadian: P.O. Box 609, Fort Erie, Ont. L2A 5X3

MARY McBRIDE

THE GUNSLINGER

Harlequin Books

TORONTO • NEW YORK • LONDON
AMSTERDAM • PARIS • SYDNEY • HAMBURG
STOCKHOLM • ATHENS • TOKYO • MILAN
MADRID • WARSAW • BUDAPEST • AUCKLAND

ISBN 0-373-28856-5

THE GUNSLINGER

Copyright © 1995 by Mary Myers.

This edition published by arrangement with Harlequin Enterprises B.V.

Printed in U.S.A.

Books by Mary McBride

Harlequin Historicals

Riverbend #164
Fly Away Home #189
The Fourth of Forever #221
The Sugarman #237
The Gunslinger #256

MARY McBRIDE

can't remember a time when she wasn't writing. Before she turned her talents to fiction, her poetry was widely published in "little" magazines and college quarterlies.

Her husband is a writer, as well. "It's wonderful," she says. "I have my own live-in editor and proofreader. The only problem is our combined libraries are threatening to crowd us and our two boys out of the house."

They live—and buy bookcases—in St. Louis, Missouri.

To all the riverboat dandies and desperadoes,
the sheriffs and scouts, the trackers and trailblazers
who ever galloped across a television screen and left
indelible hoofprints on a young girl's heart—

To Bart Maverick, Johnny Yuma, Paladin,
Ben and Hoss and Little Joe—

To all the heroes who have gone to glory...
this book is lovingly dedicated.

Prologue

Tom Bolt wore black—from the squared tips of his cavalry boots to the pinch in his low-crowned hat. Black. Like the hair on his head and the whiskers shadowing his jaw. Black. Just as the dime novels claimed, it was a fitting color for a lieutenant of Lucifer. A perfect shade for the devil's own deputy. Only instead of a pitchfork in his fist, Tom Bolt carried a .44 on his hip. The deadly metal matched his eyes.

Marcus Hale, the editor of *The Glory Gazette*, was squirming now beneath that dark and unrelenting gaze. He and Lemuel Porter, Glory's mayor, had come all the way from Kansas—by train, by stagecoach, then finally and most uncomfortably on rented mules—to this remote mountaintop in Colorado to ask the infamous, black-garbed gunslinger to serve as Glory's marshal. To ask him. To beg him if necessary. To make promises, false or true.

Mayor Porter had been blustering for half an hour now, bending Tom Bolt's ear and making promises left and right and in between.

"Law and order's what we need in Glory," Hale had offered in summation. "A dose of peace and quiet."

"We're prepared to pay handsomely," the mayor had added. "Room and board and then some. Name your price, Bolt."

He didn't. In fact, he hadn't uttered a word since his guests had lapsed into a nervous silence. The man was as hard to read as a weathered tombstone. About as animated, too, the editor noted. Tom Bolt sat still except for his right hand, which absently stroked the shaggy black-and-white coat of his dog. While waiting for Bolt's reply, Marcus Hale kept one bespectacled eye on that hard-carved, slow-moving hand.

The hand of death, he found himself thinking. Like just about everyone else in the country, he'd read the stories about that hand flashing for a gun and delivering death in the blink of an eye. Death by the dozens. A score or more. Or so the stories went. He'd printed a few tall tales himself in *The Glory Gazette*. Now, after meeting the notorious gunslinger, Hale tended to believe them. Not that Tom Bolt had been anything but quiet and courteous to his two unexpected visitors this afternoon. But the very air around the man seemed to crackle with danger, to contain the vaguest whiff of brimstone. Had he been a more religious person, the editor reminded himself, he might feel tempted right now to mouth a heartfelt little prayer of deliverance.

Instead, he shifted on the rough porch boards, thumbed his spectacles up the bridge of his nose, and watched while Lemuel Porter leaned hopefully toward the man in black as he inquired, "Well, Bolt? What's your answer?"

Tom's fingers continued to drift over the dog's sun-warmed, silky coat. Law and order. Peace and quiet. Little did these strangers know they were offering him his heart's desire. He'd come to this mountain a year ago trying to find just that, and he had in a way, Tom supposed. The peace and quiet of the wilderness. The law and order of solitude. Only he was so damn tired of being alone. Maybe, he thought, he was even going a little bit crazy with just a dog to talk to. He knew he was sick to death of staring at the four bare walls of the cabin he had built. He yearned for civilization—even the Gomorrah the mayor had described.

"Room and board will do fine," he said abruptly. "Not some crib of a hotel room, though. Or a cot in the corner of the jail house. It'd have to be a real house. A home."

The mayor sat up straight now, rubbing the palms of his hands together, bobbing his head like a windup toy. "Absolutely. Oh, absolutely."

"You'll come to Kansas, then?" the editor asked, blinking behind his spectacles as if he couldn't trust his eyes or his ears. "You'll come be our marshal?"

As he replied, Tom Bolt's gunmetal gaze scanned the mountain peaks in the distance. "I'll come. What'd you say the name of your town was?"

"Glory," the men answered in unison.

Glory. If he was going to go anywhere, Tom thought, he might as well go to Glory.

* * *

Later, a half mile down the rugged mountainside, Marcus Hale drew back on the reins and turned to his companion, letting out a cautious little whoop. "We did it, Lemuel. By God, I can hardly believe we did it."

The mayor snorted. "I knew we would, Marcus. It was just a question of salesmanship."

"Salesmanship," the editor murmured as he shook his head. "Bolt didn't even ask for all that much. Where do you figure on putting him up?"

"Zena Briggs's."

Marcus Hale stared at Lemuel Porter as if the man had taken sudden and complete leave of his senses. "She won't do it, Lemuel. Zena booted out her last boarder two years ago. Remember?"

"Oh, she'll do it, all right. Zena Briggs loves that house of hers more than anything in this world. Don't forget, Marcus, I'm the banker in addition to being the mayor." Like a banker now, Porter cocked his head and nibbled thoughtfully at his lower lip. "She's got a mortgage payment coming due, and I just might have to stop being so lenient. And she sure can't use propriety as an excuse, can she? I mean, considering her past."

"Sounds like blackmail to me."

"Why, Marcus! Shame on you." The mayor's mouth tipped up at the edges. "It's just another kind of salesmanship. That's all."

A frown dug creases above the editor's rimless spectacles. His throat tightened, making it difficult to swallow, nearly impossible to speak. "That's not all, Lemuel, and you know it as well as I do. I just hope Tom Bolt doesn't come gunning for us when he finds out we sold him a bill of goods."

"We're saving our town!" the mayor protested.

"Yeah, but not the way we told him."

Chapter One

Glory, Kansas—1879

That infernal banner was still there, draped across Front Street like a piece of dirty laundry. Glory Welcomes Tom Bolt, The Fastest Gun in The West. The town fathers had strung it up last week just in case the marshal was early, and the damn thing had sagged in the middle to the point where it was threatening to decapitate anybody on a good-sized mount.

Zena Briggs gave the banner a last malevolent glare before she ducked her head back in the window and resumed her task of bed making, snapping the sheet open with more vigor than care, then smoothing it briskly over the mattress.

"The fastest gun in the West," she muttered as she bent to square and tuck the corners. "Glory ought to be flying banners for the smartest teacher or the savingest doctor. But, no." She rolled her eyes toward the ceiling. "We have to have the fastest gun. We have to prove we're just as bad as Abilene, just as ornery and low-down as Dodge and Hays City, don't we?''

With a disgusted cluck of her tongue, she shoved the final fold beneath the mattress, then straightened up. Zena clutched at the bedpost as a wave of dizziness rolled over her. This one was worse than the one that had nearly pitched her and her armload of clean linens down the stairs earlier.

She touched her wrist to her forehead to confirm what she already suspected. She was burning up with fever. Now wasn't that just dandy? She didn't have time to accomplish what needed to be done today much less have time to be sick. The fastest gun in the West was due to arrive at any time and if she wasn't the fastest bed maker in the West, he'd have no place to sleep. And if Tom Bolt didn't have a proper place to lay his weary little head, Zena might very well be out in the street herself.

Grinding out an oath, she reached for the neatly folded top sheet and flung it open on the bed that suddenly looked so inviting. If she could just lie down and close her eyes for a minute or two, maybe she'd feel better. But then she'd have to nearly kill herself making up the time and the work. Best get it done now, she told herself. He could arrive at any time.

As if her worst fears were coming true, there was a knock on the front door downstairs.

"Hell's bells!" Leaving the bed in a jumble, she passed the mirror over the dresser without so much as a glance, trotted down the stairs and jerked open the door.

"Afternoon, Miz Zena." Billy Dakin shifted a big wicker basket onto one hip in order to doff his hat. "Miz Bird says to tell you she's real sorry but there's an extra load of wash this week."

Zena didn't know whether to feel relieved or not. As glad as she was that it was sixteen-year-old Billy standing on her front porch rather than Tom Bolt, she wasn't exactly overjoyed that Bird O'Brien's handyman-delivery boy had come bearing additional laundry from the sporting house. Of course extra wash meant extra cash, but still...

With a sigh of resignation, she pushed the screen door open. "Just set it down in the kitchen, Billy."

"Yes, ma'am." The lanky youth angled himself and the basket through the door. Once inside the house, he paused. "I don't s'pose he's here yet, is he?"

"Who?"

"Why, Tom Bolt, Miz Zena." Billy's mouth spread in a gap-toothed grin. "Shoot! I'm just so danged excited about meeting him, I could hardly get my breakfast down this morning." He peered into the parlor now, then shifted his gaze toward the staircase. "I just thought he might have snuck into town without anybody seeing him, is all."

"No. He did not sneak into town. Or, if he did, he hasn't honored me with his presence yet." Zena shook her head in bewilderment. "I can't understand what's gotten into everybody. You'd think Tom Bolt was president of the United States instead of some low-down, no-account criminal.''

"He's not.'' Billy was quick to protest. "Why, all his fights have been fair ones. The ones that weren't, well, I guess old Tom came out on top anyways.''

It was folly to argue, Zena thought, especially with Billy, whose eyes were fairly sparkling now with hero worship. "I must be the last sane person in Glory,'' she offered wearily.

"Sane maybe, but you're not looking all that well, Miz Zena, if you don't mind my saying. Could be you're coming down with that fever that's been going through town. Had it myself just the other day. You been to see the doc?''

Feeling worse now that she'd been reminded of her fever, Zena simply shook her head.

Billy shrugged. "No loss. He ain't helped anybody far as I can tell." The boy set the laundry basket on the floor, then reached into his hip pocket. "Here. Miz Bird gave me this and I do believe it helped. Couldn't hurt you anyhow. Go on. Take it, Miz Zena.''

The pint-sized green bottle was warm from riding in Billy's hip pocket. Zena turned it over in her hand, noting that it was nearly full as she read the ornate scrolled label.

"Dr. Stillwell's Amazing Vegetable Cure-All,'' Billy read aloud, tracing a finger along the script. "And look down here. It says it's particularly effective for female complaints.''

"Thank you, Billy, but I wouldn't want to take this from you. What if you get sick again?"

He bent to pick up the basket. "Aw, shoot. Miz Bird's got a whole cabinet full of the stuff over at the saloon. I'll just get me some more if'n I need it."

Zena smiled weakly. "Well, maybe I'll try it. I don't usually make use of patent medicines, but . . ."

Billy winked. "You don't know what you're missing, ma'am. You'll be feeling fine in no time, or else you just plain won't care if you're still poorly," he said, jouncing the laundry basket playfully as he headed for the kitchen.

Several hours and numerous chores later, Zena sank onto the settee in the front room. It occurred to her that she hadn't dusted in there yet, but she was just too wrung out to do it. Not that the room truly needed it. The way Zena kept house the dust barely had time to settle before she was wiping it away.

For her, it wasn't so much cleaning as it was another opportunity to run her fingertips over her possessions. Touching and tending what was hers. It was housekeeping in a very literal sense. She had spent her first eighteen years with nothing to call her own but the clothes on her back. Even those had been, for the most part, hand-me-downs and the stained and threadbare castoffs of assorted cousins.

Certainly there had been no people to truly call her own. While her mother had plied her trade in a fancy house in Richmond, Zena had been passed from one cool and disapproving relative to another. Of course, she hadn't known her mother's occupation at the time; only that she couldn't live with the pretty, lilac-scented, laughing woman who would visit her once or twice a year, then go away crying.

Crying. Zena almost felt like letting go of a tear or two right now herself. Instead she reached into the pocket of her apron for the bottle of patent medicine Billy had given her. A single little sip earlier had puckered her face and brought tears to her eyes as it burned down the back of her throat like liquid fire. But she thought it might have helped some. At least it had enabled her to finish all her chores.

She took a good-sized swig now and sat with the bottle clasped in her fist, letting her gaze stray around the room, encompassing the furniture and bric-a-brac that had come to mean so much to her. The overstuffed, silk-tasseled parlor suite that had come all the way from Cincinnati. The silk portieres. The walnut étagère with its delicately turned spindles that tucked so perfectly in the corner to display her music box collection. Four music boxes—four sweet tunes—one for each year of her marriage.

Possession was a comfort, she thought. These things, acquired as a result of her marriage to Eldon Briggs, were her sole comfort now that she was alone. People were finer comfort, of course. Zena knew that. But she had lost her people—her husband and her child—six years ago. This house and its contents were all she had left in this world, and she'd be damned if she'd lose them, too.

The next swallow of the cure-all went down easier than its predecessor. The one after that slid even more smoothly down her throat.

"I'll be damned if I'll lose my house," Zena grumbled now, feeling a fresh and increasingly bitter resentment toward Lemuel Porter, the banker and mayor whose misguided scheme for rescuing the town from oblivion had gotten her into this pickle in the first place.

The great herds of longhorns from Texas had bypassed Glory last summer in favor of Dodge City and Hays City. Nobody missed the cattle, those huge beasts who stirred up clouds of dust and stomped sidewalks to splinters. What the townsfolk missed were the cowhands and all their free-flowing cash. The Kansas Pacific Railroad missed the traffic and had threatened to close the Glory depot. Bird O'Brien, the local madam, missed traffic of another sort and was threatening to move her business elsewhere if things didn't pick up. Everybody knew that if the railroad went and the sporting girls packed up and left, no cowhand would ever set foot in town again. And everybody panicked at the prospect of Glory becoming a ghost town.

The mayor, Lemuel Porter, had panicked worst of all. He was the one who had come up with the plan to hire Tom Bolt. "Hell," he'd said, "look what Wild Bill Hickok did for Abilene. Look at Wyatt Earp in Dodge. Ask yourselves what those towns have that Glory hasn't got.'' The answer, of course, to the mayor's way of thinking, was a gunslinger—a famous one—to serve not only as their marshal but a tourist attraction, as well.

She'd laughed when she'd first heard about the harebrained scheme. But Zena wasn't laughing now. Not since Lemuel Porter—fresh from his trip to Colorado—had called on her a week ago, wheedling at first, then practically ordering her to take the new marshal in as a boarder.

Do it or you'll lose your house was what his oily words boiled down to. "And don't think you can use propriety as an excuse, Zena Briggs,'' he had warned her, "because there are still plenty of folks in town who remember how you came here and who you came with and for what purpose.''

Damn the man anyway, Zena thought as she lifted the bottle of cure-all once more to her lips. She'd never intended to refuse on the basis of propriety. She just didn't want anybody—another big-booted, clumsy, china-breaking male—tromping around her house.

Most especially she didn't want to share her precious home with a notorious gunman.

"You know how I feel about violence, Lemuel,'' she had protested. To no avail, however. She might as well have been talking to a deaf man.

The mayor had regarded her with sympathy. "We all feel bad about the way Eldon died, Zena, but it wasn't Tom Bolt who shot him, now was it?'' But the banker in Lemuel Porter was not so sympathetic and, in the end, was not to be denied.

Her last, frail hope had been that Tom Bolt might decide not to take the marshal's job in Glory, and in light of that she had postponed readying his room until the bitter end. But today, she thought bleakly, the bitter end was at hand. Not only was she ill, but she was about to open her home to and share her precious sanctuary with a violent, gun-toting criminal.

He'd probably track mud all over her clean floors. Rip her good bed linens with his ragged toenails. Leave whiskers in the washbowl, assuming he shaved at all. Break her china, too.

Glum now, in addition to feverish, Zena tipped the bottle and drained its contents. Well, maybe it wasn't all that bleak, she thought as she curled her legs up on the settee, pulled a pillow beneath her head and closed her eyes. After all, considering the man's violent reputation, how long could Tom Bolt possibly stay alive?

He stood in the doorway of the parlor a long time. It was dusk, and there was just enough light—like amethyst in a filigree of gold—to see the woman on the sofa. She was sound asleep, on her side with one arm curled beneath her head and the other drawn up almost protectively to her bosom. Her hip curved in perfect imitation of the sofa back, drawing Tom's gaze again and again.

Down the street he could just make out the raucous music at Bird O'Brien's, where his welcome reception sounded as if it were moving into a higher, livelier gear. The whole town had turned out, it seemed, to greet their new marshal. Well, not quite, he thought, his eyes once more skimming the neat decor of the parlor before returning to the softly rumpled landscape of the Widow Briggs.

She wasn't at all what he'd expected. In his experience, widows who took in boarders were half a century old and usually half a mile wide. They were matronly types with iron finger waves and whalebone figures who greeted a person with a stiff handshake and a stern expression rather than a sweet nip of uncorseted waist, a gentle flare of hip, and a tumble of mahogany hair.

Not only hadn't he expected it, but now, as the dull ache he'd come to know so well this past year suddenly sharpened, Tom wasn't at all sure that he liked it. Not when the object of his longing was the woman whose home he'd be sharing for the foreseeable future.

He closed his eyes a moment and swallowed a little groan. His dog took it as a signal of some sort and immediately nudged his cool nose into Tom's hand.

"I don't know about this, fella," Tom whispered as he began to walk quietly into the parlor.

The dog, still leery of strangers, sank down on his haunches in the doorway, tilting his head, watching.

Closer now, Tom could hear the slight rattle in the woman's breath. He'd been so overwhelmed by the sight of her that it had never occurred to him that maybe Mrs. Briggs was sick. With some urgency, he eased the saddlebags from his shoulder and placed them quietly on the floor as he knelt beside the woman. Her face, on closer inspection, appeared pale, but he wasn't sure if that wasn't just her natural coloring. Porcelain. Delicate. Like a china doll.

He didn't think she was running a fever, but leaned forward anyway to press his lips to her forehead the way his mother had always done to test his temperature. At least that's what he was telling himself as his lips touched her smooth brow where they lingered a moment after he determined her skin was dry and cool. And lingered even after he had a faint whiff of her sweet but besotted breath.

Tom sat back on his heels, grinning. "I'll be damned," he said softly, then he angled his head toward the watchful dog. "Our new landlady's skunked, partner."

The air in Bird O'Brien's saloon was so thick with smoke that Marcus Hale was wiping his spectacles for the third time. When he put them back on, he was surprised to discover Tom Bolt standing beside him. In his surprise, and because he had downed more than his customary share of whiskey, the editor draped one arm across the man's black-clad shoulder.

"Glad to have you here, Marshal. Tell me. What's your initial impression of Glory? I plan to write a piece for tomorrow's edition of the *Gazette*." He smiled crookedly. "How about a quote or two?"

"Seems like a nice enough place. Not quite the wild and woolly hellhole you and the mayor described, Mr. Hale."

The editor closed one eye in a drunken approximation of a wink. "Not yet."

"Pardon?"

"I said—"

Bird O'Brien, whose pronounced girth was equally and very distinctly divided between her bosom and her hips, managed nevertheless to insert herself between Tom and the inebriated editor. "You're a little wild and woolly yourself this evening, aren't you, Marcus?" The madam's crimson lips were smiling, but her eyes were narrowed. With one ample hip, she nudged the man away from Tom.

"I wouldn't bother buying a copy of tomorrow's *Gazette*, Marshal, if I were you," she said as she watched Hale make his way uncertainly toward the long mahogany bar. "Won't be anything worth reading."

Tom eyed the buxom, tightly corseted blonde slantways. "Hard to believe," he drawled. "For such a wild town, I mean."

If the madam heard him, Tom thought, she chose to ignore his comment. Instead, she linked a plump arm through his and plastered herself against his side. "You're welcome here any hour of the day or night, Marshal. The whiskey's on the house. The same for the girls, if you're so inclined. I told the mayor to offer you a room of your own upstairs." She tipped her face up to his and blinked her kohl-rimmed eyes. "Lemuel claimed you weren't interested in my hospitality or my, how shall I say, my amenities."

His mouth canted sideways as he tugged the madam closer against him. "I don't recall declining your amenities, Bird. The fact is you're looking at a man who's spent the past twelve months alone in a rough log shack. At the time a real house sounded like pure heaven." He chuckled deep in his throat. "Right now, though, I have to tell you, those amenities are sounding even better."

The madam raised a plucked eyebrow. "A whole year?"

"Yes, ma'am."

She fingered one of her ear bobs thoughtfully for a moment, then grinned wickedly. "Marshal, if I weren't retired from the, er, rough and tumble of everyday business, I'd surely consider it myself."

"Well, that being the case, I'd be happy to listen to any recommendations."

Bird's eyes scanned the crowded, smoky room. "What's your pleasure, Marshal? Blondes? Redheads? Big girls? Little bits?"

Tom was about to say it made no difference when a vision of his pleasure came into his head. The dark-haired, fair-skinned, sweet-hipped little tippler he had carried up to her bed. In her stupor, the Widow Briggs had clung to him like so much satin. Even after he had poured her into her pristine bed, he'd had to unlock her arms from around his neck. Cad that he was, he hadn't been able to resist taking one long, generous kiss from that pretty and defenseless mouth before leaving her. He could still taste her.

"Well, Marshal?"

The sooner he stopped tasting her, the better, Tom told himself now. Just then, toward the back of the smoke-filled room he saw a redhead whose dress was as short of satin above the waist as it was below. "That wouldn't be Nettie Fisk back there, would it?"

The madam smiled triumphantly. "The little snip wasn't lying to me, then. Nettie said she knew you from Leadville or some such place. Still, I told her not to go throwing herself at you right off the bat. Give the other girls a chance, I said. I'm glad to see she took my advice and decided to behave."

"Yes, ma'am." Tom edged out of Bird's grasp, gave a little nudge to his hat and started toward the back of the saloon. "But knowing Nettie as I do, I expect she's about reached the end of her tether with all that behaving."

Nettie had been more than a little glad to see him. The redhead had leapt into his arms and snagged both of her long legs around his waist. Then she'd promptly dug her incisors into his earlobe and suggested they head directly upstairs.

That had been Tom's intention. At least it had been foremost in his mind when he rode into Glory. What then, he asked himself, was he still doing sitting downstairs in the saloon while Nettie was drumming her long, painted fingernails on the table and, every minute or two, emitting husky and impatient sighs?

His dog had somehow managed to overcome his fear of crowds and had slipped unnoticed into Bird's. His head was on Tom's thigh now and, like Nettie, he was prone to sighing and raising bored eyes to his master.

The woman wanted him upstairs. The dog wanted him out. Tom drained his glass of beer and wondered just what the hell *he* wanted and why his thoughts kept returning to Zena Briggs.

"Tell me about the Widow Briggs," he finally asked Nettie.

"Oh, her," Nettie scoffed. "There's nothing to tell. How come you're staying with her, Tommy, instead of here? You spent a whole month in the fancy house in Leadville." She smiled wistfully, drumming her fingers on his arm now instead of the tabletop. "We had ourselves a high old time. Remember?"

"That we did, sugar."

Her lower lip fleshed out in a pout now. "So why are you boarding with that pinch-lipped, sour-faced widow?"

"Is that what she is?" Again Tom pictured the tumbled creature on the sofa, felt her clinging arms, and once more tasted that drowsy, tipsy mouth.

"Worse." Nettie sniffed. "The last man who boarded with her got booted out just 'cause he came down to breakfast without buttoning his shirt. Zena had a fit, I hear." The prostitute rolled her eyes. "I wasn't around six years ago when Mr. Briggs got shot, but I'd wager with a wife like that he probably stepped right up to that bullet saying, 'Take me, Lord, and thank you.'"

"Who shot him?"

Nettie shrugged. "Who knows? And who cares?" She tilted her head quizzically. "You worried it might have been you?"

Despite the fact that he shook his head, that worry was always there. Over the years he'd lost count of the men he'd sent to their graves. Their names, if he ever knew them, were often a blur in his memory. Too many names. Far too many graves.

He wasn't sure if his head began to throb at that moment or if it had hurt all evening and he'd only just become aware of it. He knew though that he'd lost the desire to climb the stairs with Nettie or anybody else for that matter. All he wanted right now was to return to that neat, clean little house down the street, to climb between some crisp, sweet-smelling sheets, and to sleep.

"What are you doing?" Nettie squeaked as he stood abruptly.

The dog let out with a startled little bark, too.

It was all Tom could do to summon up a grin for the redhead. He coupled it with a wink. "Save me your best, darlin'. I'll be back tomorrow."

As he shouldered his way through the crowd, he could feel Nettie Fisk's eyes burning two holes in his back. He'd make it up to her, he told himself. Lord, he'd have to. A year of celibacy was enough to qualify any man for the priesthood. And Tom Bolt, despite his black garb, was no priest.

Chapter Two

For a few moments after she awoke the next morning, Zena reveled in the warm comfort of her bed. There was just enough light to bring out the deep pinks in the cabbage rose wallpaper she loved so, and her gaze drifted from bloom to bloom like an indolent, pollen-sated bee. It wasn't like her to remain in bed once the day was upon her.

Most mornings she awoke to the remembered, nagging voices of aunt after aunt. *Up with you, Zena. There's work to be done, and plenty of it. We didn't take you in to be a layabout, girl.* On occasion, she woke to the memory of an uncle's gritty voice and rough hands fumbling at her quilt. Ordinarily then she was up and about her business like a shot. But there had been no voices this morning. Today felt different. Unaccountably sweet.

She had dreamed about her late husband last night, a dream so vivid she had actually felt his hands smoothing over her flesh and his warm mouth pressing against her own. Not that she had ever clearly seen

Eldon's face in her dream. But since he was the only man who had ever made love to her, who else could it have been?

She stretched languidly, still feeling a sensual flush brought on by that dream, thinking it had been six years since she'd even been tempted to linger abed. Eldon, bless him, had always risen first, allowing her that luxury. He'd made it plain it was simply because he was an early riser and that he wasn't doing it to spoil her. "A man hadn't ought to spoil his wife," he'd said again and again. But spoiled she'd been, with a pot of brewing coffee always greeting her when she came downstairs, and, on occasion, a kind good-morning kiss.

Coffee! Zena's contented expression changed to one of bafflement as her nose twitched. Who in blazes was brewing coffee in her kitchen? She sat up in a flash, catching a glimpse of her tangled hair and bare arms in the dresser mirror, hardly recognizing herself for a second. Where was her nightdress? What...?

In answer to her questions, a shaft of pain sliced through her head. "Oh, God," she moaned. She remembered. The frantic pace of yesterday. The wretched fever. The little green bottle with its fancy label and its syrupy, soothing contents. The very last thing she recalled was curling up on the settee.

Glancing down at her thin cotton chemise, Zena tried hard to remember coming up to bed. Her faded calico wash dress was flung over the back of the rocking chair. Her petticoat was bunched at the footboard. One high-top shoe was on the floor over by the window. She craned her neck to discover its mate—stuffed with a stocking—on the table beside the bed.

Just then, another fragrant wave of coffee tickled her nose. She may have dreamed of her late husband, she thought, but apparitions didn't stick around to fix the morning coffee. So who the devil...? Tom Bolt? It wasn't possible, was it?

Hell and damnation! Zena vaulted out of bed and dragged a hairbrush through the knots and tangles on her head hard enough to bring tears to her eyes. She retrieved her petticoat from the rumpled sheets, tugged her wrinkled dress over her head, then once again brushed the unruly mass of dark hair and pinned it at her neck. After that, she just stood for a minute, staring at the shoe on the nightstand. It was her habit to slide her high-tops beneath the bed every night. And never in her life had she tucked her stockings into them. The stockings went in the top drawer of the dresser. Always.

Of course the cure-all was to blame. Dr. Stillwell's amazing potion had put her out like a candle, apparently. How she'd ever climbed the stairs at all was nothing short of a miracle. Little wonder then that she'd tossed her clothes all over creation, crammed her stocking into her shoe, and had such—well—uproarious dreams.

She gathered up her shoes and, because she could find only the one stocking, she pulled a fresh pair from the top drawer. As she sat putting them on, Zena began to wonder if she had accomplished all that miraculous stair climbing and disrobing and shoe stuffing before or after Tom Bolt's arrival. She had no recollection of the man—of greeting him or showing him to his room or apprising him of the rules of the house. Squeezing her eyes closed, as much to reduce the throbbing in her head as to search her brain, Zena still couldn't remember a thing.

Damn that cure-all, anyway. And Billy Dakin, too. She'd give him the tongue-lashing of his young life the very next time she saw him. In the meantime, though, she had her new boarder to contend with. The new boarder she may or may not have already met.

She stood and smoothed the folds of her skirt, drawing in her breath with a sigh. It wasn't like her—not at all—to be in such a state of uncertainty. Surely she'd remember once she went downstairs and saw the man—the notorious gunman—who was evidently already making himself very much at home in her kitchen.

Tom sat at the scrubbed oak kitchen table, sipping coffee from a delicate, gilt-edged teacup. He hadn't bothered with a saucer. Actually, he hadn't wanted to bother with the widow's good china at all, but his tin cup was up in his saddlebag and he'd been loath to climb the stairs again since they creaked worse than a pond full of frogs. Considering Zena Briggs's condition the night before, she probably had a head like a swamp this morning and wouldn't appreciate additional critters to torment it.

Like every other room in the house, the kitchen was spotless. Starched, snow-white curtains framed the window glass that looked out on the backyard. Now that the sun was up, he could see the apple tree out there. The fruit was just beginning to take shape, and he wondered if he'd be here come fall when it ripened.

He wondered, too, at his conscious decision earlier to sit with his back to the door that opened onto the little hallway beside the stairs. It had been his habit for years to situate himself so that all doors were readily within his view. More than habit, it was a survival skill practiced by men who never knew from one moment to the next who'd be coming through one of those doors with revenge in their hearts or just plain mischief on their minds. This morning, however, he'd deliberately put that door at his back. It was the way to behave in a home, he told himself. This was most definitely a home. Still, he couldn't quite shake the need to glance over his shoulder every few minutes.

He reached under his vest once again to touch the tin star in his pocket—the badge that Mayor Porter had bestowed on him last night, but which he had yet to pin on his chest. Glory needed a marshal about as much as a cradle needed a spider, Tom had concluded. Aside from the shindig at Bird O'Brien's last night, the town was as peaceful as a graveyard, not at all the Gomorrah that Porter and Hale had described when they came to him with their proposition a few weeks ago.

Fine with him, he thought. The quieter, the better, but in light of that discrepancy, and because he was cautious to the bone, Tom had kept the badge in his shirt pocket. He hadn't quite made up his mind about the town or the job. In all his thirty-eight years, he'd never been on the pin side of a badge. Once he put it on, though, he knew he'd feel obliged to stay.

The floorboards creaked suddenly above his head, followed by a certain amount of stomping and the muffled sound of drawers opening and closing. Tom's mouth hooked in a grin as he brought the teacup to his lips again. Nettie was wrong, he thought. The late Mr. Briggs had most certainly not walked into a bullet to escape his wife. The man had been—before getting shot, anyway—one lucky son of a bitch.

Visions of the previous night ran through Tom's head again. The same visions that had kept him sober, celibate and hard half the night. After he had poured Zena Briggs into bed, instead of lying there like a good little drunk, the widow had slithered to the edge of the mattress and proceeded to take her shoes off. She had nearly broken the window when she tossed one over her shoulder, so he had taken the other before her aim improved.

The black cotton stockings had come next. She'd unrolled them with the methodical, murmuring deliberation that comes only from the bottom of a bottle, taking them off slowly, revealing inch after inch of pale, shapely calves and culminating in a victorious little squeal and a wiggle of her toes. That was when she'd crammed one of the stockings into the shoe he held in his hand. The other she had draped around his neck.

That memory alone caused him to shift uncomfortably in the kitchen chair now. He should have walked out right then, but how the hell could he? She might have hurt herself. Sure. And he might have missed act 2, which had consisted of more muttering, additional slithering as she yanked her dress over her head, then of course there was the wriggling out of her petticoat. It was when she commenced with the important undergarments that Tom had put a stop to it.

The only way he knew how at that point. He had kissed her. Lord, how he had kissed her—skimming her lips with his tongue, then deepening it, delving into her sweet, whiskey-tinged depths until his head was swimming, until her warm body went all boneless in his arms and he was able to lay her down and get her safely settled under the covers.

It had been the first time in his life he'd walked away from a woman. Then, not long after that, at the saloon, he walked away from a second, even more insistent one. He shook his head and closed his eyes now, wondering if a year in that damn cabin had done him permanent damage, knowing full well though it wasn't a matter of ability but desire.

The stairs creaked behind him and he took one more sip from the thin china cup before setting it carefully on the table. He drew in a deep breath, then let it out just as carefully as it suddenly became clear to him that he'd been loitering in the Widow Briggs's kitchen, postponing his decision about the town and the badge until this moment. But what that signified he wasn't sure. He wasn't sure at all, especially when his gut instinct was to get out now. And fast.

Coming down the stairs, Zena tried to keep her aching head on a level plane and at the same time peer through the balusters into the open kitchen door. All she could see was a pair of broad, black-clad shoulders, dark hair curling over a dark collar, and a black leather holster snug against a powerful thigh. It was about what she had expected, she thought, and her head began to hurt more at the sight of the gunfighter who sat at her kitchen table, the dangerous man who was invading her space, not to mention her life.

Resentment snaked through her and by the time she reached the bottom of the stairs her stomach had managed to tie itself into a hard, tight knot. Damnation!

He was rising from his chair as she charged through the door, her right arm extended almost as if she meant to hit him rather than shake his hand.

"Good morning, Mr. Bolt." Zena offered her hand only to have it disappear in his warm, firm grasp.

"Ma'am."

Unsettled by the feel of him, she became even more so at the sound of his deep, resonant voice. Had she heard it before? Then, when Zena raised her face to his, she was so startled by the familiar shape of his mouth and by the metallic gray of his eyes that all she could say was, "Oh."

"You feeling all right this morning, Mrs. Briggs?" His hand slid up her arm and tightened just above her elbow.

"Yes, I..." No. She wasn't. But that wasn't his concern. She tugged her arm away, whisked out a chair, and sat—her contact with the chair seat a bit more abrupt than she'd intended and her head throbbing harder as a result. For a moment, she had to close her eyes to keep the kitchen from spinning.

The pump handle clacked, and the next thing Zena knew, a cool, damp cloth was curving around her neck. She would open her eyes, she told herself, as soon as she was sure the room had settled down, as soon as she was sure she could deal with that gunmetal gaze and that oddly familiar mouth.

Tom sat—arms crossed, chair tipped back—contemplating her. His tipsy darlin' of the night before had been transformed. Utterly. The wild waterfall of her hair was frozen now in a dark clump at the back of her neck. The lush mouth had thinned to a dry, prim line. The boneless body he remembered so well was tense and wire tight. It was as if a butterfly had climbed back in its cocoon to revert to a caterpillar. A glistening, sensuous woman had turned into a pinch-lipped, dry old maid.

Again the Widow Briggs had surprised him. First, because she wasn't what she was supposed to be. And now because she was. The difference was intriguing, and—he suspected—more than just a snootful of applejack. Ordinarily he wasn't much for surprises, Tom thought, suppressing a grin he didn't suppose she'd appreciate.

Zena fortified herself with a deep breath, opened her eyes and met the gunfighter's steady gaze, deliberately avoiding even the quickest, most surreptitious glance at that disturbing mouth. "Perhaps this would be a good time to inform you of the house rules, Mr. Bolt."

He tilted his chair forward, leaning toward her with his elbows on the table, cocking his head slightly, waiting for her to continue.

Her brain floundered for a moment. She hadn't had a boarder in two years, and never one whose mere presence across the table seemed threatening somehow. She blurted out the first thing that came into her head. "I change the bed linens on alternate Mondays."

A corner of his mouth crooked upward. Now why was she looking at his mouth? And what was so damn amusing about changing sheets?

"Supper's at six," she said. "Sharp. I'll be bringing your noon meal to the jail house."

Now a dark eyebrow slanted up. "At noon? Sharp?"

Zena made a little chuffing sound. "Give or take a few minutes. It'll be a cold meal, Mr. Bolt, so it won't make any difference if you eat it directly or not. Suppers, however, are hot, and I'd rather not heat yours twice."

"All right," he drawled.

"What time will you be wanting your breakfast?"

"Coffee's plenty. I can do that myself."

She glanced over her shoulder at the enamel pot on the stove, thinking of Eldon puttering around the kitchen while she lay in bed listening to the happy racket. Tom Bolt, on the other hand, hadn't made a sound this morning. She didn't know if it was courtesy or an inborn stealth. The latter, no doubt, she thought as she rose and went to the cabinet, returning with a saucer, which she slid beneath his cup.

Tom studied her as she moved, seeking the warmth beneath her current chill, loosening that prim hair with his imagination, nearly feeling it sifting through his fingers. When she reached up to the second shelf, he followed the tug of her cotton dress against the fullness of one breast. He ignored the subtle insult of the saucer.

"I bathe on Saturdays," she continued, resettling herself in the chair, arranging her skirt with brisk efficiency. "Here in the kitchen. There are no locks on the doors, Mr. Bolt. Needless to say, I require privacy. I'd appreciate it if you could arrange to be out of the house then. It would be helpful, too, if you could plan your baths at a time when I don't need the kitchen."

Mentally now, Tom had her undressed and lolling in a steaming tub of bathwater, her chilliness melting and her pale complexion taking on a rosy glow. He was calculating the time till Saturday and failed to hear her next pronouncement.

"Pardon?"

"About your gun, Mr. Bolt..." Her icy blue gaze slid to his hip then latched on his face again. "I'd prefer you didn't wear it here in my house."

Up until that moment, she could have told him she required him to stand on his head and sing "The Bonnie Blue Flag" for six hours a day and he would have been more than happy to comply. The gun, however, was different.

He shifted back in the chair, crossing his arms as he extended one leg. "I prefer to wear it, Mrs. Briggs."

About to inform him that he would do as she wished while he was under her roof, Zena bit down on her lip instead. Despite the politeness of his words, the man's tone had been as steely as his eyes. His very posture in the chair, in fact, had been his answer. The gun was not negotiable. With anybody else, she might have insisted. Had the situation been different and her home not in jeopardy, she would have laid down the law and told her boarder to comply or go to the devil.

For one hopeful second she entertained the notion of doing just that. Surely Lemuel Porter wouldn't hold it against her. There had to be rules. The law was, after all, the law—whether it was in a town or a boarding-house. On second thought, however, here in Glory that was no longer the case. The law was now the man sitting across the table from her, and if the new marshal had any complaints about his room and board, Lemuel would see that Zena suffered the consequences.

But before she could tell him she would be willing—for now—to overlook the weapon, she was distracted by a soft scratching at the back door. She turned her head just in time to see a large shaggy black-and-white animal grab something in his teeth, yank on the strap or whatever it was, and pull the screen door open in a wide arc, after which the beast scuttled through the door before it slammed behind him, and stood there, in the middle of her kitchen, slashing its huge tail from side to side, dripping slobber from its sidelong tongue.

"Good boy."

Tom Bolt's rumbling praise made the tail slash even faster. It was like a machete, Zena thought. A menacing, china-smashing, vase-toppling blade. She was nearly too astonished, too horrified to speak. She stabbed a finger in the animal's direction. "What in the world is that?"

"My dog." Tom patted his knee, and the beast shambled toward him, his nails clicking on Zena's clean tile floor, his wet paws leaving little clover-shaped prints. "Sit, fella." The dog sank onto his haunches, sighed and draped his wet muzzle on Tom's leg.

"Your dog." The word emerged from her mouth as if it pained her to speak it. In truth, it did, for her head had resumed its horrendous pounding. She closed her eyes, seeking strength and perhaps a modicum of patience. "Is your..." She could barely coax the word through her clenched teeth. "Is your dog more negotiable than your gun, Mr. Bolt?"

He didn't reply. He merely sat with his hand smoothing the animal's thick coat. And Zena found herself staring at that finely shaped hand with its clean, neatly clipped nails. It was, she thought, a gentleman's hand.

She returned her gaze to his face, feeling the color steal into her cheeks as she realized he'd been looking at her the whole time he'd been petting the dog.

"I can't have that animal in my house," she said, adding a quick "I'm sorry," for she sensed the attachment between them.

"That's all right," Tom answered. "He's used to being outside. Aren't you, partner?"

The dog's tail thumped against the table leg, rattling the teacup in its saucer.

That confounded tail seemed the very symbol of her predicament. Her home was under siege—by man and beast—and there was nothing she could do about it. To end the siege would be to lose the very home she needed to protect. Zena shivered.

"He's gentle enough, Mrs. Briggs. He won't hurt you." The voice—deeper than a well—paused, but the still air of the kitchen continued to vibrate with it. "Neither will I."

Her spine stiffened. "I was concerned for my house, Mr. Bolt. Not my person. I assure you." It was the truth, she told herself. Whatever danger this man carried with him had nothing to do with her. Nothing whatsoever.

A grin broke the firm line of his lips. "I'm glad to hear that, ma'am. My reputation tends to make some folks a little nervous."

Zena sniffed. "Men mostly, I'm sure."

"Mostly."

"I don't wear a gun, Mr. Bolt. I don't even own one. The fact of the matter is, I don't approve of them. Guns have cost me dearly." Her gaze locked on his now. She was glad to see his grin had disappeared. "Guns," she repeated, "and gunfighters."

"I heard about your loss," he said quietly. "It wasn't me, Mrs. Briggs."

"No. But it was someone just like you."

If it was, Tom thought, then the gunman's gut was probably twisting now just like his own. Twisting with regret, with sorrow, and finally with a kind of futility that told him once again he would never escape that reputation, never be free. Funny. Most men were haunted by their mistakes. In his case, it was his successes that hounded him and kept him on the run.

The Widow Briggs didn't think much of him, that was clear. He could feel her disregard like a chill wind across the table. Her blue eyes grew frosty and her mouth thinned to an unforgiving line. Last night that mouth had been a warm and generous cavern where he'd lost himself, where he'd been able to forget for one sweet moment who he was and what he was. But she wasn't letting him forget this morning. The widow had been drunk last night—a valid excuse for her behavior. But his only excuse was being a fool.

He shoved his chair back from the table. "I best be getting down to the jail house."

Zena hadn't meant to be quite so blunt, but she hadn't been able to help herself. Lashing out at Tom

Bolt seemed her best defense at the time. Her remark had clearly stung him. She was about to apologize when footsteps sounded at the back door.

The man across the table moved so quickly, she never actually saw his hand move toward his gun. But it was there all of a sudden, poised, flexing slightly. His gunmetal gaze was riveted on the door. The dog, too, stared in the same direction, a growl pulsing in its throat and its lips pulled back in a snarl.

Twisting her head, Zena recognized Billy Dakin's lanky form through the screen. "It's the delivery boy from the saloon," she said in a rush of breath, then turned back to glare at the man in black. "Really, Mr. Bolt. This is my home."

His reaction surprised her. The gunfighter winced as if she had slapped him across the face. The hand hovering over the butt of the .44 shifted to the scruff of the dog's neck, the fingers burying themselves deep in the long black-and-white fur.

"It's all right, boy," he murmured.

Billy's face was pressed against the screen. "Is that him? I only just got a glimpse of him last night," the boy whispered when Zena came to the door. "Lord have mercy, Miz Zena. If that isn't the fastest damn gun in the West sitting right there at your kitchen table."

Irritated, she slapped the door open with the heel of her hand. "The wash isn't finished yet, Billy. Tell Bird—"

"Oh, I didn't come for no laundry." He stepped over the doorsill, still gawking at Tom. "I came to accompany the new marshal to his office." He touched the brim of his hat in Tom's direction.

It was then that Zena noticed the gun belt angled over the boy's lean hips. Her eyes narrowed on the holster, its leather still shining and unscratched, apparently fresh from a shelf at the mercantile. "Since when did you start wearing a weapon, Billy Dakin?"

The boy's face flared with color as he replied, "A while back. Quite a while. I guess you just never noticed."

Zena's hands settled on her hips. "No, I never. And I don't approve, either. I'll not have you coming into my house sporting a gun, young man."

Guns! Sometimes he wished the damn things had never been invented, Tom thought as he watched the stiff-backed widow accost the eager kid. She was right, of course. The boy was much too young to be packing iron, but there wasn't anybody who would be able to convince him of that. Especially now that the great Tom Bolt and his even greater reputation were in town. Hell, he ought to just go back to the mountains, grow a beard down to his boot tips, and be done with it.

Instead, he scraped his chair back and stood up. "Morning, son. Maybe we both better get our hardware out of Mrs. Briggs's kitchen before she gets any more riled and decides to take a frying pan to us." He angled his head toward the door. "You go ahead. I'll be out directly."

"Yes, sir." The boy cast the woman a wounded glare before sidestepping out the back door.

Then the widow turned her full fury on Tom. Her blue eyes flashed like summer lightning. "You needn't encourage him."

"I don't intend to." Tom reached to the sideboard for his hat and planted it firmly on his head while fighting the desire to yank the fire-breathing little female into his arms, to pluck the pins from her hair, to kiss her until she was drunk again and kissing him back instead of flaying him alive with her sharp tongue.

He strode toward her with such purpose that Zena's heart lurched and she found herself stepping back, out of his way. Considering his reputation and what was undoubtedly a lethal temper, she had probably gone too far, had probably spoken her mind a bit too freely. But she didn't regret it. Not one word. It *was* her house. For now anyway.

He stood so close she could feel the heat emanating from his body, and Zena was suddenly aware of the sheer physical power of the man. He towered over her, his shoulders looming like a slab of black granite. She refused to be afraid in her own home, however, so she struck a defiant angle with her chin, meeting his intense gaze with one of her own.

And then he did something that she hadn't been prepared for. He grinned. A funny, lopsided grin that revealed white, even teeth. A startling slash, beguiling in its warmth, bewitching in its sheer unexpectedness. She stood transfixed, her heart pressing into her throat, unable to take her eyes off that sensual, strangely familiar mouth. Why did she imagine she knew the feel of it, the warmth and the taste?

He reached into his shirt pocket. "I wonder if you'd mind doing the honors here, Mrs. Briggs." He pressed the warm tin star into her hand.

She was just a little bit of a thing, Tom thought, watching her stare at the badge a second then lift on her toes slightly to get it properly situated—just over his heart—on his black leather vest. It occurred to him when he made the request that she might take the opportunity to stab him, but her expression had softened somewhat as she concentrated on getting the pin through the worn cowhide. A wisp of dark hair had come loose at her temple. Her mouth was a soft curve now, wet by a little flick of her tongue. A glimmer of the butterfly he'd put to bed.

"There," she said, stepping back and surveying the badge, her mouth once more resuming its prim shape, her blue eyes taking on their familiar chill. He found himself wanting to shake her if he couldn't kiss her, wanting to rattle the woman inside the icy veneer, the butterfly inside the tough cocoon.

"Thank you, ma'am." Tom gestured to the dog, then moved toward the door. He paused a moment, half turned to her, and smiled to himself as he reached into his hip pocket to slowly produce the long black stocking the butterfly had draped about his neck the night before.

"This is yours, I believe, Mrs. Briggs," he drawled, looping the soft length of fabric over the doorknob, watching the chill in her eyes turn to bafflement and her mouth drop open in fetching dismay. He touched a finger to the brim of his hat, then sauntered out the door.

Chapter Three

Zena stood in the middle of the kitchen, staring at the stocking-draped doorknob, her jaw unhinged, her mind scrambling to recall the previous night. She had fallen asleep on the sofa in the parlor, then awakened upstairs in her bed. In between, she had dreamed of...

She shook her head now, trying to erase the notion that was forming there, trying hard not to think the unthinkable. It was a dream, wasn't it? It had to have been a dream. Please, Lord, let it have been just a dream.

Surely, she thought, there was some logical explanation for the stocking the gunfighter had produced from his pocket. Perhaps she had taken it off in the parlor, then dropped it on her way upstairs. That had to have been the case. Then Tom Bolt, when he went up to his room, had discovered it and put it in his pocket.

Whisking the garment from the knob, Zena stuffed it into her own pocket. She had dropped it on the stairs last night. That was the only acceptable answer. It was what she was going to choose to believe anyhow. She had too much work to do today to be wondering about stockings.

With work in mind, she went back upstairs to make beds only to find that her boarder's bed was already in order. Her own, in contrast, was a jumble of sheets and quilts. The sight of the tangled bed linens brought her up short in the doorway. Usually she slept peacefully, barely disturbing the covers, and making her bed each morning was a simple matter of smoothing and tucking.

As she stared at the bed, an image of Tom Bolt's full, sensual mouth flitted through her head causing her stomach to do a little flip-flop. It was ridiculous to even entertain the notion that he had kissed her. She wouldn't have allowed it, cure-all or not. What was even more ridiculous, she thought, was standing here like a gawky girl, wondering what it would be like to feel those finely-carved lips on her own.

With a little sigh of exasperation, she tugged the stocking from her pocket, put it in its proper place in the dresser drawer and set about making her rumpled bed.

The mid-morning sun was hot in the cloudless blue sky and a steady little breeze was blowing from the south. Weather to make a laundress smile, Zena thought. Her wash would be dry by two or three o'clock, she estimated as she pinned the last pillowcase on one of the taut lines that ran across her backyard. It struck her as odd that Bird would be going through so many bed linens now that things in Glory had slowed to a crawl. But Zena wasn't complaining. A little extra cash might just make the difference in coming up with her mortgage. How she'd love to slap a fistful of bills into Lemuel Porter's hand, then tell the banker he could stash his gunslinger elsewhere.

She'd have her house back then, not to mention her privacy. And she could stop driving herself crazy about mysterious stockings, seductive lips and beasts with destructive tails. Shrugging helplessly, she picked up the empty laundry basket, settled it against her hip and made her way through damp, flapping sheets toward the back door.

Billy Dakin was sprawled on the little porch, leaning back against a post, frowning into the pages of a book. His holster stuck out from his leg at an awkward angle. Fool boy! She only hoped he wouldn't shoot his kneecap off. Or hers.

"Don't you have anything better to do than laze around on my back porch?" she snapped, stepping over his slung-out legs to slide her basket into the kitchen. She stood over him. "What's that you're so busy reading, Billy?"

He closed the little book and turned its tattered paper cover up for her inspection.

Zena squinted and read aloud. *"Death in the Dust— The Continuing Adventures of Tom Bolt*—Testified to by his Good Friend, Philo Gordon, Journalist." She rolled her eyes toward the sky. "Oh, for pity's sake!"

"Ain't you ever read one of these, Miz Zena?"

"Dime novels?" she sniffed. "I should think not."

"Oh, they're swell stories." He opened the book to a dog-eared page. "Particularly this one. It's about the time Tom...er, Marshal Bolt, that is...faced off with Hard Jack Tillman down in San Antone. See, ol' Hard Jack, he was—"

"I have work to do, Billy." Zena yanked the screen door open. "And I expect you do, too. Bird's probably been looking high and low for you all morning. You go on back and tell her I'll have her sheets and pillowcases ironed by supper time." When the boy didn't comply immediately, Zena added a forceful little "go on, now" before she strode into the kitchen and let the screen door bang closed behind her.

When she came back out several moments later, she sighed. Billy was gone, but he had left the dime novel behind and the breeze was whipping through its pages. Zena picked it up and frowned at the cover. The sketch of Tom Bolt didn't do him justice, she thought. The mouth was all wrong. Too humorless. Too hard somehow. She lifted a finger to trace the grim and unyielding line of his lips, then, realizing what she was doing, Zena muttered an oath and dropped the dime novel into her apron pocket.

"Death in the dust, indeed," she thought. She could tell Billy Dakin a thing or two about death in the dust, and how a careless bullet from a careless man had ripped her life apart as surely as if it had torn into her body instead of her husband's. All she'd been left with then—after she lost the baby—was dust. Dust in corners. Dust on shelves. Sometimes it felt as if there were dust in her heart and if she didn't have the walls of her house for protection, she just might blow away.

The marshal's office was a single room above the dry goods store. With its entrance around the corner from Front Street and up a flight of rickety stairs, it was the sorriest excuse for a lockup Tom had ever seen. Considering he was now responsible for law and order in Glory, it might have been nice to be able to see more of the town than a snatch of dusty street between the livery stable and the saloon, and that he could only bring into view by leaning his head out the window and craning his neck.

He wasn't relishing the prospect of lugging drunk and obstreperous cowboys up those stairs, either. His dog had taken one look at them, barked indignantly, and taken off to explore the better part of town.

The boy, Billy, seemed to think otherwise. He'd walked around the pitiful room as if he were showing off a piece of elegant real estate.

"And take a look out here, Marshal," he'd said, rubbing the dingy glass with his elbow when his attempts to open the room's north window proved fruitless.

Tom had given the sash a shot with the heels of both hands, wrenched it open and gazed down on the low, rectangular train depot and the line of tracks that ran beside it. Half a dozen men were occupied with paint buckets and brushes.

"They're painting the station," Billy said. "Getting it all gussied up."

"So I see." For what, Tom didn't even want to wonder.

After Billy left, he borrowed a broom from Cy Talbert down in the dry goods store and spent his first official hour as Glory's marshal sweeping out dust and dead wasps from the jail house. His dog came back and sat whining, looking up at him from the bottom of the stairs.

"If you think I'm gonna carry you up here every day, you've got another think coming, dog," Tom called down to him. "Anyway, you're not missing all that much. I've seen better calabooses in towns half this size."

Going back inside, he inspected the cell that took up the rear of the room. The bars were bolted to the floor well enough, but the door wasn't hinged properly and the lock was worthless. To prove it, Tom walked into the cell, closed the door behind him, then reached through the bar to turn the key.

Now that was the view he was more accustomed to, he thought as he stared through the iron bars. Not that he'd ever spent more than a night or two locked up before he was let go. Mostly they kept him—like an animal in a zoo—for townsfolk to come and stare at. He drew back his leg now and gave the door a solid kick, popping the lock and sending the key and several hinge screws flying across the room.

Then he spent his second hour as marshal rehanging the cell door. With luck he wouldn't have to use it much. From the looks of things, he'd be spending most of his time warning old geezers not to spit on the sidewalk. He hoped. If he never had to touch his gun again, he'd be a happy man.

Zena strolled down Front Street, swinging the linen-covered egg basket that held the marshal's noon meal. Cold roast pork. Cabbage dressed with vinegar. Two hard-boiled eggs. Buttered bread. She planned to drop it off then go home and have a bite to eat herself. If she was lucky, the jail house would be empty and she wouldn't have to worry about looking or not looking at Tom Bolt's mouth.

She gave Cy Talbert a little wave as she passed in front of the dry goods store, then turned the corner to see the black-and-white dog lying at the bottom of the stairs. Damn! That meant the marshal was in his office.

The dog lurched up as Zena approached, slashing its tail back and forth in greeting. She felt a little more kindly toward the animal now that he wasn't threatening her china, and she reached out to pat his silky head before starting up the stairs.

Behind her, the dog whimpered. His front paws were on the first step now and he was gazing up at her mournfully, obviously afraid of the steep climb up the open stairs.

"Well, come on." She patted her leg to encourage him. "Take it slow. You won't fall."

With a little yip, he put his front paws on the next tread, then stopped.

Zena hitched up her skirt, took another step and paused, looking back over her shoulder. The dog scuttled up another two steps, then shrank down, shivering.

"You're doing fine," she told him.

It was slow progress. Zena would take a step. The dog would whine, scuttle up and promptly freeze. By the time they reached the landing at the top, the animal was a quivering wreck. Not for long, however. As soon as she opened the jail house door and the beast spied his master, that tail started slashing again and he was through the door in a shot.

Lemuel Porter and Marcus Hale were nearly bowled over as they stood opposite the marshal's big oak desk.

"Here, now. What's the meaning of this?" the mayor blustered, turning to cast a black look at Zena as she stood in the doorway.

Zena shrugged slightly as if she'd had no idea the animal had followed her up the stairs. Lemuel looked as if he had been in a foul mood even before being run over by a dog, and she didn't want to bear the brunt of his temper. Not when she needed his goodwill. She offered him a winsome smile, then greeted Marcus Hale.

"You're looking a bit peaked, Marcus. I hope you're not coming down with that fever."

The editor shook his head gingerly, as if it might fall off if he shook it too hard. "I'm afraid I did a little too much celebrating at the marshal's welcome party."

"Did you now?" Zena murmured. "Well, it must have been some party." She swung her gaze to the man in black. "Mr. Bolt, I've brought your noon meal."

He rolled his chair back and rose to his feet. "Much obliged, ma'am."

Zena edged past the mayor to set the basket on the desk. Porter immediately lifted the edge of the linen napkin to peer at the contents.

"Zena treating you all right, Marshal?" he asked, letting the napkin fall back in place, then crossing his arms and squinting up at Tom.

When her boarder failed to reply immediately, Zena's eyes shot to his face. Of course she was treating him all right! Why couldn't the man manage to say so, instead of standing there dumb as a post?

Tom hooked his thumbs through his gun belt, thoroughly enjoying the widow's big-eyed panic. Did she think he was going to produce another slim black stocking from his pocket? he wondered. "She's made me right comfortable," he said at last.

"Glad to hear it," the mayor intoned. "Well, Marcus, we best be on our way and let the marshal eat his lunch while things are quiet." He nudged the editor toward the door, then turned back. "I'll let you know what the town council decides about that ordinance you suggested, Bolt."

"Thanks. I'd appreciate that," Tom said to the mayor's departing back.

The widow was busying herself with the contents of the lunch basket. "What ordinance?" she asked him as she slid a plate of cold meat in his direction.

Tom angled back into the chair, its springs creaking beneath him as he swung his long legs under the desk. "One that would require a permit to carry a firearm in town."

Her hand stilled on the desk top and she stared at him. "Are you serious?"

"Why wouldn't I be? An ordinance like that ought to keep trouble to a minimum."

Zena continued to stare. Trouble was the reason for bringing this notorious gunfighter to Glory in the first place. Not keeping it to a minimum, but stirring it up. Did he think she didn't know that? What kind of fool did Tom Bolt take her for? But she wasn't going to be fool enough to argue with him. Let him think whatever he wanted.

"I imagine trouble follows you around like your dog," she said finally, arching an eyebrow at him as she continued to empty the contents of the basket onto the desk top.

His response was a blade-thin smile. "That it does, Mrs. Briggs." He reached out a hand, letting it drift over the animal's head. "How'd you get him up the stairs?"

"Patience, Mr. Bolt," she said with a sniff. "Something you probably don't have a great deal of." Hooking her arm through the empty basket, Zena turned toward the door. "Supper's at six."

"Sharp."

She glared over her shoulder. Why did he make her feel like a fussy old maid? Or a crotchety schoolmarm with a ruler in her fist and one foot tapping on the floor? "A minute or two either way wouldn't exactly send me into fits."

"Probably because of your extraordinary patience, Mrs. Briggs."

His mouth crooked devilishly, catching at her insides like a sharp fishhook, making her stomach quiver.

"I don't like you, Mr. Bolt."

The words were out of her mouth before she knew they were even in her head, but they didn't succeed in eradicating his grin. In fact, it seemed to increase.

"I'm getting that impression, ma'am."

"Good," she snapped. "But liking's got nothing to do with our arrangement. Even though I don't care for you, I intend to make every effort to see that you're comfortable while you're in my home. In return, all I ask is that you be prompt and courteous." And stop looking at me as if I were a chocolate éclair, she added mentally.

"Fair enough." He eased back, crossing his arms. "If I'm not sitting at your supper table at six o'clock, you can pitch my gear into the street. How's that?"

His smile, Zena noticed, had slipped a notch or two. That pleased her. But she wasn't so pleased at his offer to move out of her house. In fact, she was distinctly alarmed. She attempted to hide her fear, though. No sense letting the man know just how dependent she was on him.

"I won't be pitching anything, I assure you," she said, heading for the door. "I'll see you at supper time, Mr. Bolt. Good afternoon."

If he replied, Zena didn't hear it. Just as she was preparing to exit, the jail house door burst in, and with it, Nettie Fisk from the saloon. The redhead—decked out in tight, high-bustled green silk and a matching parasol—breezed past Zena with a quick hello and a whiff of cheap perfume. She skirted the black-and-white dog in order to drape herself on a corner of the desk.

"Tommy, just look at you behind that shiny tin star!" she cooed. "Aren't you the handsomest thing! I thought you were coming over to Bird's for lunch. Want me to peel those eggs for you, honey?"

Whether or not the marshal wanted his eggs peeled, Zena didn't wait to discover. She closed the door solidly behind her and stalked down the stairs.

Chapter Four

It was ten till six when Zena heard the front door open and softly close. She was reaching with the hem of her apron to take biscuits from the oven and, in her surprise, she stood holding the red-hot pan too long. Dropping it on the table with a stifled curse, she popped her burned thumb into her mouth and looked at the clock again. He was early. She hadn't expected that. In fact, she really hadn't expected her boarder to show up for supper at all after the lovely and very enterprising Nettie Fisk had "peeled his eggs" at lunch.

Not that she begrudged one of Bird's girls trying to drum up a little extra business on the side, especially with the handsome new marshal. Well, he was handsome, Zena admitted to herself, and Bird wasn't exactly known for her generosity with the help. Why, if it hadn't been for Eldon, Zena thought, she might very well have been the one in the high-bustled, green getup, draping herself over the marshal's desk this afternoon and offering to peel a lot more than hard-boiled eggs.

That thought, along with the vivid images that accompanied it, brought Zena up short. What in the name of heaven was she thinking? And with the same efficiency she used with a dust cloth, she dismissed the vagrant thoughts, plucking her scorched thumb from her mouth with a wet little pop and proceeding to transfer the freshly baked biscuits to a serving plate.

Feeling obliged now, perhaps even challenged, to have supper on the table promptly at six as she had threatened, she hurried to take the chops from the skillet and give the potatoes a shake of salt and pepper and one last stir.

Hands laden with dishes, she pushed the door to the dining room with her hip to discover her boarder already seated at the cherry wood table. He rose immediately—good Lord, his head barely cleared her cutglass chandelier!—and Zena couldn't help but notice the little nick on his jaw or the tiny dab of soap beneath one ear. He had shaved! Now why did that surprise her? Or please her so? It was only a courtesy that had nothing whatsoever to do with her. Nor did the faint scent of bay rum that made her want to take in a deep breath.

Without a word, he moved to take the platter of chops from her hand, and after a brief tug-of-war, Zena surrendered it rather than have her supper wind up on the carpet.

"Sit, please, Mr. Bolt. You needn't bother yourself. Your being prompt is all I ask."

"I don't much like the idea of having you wait on me, Mrs. Briggs," he said, resuming his seat.

Resuming it, Zena noticed, with uncommon gracefulness. Still dressed in black and still wearing that confounded gun, the man moved like wood smoke in a warm curl of breeze. No. More like a panther, she concluded. A sleek black cat whose grace was born of stealth rather than artifice.

For a moment her dining room seemed a truly dangerous place—bay rum and shaving cream aside—and she hurried back to the kitchen for the bowl of potatoes and another of sliced cucumbers and onions, which she placed near his plate.

"There." She surveyed the table. Satisfied that everything appeared present and in order, she let out a tiny sigh. "Will you be wanting anything else?"

"Company?"

A grin accompanied his request, flickering across his lips like a breeze-blown flame. Now why the devil was she looking at his mouth again? Worse, why was she even entertaining the notion of sitting down to supper with a boarder—and this one in particular—when it had always been her habit to eat alone in the kitchen?

It hadn't been a good idea. In fact, Tom thought as he watched the Widow Briggs prod a slice of cucumber from one side of her plate to the other, asking her to share his supper ranked high among the worst notions he'd ever had.

She sat at the opposite end of the table—as far away as she could get—her spine stiff as the chair back, her gaze for the most part on her plate where she occupied herself rearranging the food rather than eating it. But then, with her prim little mouth and her high, starched collar, she probably wouldn't have been able to swallow anything anyway.

The setting sun was glancing off the waxed cherry wood, glinting on the silverware, and catching like diamonds in the depths of water goblets. It cast the widow in a golden glow, and every once in a while ran through her dark hair like wildfire. Tom was trying not to notice.

Their conversation—what there was of it—tended toward the weather. It was just as well, he thought. He didn't want to talk about his past any more than she seemed to want to discuss hers. She was his landlady, he reminded himself. Nothing more. Her polite containment—her cocoon—was altogether appropriate. When he'd asked her to share supper with him, he'd really only been yearning for companionship after a solid year of scraping beans and bacon from a tin plate balanced on his knees. A little companionship. A little conversation. And the Widow Briggs was dutifully begrudging him a little of both. But there was all that damn sunset in her hair....

Zena's fork was poised above her plate, her head tilted to one side. She wasn't sure if Tom Bolt was ignoring her or if perhaps all those gunshots had made him hard-of-hearing. She did know, however, that she was making a mighty effort at conversation, all of it to no avail. "Does he?" she asked.

"Pardon?"

She cleared her throat with mild impatience. Having asked an idle question, she now found herself repeating it for the third time. "I was inquiring about your dog, Mr. Bolt." She angled her head in the direction of the backyard, where she suspected the shaggy beast was lurking after being shooed out of her kitchen with the business end of a broom. "I don't believe I've heard you mention his name."

"He doesn't have one."

"Oh! Well, then, I don't suppose you've had him very long." Satisfied with her own conclusion and putting an end to the subject, Zena popped a wafer of cucumber in her mouth.

"A year," he drawled.

She nearly choked. "That's absurd."

The gunfighter lifted an eyebrow, Zena's only clue that he had even heard her remark.

"Well, what I mean is, a pet really ought to have a name. It's only proper. Especially after an entire year. It's..." She struggled for a word to suit her obvious dismay. Her shock, really. "It's customary. It's... well...civilized."

"Civilized." Coming from him, the word had a bitter twist. The same bitter twist, she noted, that was shaping his lips while he fixed her with his iron gaze.

Zena felt suddenly as if she were staring down the twin barrels of a shotgun. She hadn't meant to insult the man. All she'd said was . . .

Suddenly he slapped his napkin onto the table, not with anger so much as finality. "It was a fine meal, ma'am. Thank you." He pushed his chair back and stood up. "I'll be making my evening rounds now. You needn't wait up."

Before she could reply—before she could even open her mouth—he was gone. Zena blinked as the screen door was slapping behind Tom Bolt's back.

No sooner was he outside than the confounded, unchristened cur was beside him, licking his hand and thrashing his tail against Tom's knees.

"Civilized," he spat, grinding his hat onto his head while he glared down at the dog. "Civilized." This time the word seethed on his lips like a poisonous hiss. He could tell the Widow Briggs a thing or two about civilization. Educate her in the cold, hard facts of life. The ABC's of human history outside her safe four walls and miles from her clean sheets and pretty dishware. He could draw her a map of all the sorry places where lost dogs took up with lost souls.

He glanced over his shoulder, back through the window of the little white frame house. There she sat— civilized as hell—in her orderly dining room with its table perfectly squared with the walls, its carpet not an inch out of line with the baseboards. Her spine was parallel to the chair back. On the wall behind her, framed floral prints were precisely aligned.

The sight brought an oath to his lips. He'd demanded a home as a condition of this job, and the town fathers had seen to it—in spades. They'd housed him in a damn cocoon with a damn caterpillar. An inchworm! One who thought Tom Bolt didn't measure up.

His boot heels hit the steps hard and he headed toward the saloon with long strides that forced the dog into a trot beside him. It was all he could do to nod to the people who greeted him from doorways and sidewalk chairs.

Civilization! If it existed at all, he'd like to know where. Not where a man could go away to fight for high ideals, then come back to find the charred bones of his wife and child in the burned-out wreck that had once been his home. Not where the bluebelly who held the torch got off scot-free because he was following orders. Or where some greedy Eastern scribbler carved a career out of a man's misfortunes.

For a second Tom was sorely tempted to turn around and slam back into the widow's safe cocoon, yank her up from her straight chair and give her a good shake while he told her precisely why he hadn't named the goddamned dog. It had nothing whatsoever to do with propriety or custom or confounded civilization. It had everything to do with love and loss. Once he named him, the animal would truly be his. His to lose. And Tom had lost all he was ever going to lose in this life.

In fact, the only thing he had left to lose now *was* his life. For whatever that was worth.

He might have turned back to set the inchworm straight, but at that moment young Billy Dakin fell into step beside him.

"Evenin', Marshal. Making your rounds?"

Tom's affirmative grunt did nothing to stifle the boy's eagerness. His gap-toothed grin remained in place as he loped along, trying to match his companion's strides. Tom noticed, too, that Billy was still sporting his sidearm. The shiny, store-stiff leather holster wasn't properly tied down, and it flapped against the boy's thigh like a pet lizard on a string.

Halting in front of Bird O'Brien's, Tom resettled his hat and dropped his gaze to Billy's hip. "Just what are you figuring to shoot with that thing, son?"

"I been practicing," the boy answered. "Out by Royal Creek." He whisked off his hat and slapped it against his leg. "Shoot! There's so much broken glass out there now, a fella's liable to kill himself just swimmin'."

Tom nodded. "Getting good, are you?"

Billy shifted his stance, dragging a boot tip through the dirt. "Gettin'," he said, then added quickly, "course not like you, Mr. Bolt. Nobody's as good as you."

"That's what they say." Tom crossed his arms, squinting against the sunset. "Those bottles shoot back at you before they break?"

The boy's face went blank for a moment as if he were trying to decide whether or not the new marshal was joshing him. He smiled tentatively then, shrugging. "I reckon not."

"I reckon not," Tom echoed.

What he longed to say was, "Do as I say, boy, not as I do." Not that it would have done any good. Hell, at sixteen, boys were more eyes than ears anyway. More heart than head. "Best see to that leg thong," he growled, turning his back on Billy to push through the doors of the saloon.

At midnight Tom was still there, sitting with his back to the wall, his eyes on the door, and his lap full of a girl named Hazel. Nettie, Bird had told him earlier, was "entertaining a gent" upstairs. While waiting for the redhead, Tom had probably downed a few more beers than any conscientious lawman should. Enough anyway to dull the glare of Bird's cut-glass chandeliers and nearly enough to soften Hazel's hard features and to mellow the axelike ring of her voice.

She had had a few beers, too, and she leaned heavily over Tom's arm now as much to exhibit her ample cleavage as to peer down at the dog who slept curled around a leg of the table. "Nice dog," she mumbled. "What's his name?"

A ripple of tension coursed through every muscle in Tom's body and his teeth clenched. "Doesn't have one."

"Oh." Hazel smiled sloppily as she repositioned herself on his lap, then curved her arms around his chest and plastered her cheek to his shoulder. "Imagine that," she slurred.

"Yeah. Imagine that," he whispered into the stiff curls of her sunless hair.

The year was 1865 when Captain Thomas Bolt, still garbed in Confederate gray, moved like a grim specter through the charred ruins of his home in Clay County, Missouri, gathering the blackened bones of his wife and child.

The first words of the dime novel took Zena so completely by surprise that she clasped the dog-eared volume to the bodice of her nightgown, closed her eyes a moment, then stared up at the ceiling over her bed. It wasn't at all what she had expected. Not from a cold-blooded shootist, from a man who lacked even the simple warmth required to name a dog.

After her boarder had left the table so abruptly, she had sat there, stupefied, wondering what she had said to set him off like that. The man's eyes had taken on the color and foreboding of storm clouds and his voice had deepened to thunder when he bid her a terse good-night. Her first, angry inclination had been to write Tom Bolt off as a thin-skinned, ill-mannered boor. She'd snatched his plate from the table, thinking it was little wonder that, with a temper like that, he'd left a score of dead men in his wake. It wasn't as if she'd wanted to share supper with him, for heaven's sake. Or even converse with the man. Such as their conversation had been. But there'd be a blizzard in hell, Zena had vowed, before she'd ever do it again.

Once her hands had been in warm dishwater, though, and she was running a soapy rag over her china, Zena had calmed down and reconsidered. It was hardly in her best interest to have the new marshal mad at her. There was more at stake than just her bruised feelings, after all. What was at stake was her home, her very life, as far as she was concerned. What was she going to do if the marshal's thin skin and quick temper prompted him to move out?

"Over my dead body," she'd exclaimed, wringing out the wet dishrag, drying her hands on her apron and reaching into her pocket for the dime novel that Billy had lent her. Maybe if she knew a little more about Tom Bolt, she'd know how not to offend him quite so easily. If nothing else, Zena had figured, the book might point her toward topics of conversation less explosive than the nameless dog.

But she hadn't figured on this, she thought as she lay in her bed with the book tented on her chest while she stared at the ceiling. The gunfighter had been a husband and a father. He had lost a wife and a child! It was a loss she could well understand. A loss not unlike her own.

Almost cautiously, she picked up the little volume and angled it toward the lamplight, perusing the face on the cover. Was it grief looking out from those cool gray eyes? Was it unbearable sadness that gave that mouth its harsh and forbidding little twist? And the black clothes he wore. She wondered now why it hadn't once occurred to her that they might signify deep mourning.

Or not. Zena shrugged against the plumped-up pillows. After all, she reminded herself, this was the same man who had failed to give a proper name to his poor, loyal dog. That fact alone didn't speak well of the depth of Tom Bolt's emotions. With a little sigh as much from frustration as weariness, she opened the book and read on.

Tom came up the stairs quietly, avoiding the step that creaked while keeping his eyes on the sliver of light framing the widow's door. He half expected to hear a quick rustle of covers as she hastened to douse the lamp. What he heard, though, as he reached the top of the stairs, was the slow and even breathing of someone fast asleep.

With the edges of his own brain blurred from beer and smoke and Hazel's rank perfume, he wondered if the inchworm was stewed to the gills again—a picture of dishevelment, half in and half out of her clothes and her bed. He stood there in the hallway a moment, listening to her, wondering about her, cursing himself once more for wasting another opportunity tonight at Bird's.

"Aw, don't go, honey," Hazel had whined when he put her off his lap. "I know you want me. I been sitting on that hard information all night."

True enough. And yet he'd walked away from the willing whore. To come back here.

He pushed the widow's door with the back of his hand then stood there, staring, his own breathing tattered all of a sudden and his heart battering his ribs like a fist.

Asleep, she was all white lace and lamplit hair. Sober, as far as he could tell, but sensual all the same. The pale quilt fit the flare of her hip to perfection. Perfect as the curve of a butterfly's wing.

Tom couldn't have said what drew him to her, but he stood there a long time. It felt simple as a moth's attraction for a flame, strong as a tide. It was the memory of her soft mouth and the feel of her warm, sweet flesh. Her sense of order rubbing up against the disarray of his own life. Surely it was whatever was keeping him from climbing the stairs with Nettie or Hazel.

It was all of that. And it was impossible.

Chapter Five

Verna Campbell waved from the rocker on her front porch and called out to Zena as she strode by. "Morning, Mrs. Briggs. Well, I see you're headed out to the cemetery so I know it must be the third Sunday of the month."

Zena waved back. "It's a beautiful morning."

"Seems like everybody's out enjoying it, too," Verna observed, letting her knitting collapse in her lap as she brought her rocker to a halt. "The new marshal and his dog passed by here not so long ago. Course I suppose you know that, him boarding with you and all."

A weak smile was the best Zena could offer as she continued on her way. No, she hadn't known Tom Bolt and his no-name critter had gone this way. She'd barely seen the man this past week. He came home late and left at the crack of dawn. He managed to be out of his office each day when she brought his lunch. Each evening at six, he showed up clean shaven in her dining room, thanked her for serving his supper, thanked her again when he finished it and carried his clean plate into the kitchen, then left to make his evening rounds. There had been no more requests for her company, no further invitations for her to join him in the dining room. Tom Bolt ate alone.

Her boarder was clean, courteous, and about as quiet and distant as a star. It should have pleased her, Zena kept telling herself. He was still there. She should have been thrilled that, after nearly two weeks, Tom Bolt hadn't bolted. Lemuel Porter even let her by this month a whole three dollars short on the mortgage. Her house—for the time being anyway—was safe and secure.

So why, she wondered, was she always on edge lately? Always listening for the marshal's footsteps and seeking out signs of him in her house? When she'd changed his bed linens the other day, she'd even gone so far as to bury her nose in his pillowcase—like a crazed hound she'd thought at the time—searching for his scent. Telling herself it was simply because she wasn't accustomed to having a man around hadn't done any good. It wasn't any man. It was this particular man who was working his way under her skin the way grit worked its way under the quarter rounds of her baseboards. And like grit, Zena didn't like it one little bit. Nor was she able to ignore it.

The cemetery was a quarter mile west of town near Royal Creek. When they had plotted it out, everyone had hoped that Glory's town limits would soon expand to encompass the little grove of hickory and oak. That hadn't been the case, though, and it was still a good long walk from town to visit the dear departed. Zena picked up her pace now, gazing at the sky, all summer blue without a scrap of cloud.

It was a beautiful day. She wasn't going to ruin it worrying about Tom Bolt, that was for sure. She should never have read that confounded book. It had taken her close to a week to finish the thing since Mr. Philo Gordon, Journalist, made a habit of sticking one long, fifty-cent word in just about every sentence of his dime novel. One doozy every other line that Zena would have to slowly puzzle out while her finger followed the word across the page.

Her schooling had been largely hit-or-miss while she was being shunted from one aunt to another. It was a wonder she could read at all, considering. Bird had helped her some, and Eldon, too. But for the most part, her reading had been confined to recipes and *The Glory Gazette. Death in the Dust—The Continuing Adventures of Tom Bolt*—Testified to by his Good Friend, Philo Gordon, Journalist was the first real book Zena had ever tackled.

And now she wished she hadn't. Partly because it described a violent way of life she abhorred. Oh, from the sound of it, Tom Bolt was a gunslinger who never went looking for a fight. Instead, the fights came looking for him. But in the end, he always fought, using that big .44 of his to leave his victims dead in the dust. Mostly, though, Zena regretted reading the book because it raised so many niggling little images of the man in black and set her to wondering about him more than she cared to.

When she reached the little graveyard with its delicate iron fence, Zena whisked through the waist-high gate and went directly—she could have done it with her eyes closed—to the granite stones that marked the graves of her husband and daughter. Aside from her house, this was the place she loved most, and she tended the grave site with an equal determination. A weed hardly had time to put down a root before Zena was yanking it out.

Today she had brought a jar of soap water and a scrub brush to do battle with bird droppings. Without dawdling, she pushed up her sleeves and got to work on the rectangular stones. When the granite shone once more to her satisfaction, she started pulling weeds.

Ordinarily she chatted with Eldon as she worked. Over the years it had become her habit to tell him what was going on in Glory—the comings and goings, the marriages and the births. She usually refrained from telling him of the deaths, deciding he probably already knew who'd been laid to rest nearby. Always she'd tell her late husband how everybody still missed him and claimed they'd never had a better barber.

Today, however, Zena worked in tight-lipped silence. The only news in town this month was the new marshal, and for some reason she didn't quite understand, she didn't want to babble on about Tom Bolt. Not here in this sacred place. Not to Eldon, who lay here because of a gunman just like Bolt.

After pulling weeds for twenty minutes, she sat back on her heels at last to survey the tidy little plots. Hearing a rustle in the grass behind her, Zena turned just in time to receive a wet lick on her cheek from the black-and-white dog.

"For pity's sake!" She snatched up the hem of her skirt to swipe at her face while the dog proceeded to circle the gravestones, his tail wagging briskly and his nose to the ground sniffing. He stopped abruptly, raised his head decisively, and was about to raise his leg, as well, when Zena chunked a clod of earth in his direction.

"Oh, no, you don't, you brazen, nameless critter. Scat!"

He sat instead, tilting his head, pricking his ears forward attentively. His pink tongue lolled out, then disappeared as he made a little woofing sound.

"What?" Zena grumbled, reaching out to brush a speck of dirt from the glossy stone.

The dog woofed again, its shaggy tail brushing through the grass.

"Go on with you now. I don't have any scraps to give you. This is a cemetery, not a kitchen. The only thing I could give you out here is a name. Lord knows you need one."

He scooted forward on his haunches and licked her hand. And now it was Zena tilting her head, regarding him thoughtfully. She stroked his silky coat.

"Is that what you want? A name? Seems to me it's your master who ought to be doing the naming, but since he hasn't seen fit, I guess I'll just have to come up with something." She perused the animal's face, trying to decide if he was black with white markings or the reverse. She sighed. "I don't suppose Spot would do, would it?"

His furry chin sagged in her lap and he moaned softly.

"No. I didn't think so. How about Blackie?"

All he did then was raise a single fuzzy eyebrow.

Zena sighed again. "Well, give me a little time. I'm sure there's a name that'll suit you." She angled her head to seek out the smaller of the two headstones, inscribed Ellen Elizabeth Briggs, Beloved Child. "I'm pretty good at naming," she whispered. "At least, I used to be."

She and the dog had gone only a few paces back toward town when a gunshot down by the creek stopped Zena in her tracks. The dog took off in that direction, barking. Partly out of curiosity, and partly out of wanting to help if somebody was in trouble, Zena followed him. Crouching, she fought her way through haw bushes and a tangle of wild strawberries and honeysuckle, quietly emerging at the creek to discover that there was trouble, all right, but not the sort she had expected. The gunslinger was taking target practice.

He stood perhaps ten or fifteen yards away, and apparently he hadn't heard her. He hadn't acknowledged her presence anyway, so Zena remained quiet, watching. It was, she had to admit to herself, quite a sight.

The marshal was shirtless, and his dark hair was wet, dripping every once in a while down one ropy arm or down the taut muscles of his back. Maybe he'd washed up in the creek, she thought, or maybe he just liked feeling the sunshine on his skin. There was plenty of both, she observed. Sunshine and skin. A burnished gold over sleek, hard-carved musculature. Warm. Wonderfully warm to the touch. Well, if anyone touched him. Or wanted to. Which she certainly didn't.

Still, he was nice to watch. Fast as a flash of lightning when he went for his gun. Then slow, shifting his stance, setting his black boots a bit farther apart, centering his hips then settling them firmly, flexing the fingers that hovered above the sleek black holster. He lifted his shoulders once, rolled his neck and let sunlight run like melting butter the length of his arms and back.

Much to her chagrin, Zena discovered her jaw had gone slack and her mouth was hanging open wide enough to catch flies. And dragonflies, at that. She closed it with a smart little snap and wrenched her gaze away from the gunman to his target across the creek. He was shooting at himself! One of Philo Gordon's dime novels had been skewered to a tree branch—heart high—and the face on the cover was shot through with bullet holes.

"Have you killed him yet?" she called out.

Tom knew she was there. He'd heard the thrashing as somebody came through the thick foliage, then he'd caught the glimmer of her sun-struck hair and a white wisp of petticoat out of the corner of his eye. He had ignored her, though, hoping she'd go away. Back to civilization.

He kept her at the edge of his sight now as he thumbed cartridges into the chambers of his .44. "This is a skill, Mrs. Briggs. Like anything else, if you don't practice, you lose your abilities."

"I've been reading about your abilities." She was picking her way across the narrow little creek bed, her rucked-up skirts in her fists with a few inches of dark stocking showing below quick hints of lace and ruffles.

Butterfly ruffles, Tom thought as he returned his gaze and his thoughts to reloading. He'd made himself scarce, well-nigh invisible, for the past week or so. He'd barely left a fingerprint in her tidy, civilized cocoon. What the hell did she want from him now?

With a soft little grunt, she yanked the ragged book from its branch. "We don't have so many books in Glory, Mr. Bolt, that we like to see people go around shooting holes in them."

"Positively uncivilized," he muttered from between clenched teeth.

"Pardon me?" She was tripping back across the creek, the dime novel tucked safely beneath her arm and her petticoats whispering and winking.

Tom snapped the cylinder closed. "Seems like my coming to Glory strikes you as just about as bad as the barbarians sacking Rome."

"Well, I don't know anything about that," she said with an indignant sniff. "I'm not an educated woman." She dropped her skirts, whisked the book out from under her arm and waved it at him. "But I don't approve of shooting books." She glanced at the tattered cover, then added almost under her breath, "Especially ones I haven't had a chance to read."

"You won't get an education by reading that slop." He jammed the pistol into his holster. "Believe me."

"Perhaps not," she said quietly, eyes fluttering from the book to his face. "But I might get to know you better."

He felt his jaw loosen as if a fist had just connected with it. The same invisible fist then rammed into his gut as the widow's blue eyes began their earnest, curious search of his face. Blue eyes shielded by shy butterfly lashes. Guileless. Utterly sincere. God Almighty! She meant it.

He turned on his heel and stalked away to grab his shirt from the thorny clutches of a haw bush, tearing it in the process and swearing softly as he put it on. "You don't want to know me better," he growled.

At his back he could hear her thumbing through the pages of the book.

"This one starts out just the same as the other," she said, a little trill of surprise in her voice. "The year was 1865 when Captain Thomas Bolt, still garbed—"

"Spare me, Mrs. Briggs." He stabbed his shirttails into his pants before he turned to glare at her. "I know the facts. And those, to put it mildly, ain't them."

She glanced up from the page, blinking. "You didn't return from the war in 1865?"

He shrugged.

"You did or you didn't?" she pressed.

"I did."

"Well, then. That's the truth so far." Her eyes fluttered to the open book, then back to his face. "Were you a captain in the Rebel army?"

"No," he snapped.

"What was your rank then?"

"Brevet captain."

She rolled her blue eyes heavenward. "In charge of splitting hairs?"

"Battlefield promotions don't mean very much when you're about the last man alive in your regiment."

"Still," she murmured.

"Congratulations, Mrs. Briggs. You've stumbled on the two snatches of truth Philo Gordon's pen ever put to paper." He moved toward her now, one hand outstretched. "I'll take my target back, if you don't mind."

Zena whisked the book behind her. Her curiosity, far from being satisfied, had just been irresistibly piqued. Anyway, she didn't need to look at the words to remember them. She knew Philo Gordon's prologue by heart. "You were still garbed in Confederate gray," she asserted.

He stopped, crossing his arms, pinning her with his gray eyes while his lips slid into a taunting grin. "No, ma'am, I wasn't. I ditched my uniform right after we got word of Lee's surrender. Just like every other Missouri boy who wanted to get home alive."

"Oh."

He stretched out his arm again, standing closer now so he was almost touching her. He wiggled his fingers. "My book."

Zena tightened her grasp on the bullet-riddled volume, at the same time thrusting her chin up stubbornly. "Your home, Mr. Bolt? How did you find it?"

A smirk touched his lips, working across his mouth like a spark along a fuse. "Same as always, Mrs. Briggs," he drawled. "I rode two miles west of Liberty, then a half mile north of Asa Benton's mill."

"That isn't what I meant at all," Zena replied, "and you know it." In exasperation, her hands came to her hips. "I meant in what condition—"

His hand flashed out so fast Zena barely knew the book was gone until she saw it sailing through the air, its pages spreading like tattered wings. That sight had barely registered on her when six quick shots rang out, zinging the book this way and that overhead, before it dropped—like a dead pigeon—in the creek.

Her ears were ringing from the gunfire. Only now did she think to cover them. Her own voice sounded small and distant, like a child's whimper. "Why did you do that?"

Cursing himself, Tom shoved the hot gun back into his holster. Mentally he aimed a few well chosen curses at his "good friend, Philo Gordon, Journalist." Damn the man for taking his life and turning it into nothing better than a target. For turning Tom himself into the same thing.

But it wasn't Philo Gordon who'd just scared the little widow silly, was it? It was the great, the legendary, the uncivilized Tom Bolt. All by himself. All by his lonesome self. She was trembling now, her small hands covering her ears, her eyes squeezed closed. She swayed, and when he reached out to steady her, instead of shrinking away as he expected, the widow moved into his arms.

God! Tom closed his own eyes as his cheek pressed against the warmth of her sun-dappled hair, as he breathed in the mingled fragrances of sweet soap and rich earth. He didn't dare move, hardly dared even breathe. The moment was so delicate—like having a butterfly poised on his wrist.

"I thought..." she began in a voice barely more than a whisper, "I imagined you needed comfort."

"Comfort?" he murmured against her hair, his lips shaping the word as if it were foreign and its meaning unclear. Women had offered him many things over the years, but comfort wasn't one of them.

"For your losses," she explained. "Coming home that way to find your wife and child. I . . . I imagined your pain." She sighed softly and lifted her face. "But if those were only lies, then there's no need."

The light shifted in his eyes as he gazed down at her. Zena thought it was as if a cloud had passed over the sun. Perhaps it had, for she felt a small shiver race down her spine at the same moment.

A muscle worked along his tight jaw, and when he spoke, his voice was low and rough. "There's need."

She blinked, opening her lips to speak, then forgot whatever it was she'd intended to say as that astonishingly familiar mouth closed over hers. Her first instinct was to pull away. He had misunderstood! This wasn't what she had meant at all when she had spoken of comfort!

But instead of wrenching her mouth away, she found herself angling her head, the better to receive the warmth of his kiss, the more to savor the taste of him, the soft wetness of his lips and the scrub of his whiskers. His hand slipped up, curving around her neck, bracing her for the plunder of his tongue.

Zena's heart turned over and over, spinning perilously as it plunged to the pit of her stomach. She struggled for breath only to find that Tom Bolt's breath was her own now and his strength was supporting her or else she would have slid to the ground in a quivering, liquid pool. Nobody had ever kissed her this way. Nobody. Comfort! Her late husband's kisses had been comfortable. This was as comfortable as being struck by lightning. And for a moment she wanted to stand here, wild and dizzy in the center of the storm, in Tom Bolt's arms—forever.

Then he stopped kissing her. Just plain quit, leaving the muted hiss of an oath shivering across her lips, then jerking her upright before he turned his back and stalked away.

She straightened her shoulders and attempted to re-fashion the knot of hair his straying fingers had coaxed loose, wondering all the while what she had done to set him off again. He was behaving as if she had hit him rather than returned his kiss. But then, maybe she hadn't, she thought. Or at least not returned it to his satisfaction. Good Lord, what might the man have done if she had denied him rather than merely disappointed him? She glanced a little nervously at the gun on his hip.

Her heart was still thumping wildly and her face still tingled from the scrape of his beard. Summoning as much righteous indignation as she could under the circumstances, Zena called out to him. "I believe our notions of comfort are quite different, Mr. Bolt."

"It won't happen again, Mrs. Briggs." He swiped his hat from a tree stump and slapped it against his leg. "Ever."

She should have just said "fine" and had done with it. But the man's all-out, dead-certain, almost brutal resolve to never kiss her again caused a very real indignation to flare in Zena.

Maybe she wasn't the most experienced woman in Glory or in all of Kansas for that matter. Maybe she didn't know how to do all those fancy, heart-slamming things with her teeth and tongue. Maybe the fastest gun in the West found her woefully deficient. But Eldon Briggs had never complained.

"It's your loss, Mr. Bolt," she snapped, then whipped her skirts around and strode with as much dignity as possible through a blur of hot tears and the tangle of vines and branches.

Zena's skirts billowed around her as she sank down before the gravestones. She had stumbled back to the cemetery, hoping to get her emotions under control before returning to town. She was mad. She was mortified. Most of all, she was ashamed of herself for finding such pleasure in Tom Bolt's arms.

Not that she'd have to worry about a repeat performance! Her shame was dismally compounded by the gunslinger's adamant rejection. She rubbed a knuckle beneath one wet eye as she sucked in a ragged breath. She felt like digging a hole right next to Eldon and the baby, then climbing in and pulling the ground over her head like a dark blanket. But only after she'd dug another deeper, darker hole and planted the fastest gun in the West six feet beneath the ground.

"He can just go to blazes," she hissed through trembling lips.

"I expect to, Mrs. Briggs."

Black boot tips seemed to materialize out of thin air beside her. Zena was too startled to speak or even to move as the gunfighter squatted down by her side. His dark, graceful hands dandled his black hat between his knees. The dark fabric of his pants strained across his powerful thighs. His black gun belt and holster made an audible creak. Dark as death, and yet Zena was aware of heat emanating from a very live body. For an instant she bitterly resented his presence—so masculine, so brimming with life and heat—here in her sacred place, but when she turned to tell him so, the hard expression on his face kept her mute. His deep gray gaze was riveted to the smaller of the two headstones.

"Your daughter?" he asked quietly.

Zena nodded, staring down at her folded hands through a fresh film of tears, snagging her quivering lower lip with her teeth. These weren't tears she intended to share with anyone, least of all this hardhearted gunslinger.

"I had a son." His voice caught in his throat like a dry leaf on a bramble.

Her eyes snapped back to his face. Dark. Somber, she realized now, rather than hard. Drawn with grief etched deeply as an epitaph.

He shifted slightly on his haunches, giving the hat a little toss and catching it again in his strong fingers. "So you were right. About the book anyway. There is some truth strung through all that tripe." He slanted her the merest hint of a grin. "I guess you were right about the other, too. But, lady, you better believe that my loss is nothing but your gain."

Chapter Six

Tom looked into her glistening blue eyes, momentarily drowning in them, in the shimmering swirl of emotions he read there. There was grief. Anger and shame, as well. Most of all, there was confusion. She didn't need to speak what was so clear in those blue depths. The butterfly had ventured out of her cocoon for a kiss, only to be rejected. He needed to set things right with her. For her sake, as well as his own.

He reached out, feathering a fingertip along the curve of her lips. "You're not the kind of woman a man can just kiss," he said softly, "or make love to and then walk away. You're a woman a man wants to stay with. And, Zena, I can't stay. That's why I stopped kissing you, and why I won't do it again. That's the only reason." He sighed roughly. "God knows I loved every second I held you in my arms."

Color stole across her smooth cheeks. She turned her face away and, when she spoke, a trace of her former brittleness crackled in her tone. "I expect we both forgot ourselves down there by the creek. Just plain lost sight of who we are and what we are. Thank you for remembering, Mr. Bolt, and thank you for reminding me.''

"You're welcome." He chuckled deep in his throat. "Now that we've kissed, though, you might consider calling me Tom. Don't go all the way back in your cocoon, butterfly. We might as well be friends, seeing as how we're not going to be lovers.''

A thin smile threaded across her mouth. "All right. Tom." She turned back, tipping her face up. Her expression was earnest and grave. "I'm truly sorry about your little boy.''

Settling onto the ground beside her, he leaned back on one elbow and slung out his legs. It had been so long since he'd talked about his son that Tom barely knew what to say. And it surprised him all of a sudden to find that the scar he thought had healed and hardened and virtually disappeared was still there, still able to twist inside him painfully.

"That was a long time ago," he said, pulling a weed, thinking it was probably the only one the widow had overlooked in the vicinity of the two graves. "Fourteen years. He was just a little sprout, two or thereabouts, when he died." He stuck the weed in a corner of his mouth. "Now that I think about it, Tommy'd be just about Billy Dakin's age today.''

"Tommy," she murmured. "He was Thomas Bolt, Junior, then?''

He nodded. "Hannah wanted that. It was her idea.''

"Your wife?''

"That's right."

Another ancient scar pulled up now and twisted tight. Hannah. Hannah with her tiny hands and her soft hair the color of flames. One long flame of braid rippling down her pearly spine or grazing his shoulder in their bed. For years he hadn't been able think about her without picturing all that beautiful hair on fire. So he'd just plain quit remembering.

"Hannah died, too?" Zena asked. "In the fire? Or was that something Philo Gordon made up?"

"She died, too." He shunted the weed to the other side of his mouth. "The rest wasn't quite the melodrama that ink-stained viper made it out to be. I buried them, saw to it that their graves were properly marked, and then I went after the man who killed them."

Zena's voice was little more than breath. "Why? Why did he do it? Why would any man burn down a house with a woman and a little boy inside?"

He shrugged. "War. Insanity. Back then, with the war going on, Missouri was like a patchwork quilt of blue and gray, with one county supporting the Union while the next was Confederate. When the order came down that the Federal troops were supposed to move everybody out of their homes in Clay County for suspected rebel activity, Hannah wouldn't budge."

"I don't blame her," Zena interrupted softly.

"She must have been asleep, both Hannah and the boy, when they torched the place. Nobody knew the details, except for the name of the officer in the local militia who gave the order. He was a no-account named Jack Soames, a Clay County boy himself who sided with the North and never did have any use for me or mine. I guess it was his way of killing me, by destroying what was mine." Tom stared at the clouds reflected in the polished granite headstones.

"And you killed him." Zena's voice was level, without accusation, as if she were just taking up the story.

"Yes, ma'am," he said bluntly. "That I did. I would have killed him twice—once for Hannah and once for the boy—if I could have. It should have ended right there, but by the time I caught up with him in West Texas, Soames had earned himself a bit of a reputation as a shootist."

"Which you inherited then," Zena said.

Tom smiled grimly. "Lock, stock and both barrels. I was good with a gun. Always had been, and then I had four years of practice during the war. But after word got around that I had taken down Jack Soames, I had to get even better if I wanted to stay alive." He plucked the weed from his mouth now and pointed it at her, trying to work his mouth into a full-fledged grin. "The rest, as they say, is history. Most of it Philo Gordon's. Most of it trumped up and tricked out to make people buy those books of his and put a lot of money in his pockets. The best thing you can do with one of those dime novels of his is keep it handy in the privy."

"Or use it for target practice," Zena added with a little laugh.

"That, too." Tom angled his head toward the grave markers. "Tell me about your daughter," he asked. "Did she have her mama's dark hair and pretty blue eyes?"

The question took Zena completely by surprise. Although she had named her daughter with great deliberation, in the six years since the baby was born dead, not once had Zena ever tried to imagine Ellen Elizabeth Briggs as a living, breathing, dark-haired, blue-eyed child. The baby had survived more like a spirit in her mind and her heart, a disembodied creature of mist and memory. A dream that hadn't come true.

Zena shook her head now, as much to clear her thoughts as to answer Tom's question. "My little one never had a chance. She was born dead, right after her father was killed."

He closed his eyes, and his mouth twitched. "I didn't realize that. I guess I thought..." He regarded the headstone again. "I thought she'd lived, for a while anyway, considering the name."

"Everybody ought to have a name, Tom," she answered quietly, firmly. "Even..."

"Even my confounded dog." He levered up, frowning as he brushed grass and dirt from his sleeve. "Seems like you're accusing me of being an uncivilized barbarian again."

"I wasn't," she answered quickly. "I know you're not." Zena reached out her hand to touch him. For a moment he merely stared at her hand where it rested on his arm, and Zena found herself wondering how long it had been since anybody had simply reached out to this man instead of shooting at him. "Now that I know you better, I'm sure you're not," she added.

"Don't be too sure, butterfly." He clasped her hand, stood, and pulled her to her feet.

"It strikes me," she said as she brushed off the back of her skirt, "that you've been the victim of circumstances beyond your control."

A brilliant white grin blazed across his face and he covered his heart with his black hat. "Why, Miss Zena!" he drawled. "Nobody's ever called me anything half that nice."

"It's true," she protested. "You shot a man with a reputation and it became your own, forcing you to defend it. Seems to me it's a bit like a prize fighter who wins and then must stand and face all comers."

"Something like that," he agreed. He nodded in the direction of town. "If you're all done out here, I'll walk you back to town."

She glanced down at Eldon's large headstone and the smaller one beside it, realizing this was the first time she hadn't felt overwhelmed and weighted down by sadness when preparing to leave the cemetery. She wasn't sure just what it was that she did feel. There was a kind of lightness in her heart that kept working its way up her throat, urging her to smile. Was it happiness? she wondered. It had been so long since she'd thought of herself as happy, Zena wasn't really certain what it felt like anymore. Or, for that matter, why getting to know this gunslinger a little better would account for such feelings.

"Yes. Thank you. I believe I am all done here," she said, smiling up at him as she threaded her arm through his and they began the long walk back to Glory.

The black-and-white dog caught up with them not far beyond the cemetery and showered them with creek water when he stood and shook his shaggy, wet coat with head-to-tail enthusiasm. They took their time getting back to town, pausing now and then to laugh as they tossed sticks for the playful, tail-wagging animal.

Zena couldn't remember a prettier day. The sky was a deep, summertime blue even though it was still only late spring. Clouds stood out against it, distinct and perfectly white, like fresh laundry on a line. She was happy, she decided, although she was at a loss to say why. Probably it was just a fortuitous combination of sky and sunshine and silky breezes. It was pleasant, too, she thought, to stroll once more with her arm hooked through a gentleman's. She had to remind herself more than once that her escort was no gentleman, but rather a notorious gunman. Even if Philo Gordon's stories ran far short of the truth, Tom Bolt's was still a name written in other men's blood.

Once again, as they passed by Verna Campbell's house, the elderly woman called from her front porch. "Nice to see you again, Zena. Afternoon, Marshal. Lovely day, isn't it?"

Zena merely smiled and nodded in passing. Verna was a fixture in Glory. She had been here forever it seemed—longer than Zena anyway—and the woman didn't miss much from the vantage point of her front porch. Not that she was a gossip exactly, but . . .

Zena stumbled, and Tom tightened his hold on her arm.

"Careful," he murmured, his gray eyes searching her face from the shadows cast by the brim of his hat.

She told him she had stepped on a rock. It wasn't true, though. It was more as if a rock had just landed in her stomach, sending little shivering ripples all through her. Thin circles of panic, widening and racing over one another. In her eagerness to get to know the marshal better, Zena hadn't given a single thought to how much he might already know about her. After all, it wasn't as if he'd just arrived. He'd been in Glory a few weeks now, long enough to have had one or two good earfuls of the local gossip.

Tilting her head, she glanced at him. Those steely eyes shifted briefly in her direction, softened a moment, then stared straight ahead.

What was it he had said to her about not kissing her again? Something about her not being the kind of woman a man could make love to and then just walk away. Zena looked at him again, wondering now if he had meant to be ironic. If that remark had been intended to taunt her rather than reassure. What exactly did the marshal know about her past? And how the devil was she going to find out?

Her thoughts were interrupted by Billy Dakin, who suddenly appeared as if out of nowhere, his eyes big and wild, his holster flapping against his leg.

"Stranger's come to town looking for you, Marshal." Billy sucked in a breath. "Mean lookin' fella if ever I saw one."

Tom stopped dead in his tracks, his eyes swiftly taking in all of Front Street, its sidewalks and doorways and windows. When Zena felt his arm stiffen under hers, she followed the direction of his gaze.

The man leaning against the hitching rail outside Bird O'Brien's was more than mean looking. He looked deadly with a sweat-stained tan Stetson pulled low over his face, with smoke from a clenched cigar trailing up and wreathing around his head, with sunlight glinting off a gold tooth and off the fast-draw rig he wore on his hip. The stranger nodded slowly in their direction, then straightened up, spat contemptuously on the sidewalk before he pushed through the batwing doors of the saloon and disappeared.

"You know him, Marshal?" Billy asked, his voice high and tight.

"I know him," Tom growled.

"You gonna kill him?"

Zena gasped. "Billy! For shame!"

"Well, tarnation, Miz Zena, that's why we brung Tom Bolt and his big reputation to town in the first place, ain't it?"

If the marshal's arm had felt hard under her arm before, she sensed it turn to stone now as Billy blabbered on.

"You gonna go in there and get him? Lemme go with you, huh, Marshal?" The boy tapped his gun. "I'm ready as I'll ever be. Lemme help you."

To Zena's astonishment, Tom grinned and said, "Much obliged, son. I believe I could use your help."

Billy straightened his shoulders and appeared to stand several inches taller. "Yessir."

"I want you to see that Mrs. Briggs gets home safe. Right now. Will you do that for me?"

Zena and Billy protested in unison. She didn't want to go home any more than the boy wanted to escort her there. The marshal cut Billy off with a terse "Now, Billy." Then he turned to Zena and as he spoke he eased his arm from hers.

"Go home, butterfly. I'd appreciate it if you'd take my dog with you and see that he stays out of harm's way."

"Harm?" Her voice had a frantic edge. "What in the name of heaven...? You're not actually considering...?"

He stilled her lips with a finger. "Shh. I'm just planning to do the job I was hired for."

"You were hired to be a gunslinger," she replied. "Plain and simple."

His gray eyes flicked toward the badge on his vest. "Not according to this." His voice lowered ominously. "Don't argue with me, Zena. Not now."

From the steel glint in his eyes and the set of his jaw, she knew any protest would be useless. "I wouldn't dream of it," she snapped, turning her back on him.

If he was in such a damn rush to kill or be killed, then let him. At least she could make sure young Billy wasn't anywhere nearby once the bullets started flying. She grabbed his hand and tugged the reluctant young man down the street, away from Tom Bolt and the danger he seemed so eager to court.

Tom stood in the middle of Front Street, loading the revolver he had emptied earlier on the flying dime novel, cursing under his breath. The sight of Pawnee Jack Smith had confirmed what he had only suspected. The town fathers of Glory craved law and order about as bad as a kid craved a toothache. He'd given them the benefit of the doubt till now. He'd made do with the ramshackle jail house. He'd even swallowed that story about the town council not being able to convene to make any new ordinances. But Pawnee Jack's showing up put the lid on all his hopes. It was no secret the great Tom Bolt was in Glory, and the town was open for business. Bad business.

The widow had known all along, too. *You were hired to be a gunslinger, plain and simple,* she had said. No wonder she regarded him as just a shake removed from Attila the Hun. What he was, though, was just a damn fool for thinking he'd ever shed his reputation.

He walked into the saloon, and stood just inside the doors while his eyes adjusted to the dark interior. The buxom Bird approached him immediately.

"I've got a substantial investment in glassware in here, Marshal. I'd appreciate it if you'd conduct your business outside."

Tom nodded. "Where's Smith?"

"Upstairs," Bird replied. "With Hazel and Fat Alice."

A little smile stole across his lips. Pawnee Jack Smith might have had a face like a weasel and the disposition of a rattlesnake, but, as Tom recalled, when the man was anywhere near female flesh, he also had the self-control of a jackrabbit.

"Outside, Marshal," Bird reminded him.

"Yes, ma'am." He drew his gun, held it against his leg and moved for the stairs.

"What's happening now, Billy?" Zena sat on the edge of the settee, her hands fisted in her lap. The dog was curled in a ball of black and white by her feet.

"Nothing." The boy leaned farther out the parlor window. "Nothing at all. The marshal went into Bird's. Ain't hardly nobody on the street. Them that are are trying to make like they're invisible around corners and behind lampposts." He craned his head back in Zena's direction. "You oughta come watch, Miz Zena. There's sure to be some fireworks soon. Hot damn!"

She rolled her eyes and clasped her hands more tightly. "I'll depend on you to keep me informed." As these things tended to progress, she expected Tom and the ugly stranger to stride out into the middle of Front Street in a matter of moments. Shots would ring out. Probably two. Death in the dust.

But instead of shots, a blood-chilling female scream rent the afternoon silence. The dog sat up fast and Zena put out a hand to hold him. "What in the name of heaven was that?"

"Sounded like Fat Alice," Billy said from his perch on the windowsill. "I still can't see...wait a minute. A window just opened upstairs at the saloon, and...what in tarnation? A shirt and a pair of pants just came sailing out."

No sooner had Zena echoed "pants" than Billy cried out, "Now there's a pair of long johns flying over the balcony rail. And a hat. And now... Holy hellfire!"

"What?"

"That desperado just got pitched out the window. Stark nekked."

"Good Lord!" Zena rushed to the window, jamming her shoulders alongside Billy's in the open frame.

The boy turned his astonished face in her direction. "I don't know if you oughta be watching this, Miz Zena."

But Zena's eyes were glued to the second-floor balcony of Bird O'Brien's. The window behind the naked man slammed shut now. He banged on it with both fists as the drapes fell back. He cursed at the top of his lungs, then he turned toward the street. A chorus of laughter rose from every doorway and lamppost as the citizens of Glory popped into view, all of them with their faces turned up as if they were watching a fireworks display.

"Gol dang it," Billy breathed. "Excuse me, Miz Zena, but that's the knobbiest, sorriest, *ugliest* human body I ever did see. He don't look so dangerous without clothes, does he?"

She stifled a giggle as she watched the naked desperado bend slightly at the waist, his hands splaying out in an attempt to shield his private parts from the crowd below.

"Ain't all that much to see, Smith," somebody shouted up to him.

Then the saloon doors swung open, and out poured all the customers along with Bird and her bevy of bright-dressed girls. Everybody was out on Front Street now, laughing and looking up. Hardly anybody paid any notice to the marshal when he sauntered outside. Hardly anybody but Zena.

She watched him intently as he angled one lean hip onto a hitching rail, settled his hat more firmly on his head and then casually crossed his arms, gazing upward with all the rest. She noticed, too, the fast-draw rig that was now draped over one of his broad shoulders. The marshal had disarmed the gunfighter. Disarmed him, and then some.

The laughter of the crowd increased, and she returned her gaze to the balcony where the naked wretch was now trying to shimmy down a post to the street below.

"Take care you don't get any splinters in that little thing, honey," one of Bird's girls yelled.

Billy angled his shoulders now, blocking Zena's view. "You best not watch, Miz Zena," he said with some authority.

She bit down on a grin and managed to say, quite seriously, "I suppose you're right, Billy." Then she returned to the settee. Smiling.

It was well after midnight, judging from the ragged strains of music that filtered down the street from Bird's, when Tom came home. From her open window, Zena heard the front door open and close softly. Then, when she heard the soft creak of the stairs, she tossed back the covers and rushed to her closed bedroom door.

Her hand was on the knob and her heart was thumping against her ribs when she realized she was wearing only her thin cotton nightdress. What in the world did she think she was doing?

His footsteps paused at the top of the stairs.

"I kept your supper warm," she said softly through the door, pressing her forehead to the wood's cool surface.

There was no response for a moment, but then his voice came from mere inches away, just on the other side of her door.

"It's late."

From the deep, whiskey tinge of his voice, she knew that the marshal had drunk his supper tonight. Plenty of it, too.

"Go back to bed, butterfly."

So close! Her heart leapt into her throat, fluttering there, and Zena couldn't speak, imagining Tom on the other side of her door, his forehead pressed just above her own, his fingertips touching the smooth, cool oak.

"I wanted..." she began, but her voice failed her.

"What?" came the deep whisper. "What did you want?"

She cleared her throat. "I wanted to commend you for this afternoon, for the way you avoided violence. I was...well...surprised."

He laughed softly. "So was I."

Her eyes were closed now. "You did yourself proud, Tom. I...I just wanted you to know that."

On the other side, Tom closed his eyes and let out a rough sigh. The dark hallway seemed to shift perilously under his feet so he leaned his forehead against the door. "I didn't do anything, butterfly. Save your congratulations for Fat Alice."

"I don't understand."

No, he thought. She wouldn't. And he was at a loss to explain to the sheltered butterfly that over the years he had garnered some knowledge of Pawnee Jack's proclivities in bed. To put it bluntly, the man was an unnatural goat. But Fat Alice was no she-goat, and she outweighed him by a good fifty or sixty pounds. So he had merely followed Smith up the stairs, then bided his time in the hall until events unfolded, so to speak, and Fat Alice had bellowed.

Tom smiled a bit sloppily now, remembering the sight of Alice, standing like a big pink mountain, cramming Pawnee Jack through the window. All Tom had done was reach in and lift the man's fancy gun belt from a peg on the wall.

"You disarmed a dangerous gunman," Zena whispered through the door.

"More or less."

"Without resorting to violence," she added. "I thought you behaved heroically."

His grin faded. Some hero. "It doesn't always work out that way, Zena," he muttered. "Go back to sleep now."

"All right. Tom?"

"What?"

"You're a fine lawman."

"Yeah. Good night, butterfly."

Chapter Seven

With a lunch basket in one hand and a hot pot of coffee in the other, Zena could barely hitch up her skirt to keep from tripping on the stairs to the jail house. Precarious as her balance was, she halted halfway up to look back at Tom's dog. Fool animal! He still wouldn't attempt the open staircase without twenty minutes of cajoling.

"Come on, Silky," she called.

The dog stared up at her blankly, making no effort to mount the stairs.

Zena sighed. For a month now she'd been trying out names on him to no avail. He simply wouldn't respond. Or, if he did, it was to growl or grunt, and in one case to cover his ears with his paws. His reaction or lack thereof only made her more determined than ever to come up with the perfect name for the black-and-white beast.

"That a boy, Skunk." She clucked her tongue. "Come on."

He folded his back legs, sitting, stirring up dust with his tail.

Exasperated, Zena turned and continued up the stairs. Once inside, she set the basket and coffeepot on the marshal's desk, then went to the window.

They'd finished painting the train depot weeks ago. It sat beside the tracks, gleaming white in the summer sun. Now the air rang every day with the sound of saws and hammers as they hurried to construct the new cattle pens nearby. A herd of Texas longhorns, the first of the year, was due in any day. A few land speculators from the East had been snooping around, hiring buggies and putting their heads together with Mayor Porter. The laundry from Bird's had increased from two baskets a week to three. Glory, to all appearances, was booming. All of it thanks to the fastest gun in the West.

She caught a glimpse of him now, scrunching his head down a few inches to clear the door frame as he came out of the telegraph office in the depot, then straightening up and launching into that long, smooth stride of his that she was beginning to know so well. Much as she loved watching him, Zena stepped back from the window. Tom seemed to have a sixth sense when it came to people looking at him. And he caught her much too often.

Too often for what they were to each other. Landlady and boarder. Acquaintances. Possibly friends. Certainly not lovers. He'd kept his promise not to kiss her again.

Irritated at the direction in which her thoughts were straying, Zena went to the desk, emptied the lunch basket and arranged the meal on a small linen cloth. Then she rearranged it, moving the sweet pickles to the left and the hard-boiled eggs to the right, refolding the checkered napkin. Dawdling, she knew very well, and yet she couldn't help it. It was always so good to see him in the middle of the day, standing at first like a black shadow in the bright doorway, then moving into the room with the slow grace of a panther.

She turned toward the door in anticipation, her fingers toying with a button on the bodice of her dress, then flitting up to make certain her hair was somewhat in place after a morning spent over a steaming tub of wash.

The nice thing was, she thought, Tom never seemed to notice if her dress was damp from doing wash or her hair was bedraggled or her hands red and raw. Those gray eyes of his were always appreciative, as if she were indeed as beautiful as . . . well . . . a butterfly.

Her fingers began drumming on the desk top. If she didn't get the rest of the wash hung soon, it wouldn't be ready to iron. Then it would be well nigh six o'clock and dinner would be only half-done. Where in tarnation was he? It shouldn't have taken those long legs of his more than a minute or two to cover the distance between the depot and the jail house.

And why in tarnation was she being so silly, hanging around the marshal's office like a schoolgirl when she ought to be home hanging wash? With a little shrug, she picked up the empty basket and headed for the door. The noontime sun made her blink as she came outside. She had expected to be met by a happy wag and a woof from the nameless hound, but instead, at the bottom of the stairs, she was greeted by the sight of Nettie Fisk—in skimpy green silk—twined like a honeysuckle vine around Tom. It was hard telling who was kissing the daylights out of whom.

It wasn't so hard, though, to see that there wasn't a speck of daylight between them. And when Tom's hand slid up Nettie's thigh, grasped her rump and pulled the prostitute even closer, Zena had seen quite enough.

She slammed the jail house door and stomped down the staircase. "Don't mind me," she snapped as she whisked past the two lovers. If either one of them was aware of her presence, she didn't know. If they broke the kiss long enough to acknowledge her passage, she didn't care. She hurried home as fast as her feet would carry her.

Ironing didn't help to cool her temper or lift her spirits. It did, however, give her time to ponder her bruised feelings and to try to define them.

"I am not jealous," she hissed as she repositioned the sheet on her ironing board.

The dog, sprawled on the kitchen floor just inside the back door, lifted his head and looked around as if to see who she was talking to.

Zena scowled at him. "Jealousy is an ugly, wicked emotion, and I'll have no part of it." She sprinkled the fabric vigorously and it steamed when she put the hot iron to it once more, pressing down hard. "Besides, it's obvious your master prefers Nettie to me. So, let him, I say. He's entitled to his preferences. We all are."

With a sigh, the dog lowered his muzzle to the floor while his eyes remained on Zena.

"I have my own preferences," she continued. "Steady and dependable men. Men with gentle dispositions. Like Eldon."

Her late husband's name caught in Zena's throat. It had been weeks since she'd even thought about him. Instead she'd been lying awake at night, dreaming about Tom Bolt. When she wasn't dreaming, she was reading the books she'd surreptitiously borrowed from Billy. Reading how the man moved from town to town, from gunfight to gunfight, from woman to woman.

Her eyes narrowed on the dog, as if he were partly responsible for his master's behavior. "He's had his share of women, hasn't he?" She sniffed, recalling Philo Gordon's vivid descriptions of the gunslinger's manly desires and obvious prowess. "More than his share. Enough to satisfy a regiment."

She put the iron back on the stove top and folded the warm sheet.

"Well, anyway, I'm not interested in any man who visits Bird's," she announced to the dog and the room in general. Her words seemed to hover in the hot kitchen air, buzzing like flies.

What was she saying? She had married a man who visited Bird's. Visited *her* there, as a matter of fact.

She tossed the sheet into the basket of finished laundry. Maybe it was time for her to pay a visit to her former place of employment, she thought, just to see what was going on there that wasn't going on here.

It was Nettie Fisk who answered Zena's knock on the back door. The redhead's smile evaporated as soon as she saw who was standing there. She gave her long hair a contemptuous toss, then turned and walked away, leaving Zena standing out in the back alley until Bird appeared.

"You ought to have let Billy bring that back," the madam said, pointing a long, crimson-tipped finger at the laundry basket in Zena's arms. "That's what I pay him for."

"I'd like to talk with you, Bird." Zena shifted the heavy burden onto her hip. "May I come in?"

The buxom blonde made a clucking sound with her tongue then stuck her head out the door and looked up and down the alley. "It's not right, your being here," she cautioned, motioning Zena inside. "I told you ten years ago, the day you walked out, you'd be foolish to come back even for a visit. 'Let folks just forget,' I said, didn't I?"

Zena laughed as she set the basket on a chair. "I keep forgetting just what a mother hen you are."

Bird closed the back door and latched it. "There are some who need it more than others, my girl."

"Does Nettie Fisk?"

One of Bird's plucked eyebrows assumed a higher arch. "Why would you care anything about Nettie?"

"Just curious," said Zena with an air of feigned nonchalance she hoped would sound convincing.

"Nettie looks out for herself," Bird replied. "I can't say I like her much."

"The marshal seems rather fond of her."

Now Bird's other eyebrow climbed to match the first. "Is that what this is about?"

It was, but Zena hadn't expected to let the curious cat out of the bag quite so soon. She felt her face begin to prickle and burn.

"Sit down," Bird commanded.

Zena did as she was told, shoving the laundry basket onto the floor. Bird aimed her bustled backside onto another chair, spent a moment or two readjusting her low-cut bodice and the silken gathers of her skirt, then tapped her long red nails on the table.

"I don't ordinarily pass on information about my customers' comings and goings," she said, "but I will tell you this. Tom Bolt hasn't been upstairs with Nettie or any of my girls. And don't look so surprised. The word around here is it's because there's a certain widow who's, well, taking care of his needs."

Zena felt her eyes nearly pop out of her head. "I'm not," she blurted.

The madam didn't say anything. She just sat there, her gaze cool and level, making Zena squirm like a child caught in a lie.

"I'm not lying, Bird." Her face felt on fire now and her tongue tripped over her teeth as she tried to explain. "It isn't that . . . that I haven't thought about it. About the marshal, I mean. Only . . . only he doesn't have any interest in me. Not that way. I think he regards me as much too prim and proper. Or . . . or else . . ." Her voice shrank to a dull whisper. "Or else he knows I used to be a whore and he doesn't want to have anything to do with me."

Across the table, the madam exploded with laughter, so much so that her ample bosom was barely contained in her dress. "Oh, honey, that's rich," she finally managed to say, wiping tears from both eyes. "You used to be a whore the way I used to be Queen Victoria."

"Well, I was."

Bird shook her head. "Yes, you were, Zena. For all of five minutes. Eldon Briggs took you up those stairs out there, talked to you, maybe kissed you a little, then proposed marriage. He didn't even take you till your wedding night, and I know that for a fact." She tapped a finger just above her cleavage. "Don't forget who used to do the laundry around here in the old days."

Glum now, Zena crossed her arms and chewed her lip until Bird broke the silence.

"I don't know what to tell you, honey. The marshal has a few beers every night, plays cards once in a while, but mostly he just sits by his lonesome back in a corner, keeping his eyes on the door and his hands to himself. Maybe the man's sworn off women. Maybe his equipment isn't working right, although Nettie swears that can't be the case." Bird shrugged. "All I know is he's not using it around here."

At supper that night Tom didn't know what to make of Zena's mood. She wasn't mad exactly, and she didn't strike him as sad, just quiet and self-contained. They had been having supper together ever since that afternoon at the cemetery. Neither one had said anything or issued an invitation; it just seemed to happen. Tom was glad. He liked seeing her pretty face down at the other end of the table each evening. Usually, though, her mood was bright. Not now though. This evening she was like a chrysalis deep in a cocoon, lost in her own thoughts. Disapproving, perhaps.

He wondered if she was thinking about this afternoon when Nettie had had him plastered against a wall. The redhead was persistent, he had to say that, and any man would have to have ice water in his veins to resist her completely. He hadn't resisted—completely. Hell, his body was still ringing like a damn bell.

"You're quiet this evening," he finally said.

Her eyes snapped to his. Then her tongue snapped. "Am I?"

Oh, Lord, Tom thought. He was walking right into this like a blind man in a mine field. He put his fork down. "What's on your mind, Zena?"

"Nothing."

Her lips were beginning their thinning process now. She hadn't done that in quite a while, and Tom realized he'd forgotten how that lush mouth of hers could tighten down at the corners and nearly disappear in the middle. She continued to eat, but it was a wonder she could even get a fork between those battened-down lips.

"Something's bothering you," he pressed.

Her fork clattered onto her plate. "If you must know, I don't approve of your behavior this afternoon."

It didn't come as a surprise. Tom couldn't say he particularly approved of the spectacle he and Nettie had made outside the jail house, either, but he hadn't been using his head at the time. What did surprise him, though, was his sudden urge to pursue the subject, to prod and press the inchworm until that prim exterior cracked or even exploded.

He cocked his head. "My behavior, or who I was behaving with, or where we were at the time?"

"Both. All of them."

"What if it had been you, butterfly?"

"I beg your pardon?"

He folded his napkin with slow deliberation and placed it perfectly parallel to the edge of the table, precisely an inch from his plate. Then he pushed his chair back and stood. "You heard me. I asked, what if it had been you?"

Zena squirmed beneath his unrelenting gaze. "I wouldn't. Not there. Out on the street for all the world to see."

"Where then?"

"What?" Her voice was little more than a dry croak. She could hardly swallow, watching Tom coming toward her with an expression on his face so intense she didn't know whether he was going to strike her or spring on her like a black panther. Or—her heart somersaulted in her chest—ravage her with kisses.

"Where would it be civilized and suitable to behave that way?" he asked, standing beside her chair now.

Zena dropped her gaze to her lap and whispered, "In private, perhaps. At home."

"Home?" he pressed, his voice a low taunt, one hand gesturing to encompass the room. "Here?"

"I . . . I suppose."

"I didn't quite catch that," he purred.

"Yes. Here."

"Now?"

Her chin snapped up, and her mouth opened to protest but there were no words. She was caught in the gray glint of his gaze. Her heart fluttered wildly, and she felt like a butterfly, shivering as the net swooped toward her, as the gunfighter scooped her up in his arms.

"Now," he rasped just before his mouth closed over hers.

Instinctively Zena's hands balled into tight fists against the hard curve of his chest. She twisted her head to escape the fierce possession of his lips, but a strong hand at the back of her neck prevented it. His hot breath seared her cheek and an insistent thumb on her jaw repositioned her mouth below his.

"Open for me, butterfly," he whispered hoarsely against her lips, tasting her, teasing the seam with his tongue.

"Yes." The word had barely been spoken when he deepened the kiss hungrily. Zena's arms rose to curl around his neck, holding on as waves of pleasure swept through her.

His fingers tore through her hair, scattering pins and sending her thick tresses cascading down her back and spilling over his hands. Even as he was drowning in the sweet depths of her mouth, Tom was cursing himself. But wrong as it was—wrong as anything he'd ever done in his life—he couldn't keep his hand from seeking the soft swell of her breast or dull the hot blade of desire when her nipple hardened to his touch.

She moaned softly, and he widened his stance, allowing her to move her hips into the cradle of his, absorbing her motions, being absorbed by them until his brain was nothing but mist and fire, hot longing and cold, cold restraint.

He'd never wanted a woman so badly in his life, he thought, and it had nothing to do with his celibate state. He could have bedded all the whores at Bird's a dozen times each and still have felt this piercing need for the lovely widow all warm and willing in his arms now. If this was love, he thought grimly, it had come to him on the wings of a butterfly, and much too late.

He broke the kiss, setting her away from him, then nearly knocked her over as he shoved past her on his way to the stairs, which he took in a few long strides.

Weak-kneed, Zena leaned a hip against the table as her glazed eyes tried to bring the dining room back into focus. She wasn't sure if she had done something wrong to cause Tom to leave her so abruptly and go tearing off to his room, or if she'd done everything right. She didn't know how these things proceeded between two people. Between two lovers. For surely they were much more than friends after that soul-searing kiss and the way his hands had moved over her with such ardent possession. Surely he knew that she was willing to consummate this passion. More than willing. Eager.

Overhead, she heard the ring of his boot heels and the sound of drawers opening and closing. Was he getting ready for her? Waiting for her to come to his room so they could consummate this sudden and astounding passion, properly, in his bed?

Not knowing what was expected of her now, Zena climbed the stairs. She stood outside his door, taking measured breaths, trying to sort out her tangled emotions. Her head had never led her astray, but now it was her heart that seemed to be propelling her toward something she might bitterly regret.

She put her hand on the doorknob. Regret kissing Tom Bolt? Regret loving him? "Never," she whispered. Then she smiled, twisted the knob and walked into the room.

He was packing!

Chapter Eight

He was leaving! She could see it in the hard set of his jaw and in the way he was stowing his shaving gear—with grim finality—in his saddlebags.

Unwilling to believe her eyes, Zena gasped. "What in the world are you doing?"

"What does it look like?" he snarled, closing the flap on one of the bags and wrenching its buckle tight. "I'm leaving, Zena."

"You can't." Dozens of reasons raced through her brain right then—how she loved listening to the way he hummed softly while he shaved, how she had become accustomed to having him across the table from her at supper whether his mood was hot or cold, and how she just loved looking at him and feeling her heart catch in her throat. But one terrible reason hovered above all the rest. If he left, she would lose her home. Quite suddenly, Zena wasn't sure which would be worse. Her hand fluttered to her mouth. "Oh, please, you can't."

He ignored her for a moment, shoving spare clothes into his saddlebag, then he stood before her, black as night, his face as hard and implacable as she'd ever seen it. He dragged in a long breath, then let it out with a rough sigh as he took both of her hands in his. "It's for the best. Believe me."

"Best for whom?" she wailed. "I know it's not best for me."

"For me then." He lowered himself onto the edge of the bed, leaning forward, his elbows on his knees. "I'll take my gear down to Bird's tonight. She offered me a room when I first came to town."

"I see."

"No, you don't." He shook his head wearily. "But it doesn't make any difference."

Zena sat beside him, biting her lip, afraid to tell him the truth, but at the same time terrified not to. What if she told him his leaving put her house in jeopardy, and he went ahead in spite of it? Her losses would be compounded then. She wasn't sure she could bear it.

"If you go," she began in a voice barely more than a whisper, "If you go...Lemuel Porter and I had, well, an understanding about your staying here. If you go, he and his bank are going to take my house away from me."

He turned his head to simply stare at her, his face expressionless as a stone, his eyes hard and cold as granite. The grave and heartless face of a gunfighter. It occurred to her that this was probably the look that a score of men had witnessed just before meeting their deaths.

The look rattled her. Hands twisting in her lap, Zena began to stammer. "Well, I hadn't had a boarder in several years. I didn't want one. But Lemuel said I had to or else he'd stop being so lenient about my mortgage payments." She paused to take in a breath. "Of course, that was before I got to know you." And before I found myself falling desperately in love with you, she wanted to add.

He didn't say anything, but kept staring at her with those gunmetal eyes of his glittering, not with warmth, however. For the life of her, Zena couldn't figure out what emotion was sparking that odd and somehow threatening light. When he finally spoke, there was a gravelly quality to his deep voice.

"That's what this was all about then? Keeping your house?"

"Yes," she murmured, then bit her lip and corrected herself. "Well, not exactly."

His mouth twisted in a bitter smile and his lips barely moved as he echoed her words. "Not exactly? How far would you have gone, Zena? To save your precious house, I mean?"

Her jaw went slack at the accusation and her eyes widened. "I never...I wouldn't..."

"How far, Zena?" he growled, grabbing her by the shoulders and giving her a shake. "A kiss seems a pretty small price to pay for a whole damn house."

"It wasn't..."

Furious now, so furious he was afraid he might truly hurt her, Tom let her go. He ripped his fingers through his hair, cursing. What kind of fool had he been to imagine Zena Briggs as a butterfly, wound tight in her neat cocoon? The woman was a spider—and a black widow to boot—who had let him into her web and then woven the doors and windows shut.

All for her damn house! Had his kisses turned her stomach? And, dear God, if he hadn't stopped a while ago, would she have let him make love to her tonight, gritting her teeth all the while and hating every second, every touch?

He looked at her now with her dark, beautiful hair spilling over her shoulders and her blue eyes brimming with tears that only a few minutes ago he would have been happy, even eager to kiss away. The fierce hurt inside him was goading him to test her will, to see just how far the Widow Briggs would go to preserve her precious sanctuary. He fought down the urge to kiss her, to consume her with all of his passion and rage, to make her love him more than she loved a damn house. He was tempted to make her pay dearly for the desires that had nothing to do with him. And yet he knew he couldn't.

If he ever hurt this woman, he thought grimly, it wouldn't be on purpose. He'd die before he hurt her. Maybe, with luck, he would.

"Your cocoon is safe, butterfly," he told her quietly.

Her tears brimmed over now, catching in the corners of her smile. "You'll stay? Here? With me?"

Tom nodded. For as long as he stayed in Glory anyway, he thought. For as long as he could stay here and alive.

Down in the kitchen, Zena could hear Tom's footsteps overhead, moving methodically, putting back what he had packed. Every once in a while a drawer slammed, hard. After he had promised her he wouldn't leave, and after she'd stopped crying those silly tears, she had tried to tell him it wasn't just the house she was afraid of losing, but he had refused to listen. In fact, he'd gotten downright furious all over again and told her to shut up and get out of his room. Then, when she'd reached out to touch his arm in gratitude, he had exploded like a bomb and practically shoved her out the door.

But he was staying! She smiled as she took a plate from the rinse water and rubbed it dry. The marshal was staying. Lemuel Porter wouldn't be knocking on her door with an eviction notice tomorrow, telling her she hadn't lived up to her part of the bargain. As for Tom, if he had gotten it into his head that everything she had done was for the sake of her mortgage, that every kind word and every kiss had been calculated for that reason alone, she'd just have to set him straight. The truth of it was that she had almost forgotten about her bargain with the banker until Tom had threatened to leave.

When she lifted up on tiptoe to put the dry china plate on its shelf in the cupboard, the sight of all that delicate dinnerware made her frown. It looked so fragile, so breakable. One good tug on the shelf, one violent movement could bring the whole thing down with a resounding crash. What was she doing being so glad this violent, gun-toting man was sharing her home? Worse, what was she doing even considering loving him, opening her body as well as her heart to him?

Her heart, she thought as she stared at the contents of the cupboard, had to be at least that fragile. Why in the world would she even dream of offering it to the infamous Tom Bolt? To a man whose sensibilities were so hardened by now that he couldn't even bring himself to christen a dog? Whatever was she doing, loving a man who couldn't possibly love her back?

She gave a little start when she heard the screen door bang shut. Slamming the cupboard closed a little harder than she'd intended, Zena rushed to the front door.

"Tom," she called a little breathlessly to the dark figure already at the bottom of the porch steps.

He stopped but didn't turn around, and Zena could see his shoulders lift and his back expand as if he were drawing in a long, slow breath. Then he answered her coolly. "Don't worry. I'm just headed for my evening rounds."

Those, Zena knew by now, consisted of one brisk walk down Front Street and one long evening at Bird's. "I wasn't worried." She wrapped her arms around herself against the early evening chill, adding quietly, "No more than usual anyway."

He didn't reply, but shrugged slightly and started toward the saloon. Zena stood there watching his black-clad form beginning to blend with the oncoming dark.

She was about to turn and walk back into the house when a shrill voice called out from down the street.

"You! Tom Bolt! Say your prayers, mister."

What happened next was like watching a nightmare taking place before her wide-open, horrified eyes. Tom dropped to the dirt at the same instant shots were fired and bullets bit into the street, sending up little plumes of dust just inches from his body. She never saw him reach for his gun, but it was in his hand all of a sudden and he was rolling over and over, twisting toward the sidewalk while his Colt exploded again and again, fire flashing from its muzzle like the hot red tongue of a dragon.

For a moment everything was quiet, except for the sound of her own hitched breathing. And then, down the street, a man staggered from the doorway of the mercantile and fell to his knees on the sidewalk. At first Zena thought he was wearing a red shirt, but when he crawled into the lamplight, she saw it was a white shirt soaked with blood.

Her stomach wrenched. She closed her eyes and clasped her arms more tightly around herself, trying to erase the sight from her mind, trying to force back the bile that was rising in her throat, trying to believe that

Tom was all right. With every ounce of her being, willing him to be all right.

By the time she opened her eyes, she couldn't see Tom anymore for the crowd that had flocked around him. Dear God! A second later she was running down the street, then clawing at sleeves and shouldering her way through the crowd, barely able to see now through the tears that blurred her eyes.

He stood there—dusty as the street itself, his sweat-beaded face streaked with dirt—surrounded by gawkers and backslappers, trying to reholster his revolver, but unable to for all the hands that were reaching out to touch the gun and to grab at his sleeves. He stood there alive and, for all that she could see, unharmed. Zena let her breath out now in pure relief.

"Thank God," she whispered.

"I'd say we ought to be thanking Tom Bolt instead, Zena." Lemuel Porter jostled her arm, then appealed to the crowd. "What do you say, folks? Three cheers for our marshal, Glory's great and undefeated Tom Bolt. Hip, hip, hooray!"

While the crowd took up the mayor's cheer, Zena moved toward Tom. She found she wanted to touch him, too, not to claim a piece of his fame, but rather to further reassure herself that he was still warm and solid. When she reached out her hand, though, he drew away.

"Don't," he told her sharply, stabbing her with a look as hard and cold as the blade of a knife.

"Tom, I just..." Unable to refrain, she reached out to him once more.

This time he caught her wrist, gripping it hard. "Don't," he warned her again.

"But why?" She couldn't understand why he was refusing her, why he was glaring at her as if she had been the one shooting at him. "Why?"

He answered her in a voice so low only she could hear.

"Don't touch me, butterfly. I'm dirty."

When he released his grip on her wrist and turned away from her, Zena knew he meant more than just the dust covering his clothes.

That night she couldn't sleep. No amount of tossing and turning induced an ounce of comfort or a moment's respite from her worries. The music coming from Bird's was louder and more raucous than usual, and there were continual hoots and hollers on the street. Zena kept jamming her fist into her pillow. Once she even stalked to the window, sorely tempted to yell for the whole town to settle down and be quiet.

It wasn't right, celebrating death like that. It just wasn't decent. She had said a prayer for the stranger in the blood-covered shirt, the man whose name nobody knew, whom they had carted off unceremoniously to the undertaker's. And she had prayed for his killer, too. For Tom. For the man who had had no choice but to kill or be killed this evening. She had witnessed it herself, and she understood. But still...

She must have drifted off, for she woke with a start when she heard the stairs creak. The footsteps coming up were heavier than she'd ever heard before, as if the incident tonight were a burden on his shoulders. Or maybe that was just her imagination running away with her, she thought. Perhaps the heavy tread was simply the result of too much whiskey down at Bird's. Whiskey to wash away the dust and the dirt.

She got out of bed, then tiptoed to the door, listening as Tom's door closed with a little click. Silently she went out into the dark hallway, all the while asking herself just what it was she thought she was doing, and not being able to come up with an answer. Only a feeling. An urgent need to go to him.

He always hung his gun belt on the bedpost, and she listened for the dull thump of the heavy holster making contact with the wood. Next came the distinct and separate thuds of boots hitting the floor. She crept a little closer to his door and heard the sound of water splashing from pitcher to basin.

Ordinary sounds, she thought. Like a man coming home from a long day's work. Taking off his boots and washing up. An ordinary day. Only it wasn't. There was nothing ordinary about it. Those mundane sounds disturbed her, echoed hollowly in her heart. Tom Bolt had killed a man today. Had he gotten over it so quickly? Was it over and done with tonight? Just another notch on his gun?

Her mouth turned down in dismay. She couldn't pretend to understand a man of such ingrained violence, and she wasn't sure now that she even wanted to. Again she recalled that a man just like this one had, with a single errant bullet, taken all that was dear to her. She was about to return to her room and leave the gunslinger to his casual washing up, when she heard a low, gut-wrenching moan.

Zena stopped dead in her tracks. What she heard next was a distinct and almost painful retching, followed by a string of muted curses. She crept closer, hearing the ropes creak under his mattress and then the thud of a big fist in a pillow. Then a sound—what was it?—that drew her like a magnet mere inches from the door.

She pressed her ear to its smooth surface. She held her breath, and then her heart held still as she listened to a choked, almost strangled, noise that sounded for all the world like somebody crying. And then there was nothing. Just black silence.

Chapter Nine

It wasn't too long after sunup that Zena was pouring a practice griddle cake in her cast-iron skillet. She had stayed awake all night in order to get down to the kitchen before Tom did the next morning. After a night like that, she thought, a man shouldn't have to fix his own coffee. He ought to have a good breakfast, too, to put back what he'd lost. Lost from his stomach, not to mention his soul.

How she'd wanted to comfort him, to hold him in her arms, to soothe away his tears and his pain. But she hadn't. He had warned her earlier not to touch him, and she didn't think he'd appreciate a witness to his agony. Sadly, too, he might believe she was just using it as another opportunity to secure her house.

Well, she'd take care of him this morning, she thought, as she watched the batter come to a bubble in the skillet, then flipped the pancake over. When it was done, she put it on a tin plate and stepped out the back door, scanning the yard for a moment before calling out.

"Here, Ebony. Come on and get your breakfast, boy."

The dog regarded her with mild indifference as it lay by the pump. His tail gave two quick thrashes, then settled down.

"Ebenezer," Zena called. "That's a good dog. Come on."

The animal didn't move. With a sigh and a vow that she would indeed find the perfect name for the beast, Zena put the plate down on the porch boards and went back into the kitchen.

A deep voice greeted her. "Good morning."

Tom was standing at the stove, pouring coffee, looking only slightly pale beneath his shadowed cheeks and jaw, looking less like the victim of a rough night than a man who was ready to begin an ordinary day. If she hadn't heard his grief with her own ears, she'd be tempted to believe the gunfighter had no feelings at all beneath that hard mask he wore.

But she *had* heard, and it was difficult not moving to put her arms around him now, so instead she went to the cupboard for a saucer and placed it on the table, then came back to give her batter a brisk stir. "I'm making griddle cakes for you."

He sipped from his cup, eyeing her over the rim. "What's the occasion?"

She gazed at him a moment—on closer inspection she noted his wrung-out, red-eyed visage—and yearned to tell him what was in her heart, but she wasn't even sure she knew. "Just breakfast," she said with all the brightness she could muster. "Go sit and have your coffee while I get it going."

Tom pulled out a chair, straddled it and sat. The last thing he'd expected this morning was to come downstairs and find the butterfly flitting happily around her kitchen, her thin cotton wrapper clinging softly to her body and her hair spilling down her back in a long, loose braid. He had thought to encounter the inchworm, measuring him with her cool eyes and the fine line of her mouth, measuring him and making it plain she found him worthless. She wouldn't have been far off the mark, either, he thought, taking another sip of coffee then placing the china cup carefully in its saucer.

No, that wasn't quite true. He was worth a great deal to Glory. The mayor had told him so last night. So had the editor of the *Gazette* and a dozen other backslapping, hand-shaking idiots. And, he remembered grimly—as if he could forget—he was worth a whole damn house to the Widow Briggs.

She was stirring up a little storm, then pouring batter and catching the last drip on her finger and licking it, sending a shower of sparks through Tom's body. He kept forgetting she wasn't a butterfly at all, but a spider who kept spinning silken, sticky threads he couldn't seem to find his way out of. This warm show of domesticity was designed to keep him here, and nothing else. How she must hate it, especially after the gun show last night.

Last night! Hell, he was lucky to be alive, so why didn't he feel lucky? All he felt was old and worn-out. Too tired and sick at heart to keep doing what he'd had to do out on the street, but not ready to give it up yet when that meant giving up his life. Not yet.

What he needed to do was get out of Glory. Now. Before more men came to try for a different kind of glory by killing him and taking on his reputation. That's about the way he had put it to the mayor last night when he'd handed him back the badge in a dark corner of the saloon.

Lemuel Porter had acted as though the tin star were burning a hole in his hand. He jabbed the pin back through Tom's vest. "You can't quit. We had a deal, Marshal."

Only a miracle had kept Tom from sinking his fist into the man's belly. "You've been making deals with just about everybody in town, Mayor, or so I hear."

"I take it Zena's been talking out of turn?"

"You take whatever you want, Lemuel, and put it wherever you want. If I had known you were making her have me as a boarder against her will, I'd never have moved in there. So your deal's off. And so am I just as soon as I can get my gear together."

Hell, Tom thought now, he should have known better. He might be good with a gun, but he was no match for somebody who was good with money and the power that went with it. Not in this case anyway.

The mayor's expression had hardened like the face on a coin. "If you don't want to stay at Zena's, it's fine with me. I won't hold that against her. But the day you leave Glory, Bolt, I'm not only taking the Briggs place, I'm burning it to the ground."

Tom had tried not to flinch. "Not a very good way to treat an investment, Lemuel."

"You're my investment, Marshal. The whole town's placed its stock in you, and you're not going to let us down. Are you?"

The only one he couldn't let down was the butterfly, Tom thought now. And damned if he knew why.

She placed a stack of pancakes on the table before him. The steam rose, tickling his face. The rising warmth and aroma called to mind so many other mornings. Home. Hannah and the boy. All that he had ever lost. The butterfly he'd never have even long enough to lose. God.

His stomach clenched and he thought he was going to be sick again so he pushed his chair back and headed out the back door.

Zena was closing up the warming oven when there was a knock on the back door. Billy walked in, a basket brimming with dirty laundry in his arms, his nose twitching. "Griddle cakes! Lordy, don't those smell good."

The boy was hunkered down at the table over a syrupy plate when Tom came back in. "Mornin', Marshal," he mumbled out of the side of his full mouth. "You eat yet?"

"Not much appetite this morning," Tom said, sending Zena an apologetic little smile.

Billy forked in a last bite of breakfast, then jumped up, wiping his sleeve across his mouth. "I'm ready whenever you are."

Zena glanced from Billy to Tom. "Well, now, what are you two up to this fine Saturday morning?"

Tom shrugged as the lanky youth gave his holster a pat. "The marshal's taking me out to the creek for some target practice."

She was shocked. No, dammit, she was outraged that Tom would even consider such a thing especially after last night. What did he think he was doing, egging Billy on this way? She was about to give the gunslinger a good piece of her mind when he told the boy to wait for him outside.

After the door banged shut behind Billy, Tom said, "If he doesn't get a little guidance, Zena, he's going to get himself killed."

"Guidance!" She nearly spat his word back at him. "Why don't you guide him properly and tell him to quit wearing that confounded firearm?"

His mouth quirked into a lazy grin. "When was the last time you tried telling a sixteen-year-old boy to do something?"

"Well, stop setting him such a bad example." She crossed her arms and glared at him. "Quit wearing your gun and maybe he'll do the same."

He laughed, a short, almost brutal little gust of laughter, then pinned her with his steely gaze. "I appreciate the advice," he growled. "And I just might take it one of these days, lady. Whenever I get good and ready to commit suicide, that is."

The back door was slamming behind him before she could reply.

"Suicide." The word escaped Zena's lips in a soft hiss as she leaned back in the warm hip bath. She'd barely been able to think of anything else all morning while heating kettle after kettle of water for her bath.

Tom was right, of course. If he hadn't been wearing his gun last night, he'd be dead this morning. That notion sickened her, but what disturbed her almost as much was his saying he just might do it one of these days. If he hated his reputation so much, she wondered, why didn't he just go off where nobody could follow, the way he had before?

She frowned as she soaped her washrag. If Tom quit being marshal and just left town, surely Lemuel wouldn't hold Zena to account. How could he take her house for something that wasn't her fault?

"Oh, who cares about a damn, empty house anyway?" she snarled, nearly grinding the rag over the soap now.

You did, Zena, she told herself. After losing Eldon and the baby, the house had meant everything to her. It came to be like a living thing, requiring love and constant care, demanding her thoughts and her energy, not to mention the hard work necessary to scrape together each month's mortgage payment.

But somehow that had all changed with the arrival of the gunslinger. Her thoughts had turned to Tom more and more, and as the marshal was taking up more and more room in her heart, her house and her precious possessions were slowly being eased aside. She tried to recall the last time she had even looked at her music box collection—those treasured mementos of her four years with Eldon. It had probably been a week or two since she'd even thought to dust them.

If Tom left now, the house would feel like a dry, empty husk rather than a warm cocoon. And he would go. Dear God, he *should* go rather than stay here just to be a tourist attraction and a magnet for every crazy, quick-drawing fool west of the Mississippi and north of the Rio Grande.

If he stayed...

Zena sighed, slipping down a bit farther in her bathtub, losing herself in vague and impossible dreams.

The day had turned hot with a big, relentless circle of sun and a stiff breeze coming in off the prairie. Tom had left Billy Dakin at the creek. The boy was determined to shoot up every bottle and tin can in Kansas. He was getting fairly proficient, though, Tom had to admit. Not all that fast maybe, but accurate. Dead on target. In the long run, that lethal accuracy counted for a lot more than speed. And, God, in the long run, how he hoped the boy would use his head half as much as he was dying to use his gun.

"Come on, fella," he called now to his dog who had chased a squirrel up a bur oak at the edge of town and was looking like he was about to sit and wait till the red-tailed varmint came down. "Let's go home, boy."

Home. The word came so easily, Tom thought. Too easily. Hell, it wasn't his home. It was Zena's. She'd spent the morning trying hard to keep it, too, with hot coffee and griddle cakes. It was plain she didn't know she wouldn't lose it if he made the move down the street to Bird's. As far as he could see right now, that didn't make much sense. It might take care of the persistent ache in his groin, but he was on his way to being a corpse whether he stayed at Zena's or Bird's or any-place else in Glory. Being a corpse, or creating more for the undertaker the way he had last night.

The dog raced ahead of him now, sniffed around Verna Campbell's flower garden, then lifted his leg on the petunias.

"Scat!" The elderly Mrs. Campbell shot from her rocker on the porch, a rolled-up copy of *The Glory Gazette* in her fist. "Go on with you."

The animal did exactly that, scuttling away in a flurry of black and white as Tom halted in front of the porch. He touched the brim of his hat.

"Afternoon, Mrs. Campbell."

"Oh, Marshal," the woman said, somewhat flus-tered. "I didn't see you there." She fidgeted with the paper in her hand. "I wasn't going to whack him. Just figured on spooking him away from my petunias be-fore he drowned them."

Tom grinned. "Yes, ma'am."

She unfurled the newspaper, waving it at him like a flag. "Have you seen this morning's *Gazette?* That must have been quite a spectacle last night. I don't know how I managed to sleep through all that gunfire, but I did." She clucked her tongue. "Such a vicious man."

Tom winced imperceptibly, thinking she meant him, but then the woman leaned over her porch rail and positively beamed.

"Glory's in good hands, Marshal Bolt," she asserted. "We're all right proud of you."

"Thank you, ma'am." The words stuck in his throat like dry bread crust. He didn't know if the man he had gunned down was vicious or not. He didn't even know his name. All he knew was that Tom Bolt and his reputation remained unscathed and that more nameless, *vicious* men would be headed for Glory—if they weren't already here, hiding in shadowy doorways, invisible behind window curtains, sighting down from rooftops.

"You keep up the good work, now, you hear!" Mrs. Campbell called after him as he continued down the street, alert as always to the possibility of danger, his right arm never truly relaxed and his hand forever the merest blink of an eye, a fraction of a heartbeat from the butt of his Colt.

It was, he thought, a hell of an existence, always being strung so tight. Maybe he relaxed some when he slept, though he wouldn't have put money on it. Even asleep, there seemed to be a part of his brain that kept watch. He'd been doing it so long it was just second nature now. But he was starting to wake up tired, too. It wasn't like he was a twenty-year-old kid anymore.

Hardly a kid. He was thirty-eight, and all he had to show for living that long was a damn reputation—one he'd gladly pass along to any man if he only didn't have to die to accomplish that.

Just quit wearing your gun, Zena had told him. He shook his head. Just quit living, she might as well have said.

Six more people stopped him with congratulations in the space of half a block, so that, by the time Tom reached Zena's back door, his jaw ached from clenching his teeth so hard and his mood was as black as any midnight.

He was more than half tempted to collect his gear, leave the damn tin star on the dresser upstairs, tip his hat to the butterfly and get the hell out of Glory. By God, let her suck up to Lemuel Porter in order to save her confounded house. Why she hadn't done that already was a mystery to him.

Jerking open the back door, Tom stalked into the kitchen, then stood there, stunned, absolutely still, as if riveted to the floor by a bolt of lightning.

She was caught in daydreams and cooling bathwater, and like a startled rabbit trying to blend in with its surroundings, Zena sought refuge in stillness. She barely breathed as she reclined against the high back of the tub, but her heart was picking up speed, nearly clanging against her rib cage. Any minute, she thought, the metal bath tub would begin ringing like a bell.

Through the screen of her damp lashes, she could see Tom just inside the door. The curtains were drawn, but even in the dim light she could read the intensity of his gaze, the hard slant of his mouth and the stark longing etched on his face.

The humid, soap-scented air of her kitchen seemed to fill with palpable desire. The ticking of the clock and the tinny drip from the pump gave way to the sound of her heartbeat hammering in her ears, to the measure of Tom's tattered breathing and the slow rise and fall of his chest.

Like hot, noonday sun, his steady gaze was pouring over every inch of her, searing her at the same time it was caressing her, burning and blanketing. Almost against her will, Zena could feel a heavy ripening in her breasts, feel them burgeoning to rigid peaks while, deep inside her, desire unfurled like shimmering, translucent leaves.

Her heavy lids lifted to his face, and Tom could see that her eyes were a deep sapphire now, slumberous, drugged with desire the way he had first witnessed them the night he arrived. A dreamy smile—one part shy and three parts pure temptation—teased the corners of her mouth.

He dragged in a raw breath. "Kinda tough on a man's pride, Zena," he drawled, "being seduced on account of real estate."

Her lower lip snagged between her teeth and she shook her head. Her sleek arms rose to cover the lush slope of her breasts, as if she felt she had to protect herself from him somehow.

"It isn't about the house," she whispered. "Not anymore. It's about us. About you and me." She sighed softly. "I don't blame you for not believing me. There's no way I can prove it."

And now Tom shook his head. Damned if he'd ever been in such a fix in his life, not knowing whether to go or stay, to yank her out of the tub and take her right here on her clean kitchen floor or to get the hell away from her as fast as his wobbly knees would allow. What was he doing, making this beautiful, infinitely desirable and now obviously desirous woman come up with a list of reasons why he ought to make love to her? Insisting that she swear on a foot-high stack of Bibles that her motives were pure and it was only him she wanted. Demanding that she prove the unprovable.

Or was it?

He moved across the room with such violent purpose that Zena shrank back against the metal edge of the tub, regretting her flagrant, impetuous attempt to incite his passion. But he passed her without so much as a glance to race up the stairs and return a moment later, his saddlebags over his shoulder.

"Proof," he said through clenched teeth as he passed her on his way to the door. "You're about to get more than you bargained for, butterfly."

The door had hardly closed behind him before Zena was up and out of the tub, snatching a towel around herself, then running to the front window in time to see Tom stride into Lemuel Porter's bank like a man on a mission from the Almighty. Or, she thought, like a black-clad henchman of the devil.

Chapter Ten

"How much does she still owe you?" Tom slammed the heavy saddlebags onto Lemuel Porter's desk.

"Now see here," Mayor Porter sputtered as he righted the blotter and moved the inkwell a safe distance back from his paperwork. "What's the meaning of this, Bolt?"

"How much does Zena Briggs have to come up with before that house of hers is free and clear?" Tom put a boot up on the chair opposite the banker's. Bracing an arm on his knee, he leaned menacingly over the desk. "And don't tell me you don't have the figure right handy in that cast-iron trap you use for a brain, Lemuel."

The man's jowls shook and his fingers whitened on the pen in his hand, but he cleared his throat and asked almost sheepishly, "Who wants to know?"

"You're looking at him."

"Well, I..."

"Now," Tom thundered.

"Four hundred thirty-two dollars." Porter shrugged his beefy shoulders. "Give or take a few cents."

"I'll give 'em."

"I beg your pardon?" The banker ran a thick finger under his collar, then gave the knot of his striped tie a little tug. "I don't understand."

Tom lowered himself into the chair and pulled the saddlebags onto his lap. "I'm paying off Mrs. Briggs's mortgage," he said as he unbuckled a flap and thrust his hand into the bag. "I want the paperwork done today so you might want to get that started, Lemuel, while I'm counting out the money." He arched one dark eyebrow in the banker's direction. "Gold's all right, I guess?"

Porter blinked. His mouth opened, then closed and slowly curved upward. "Fine," he breathed. "Gold'll be just dandy. I'll go get the papers."

Tom was still in the bank. Zena was sure of that because she'd raced from the parlor window upstairs to her bedroom window, tripping over the towel, grabbing clean clothes from her dresser drawers as she passed. With one eye on the closed bank door, she jerked on her petticoat and knotted the tapes, then dragged her dress over her head and worked the buttons blindly.

She had a good idea what he was doing in there. Right now he was probably ripping the badge from his vest and tossing it in Lemuel's fat, flustered face. On the other hand, she hadn't the vaguest notion what she was doing climbing into her clothes as if her house were going up in flames. She wasn't going to run after him. Was she?

No, she wasn't, she vowed as she thumped a hip on the windowsill. He'd made it perfectly plain he didn't want her, or for that matter any other female in Glory. He didn't want to kiss her. He refused to take any kind of comfort from her, including griddle cakes. And then, like a fool, she'd gone and offered herself anyway, sitting down there in the kitchen—naked as the day she was born—like a backwater Venus in a tin clamshell.

He thought she was just a schemer, a conniver who only cared about four walls and a roof, who only cared about him for the sake of her property. She pushed off the sill now and stomped to the bed. He'd be coming out of the bank any minute and heading for the livery. Then he'd be riding out of town. She didn't need to watch. She'd be able to hear the hoofbeats, to feel every one of them like the beating of her own heart.

Grabbing a pillow from the head of the bed, Zena buried her face in it. Let him go, she told herself. Good riddance, too. If he could leave her so easily, then she was better off loving empty rooms. At least they didn't have anywhere to go.

"Zena!"

The front door slapped shut and Tom's deep voice thundered through the house. She barely had time to scrub a corner of the pillowcase over her wet face before he was looming in the doorway like a black specter.

"Here." His boot heels rang on the hardwood floor as he strode to the bed. He grasped her wrist then and pressed a paper into her hand. "Now it's just you and me," he growled. "If you're still interested, I'll be across the hall."

He was gone then as quickly as he'd appeared, leaving her room nearly vibrating with the sound of his voice and his fierce energy. Zena stared at the empty doorway a moment before her gaze drifted down to the paper in her hand.

It took her a long time to make sense of the document. As difficult as it was for her to read print, it was nearly impossible to decipher script, especially the scrawl of Lemuel Porter's crabbed hand. There were endless run-together words like *whereas,* and *heretofore,* and *abovementioned.* She kept losing her place even though she trailed her fingertip across each line. Each time she thought she knew what it meant, she'd go back and begin once more.

It read for all the world like a paid-up mortgage, but she struggled through it again—out loud—just to be certain. There was no mistaking the signatures at the bottom, however. Beneath Lemuel's little chicken scratch was a dark and distinct slash of a name. Thomas Bolt.

Across the hall, Tom leaned back against the headboard—one leg slung over the other, arms crossed, his hat slanted over his eyes—looking relaxed despite the fact that he was wound tight as a watch spring. And winding tighter each minute the butterfly delayed.

What was it they said about juries? he wondered. Something about the longer they deliberated, the worse it was for the defendant. Zena had taken enough time to send him to the gallows—twice.

He scraped his hat off, ran his fingers through his hair, then hid again beneath the felt brim. Of all the damn fool things!

Well, hell. It was as black and white as the mortgage paper itself. She'd come to him or she wouldn't. He'd stay or he'd go. Tonight he'd be sleeping with Zena's soft body in his arms or he'd be ten miles west of Glory, bedded down on hard ground. And beyond that...?

Beyond that he couldn't even fathom. He was used to taking one day at a time, one night at a time. Tomorrow wasn't a word or a notion that came easily to gunfighters. He'd told her that, hadn't he? That she wasn't the sort of woman a man could kiss and leave? That she wasn't some dance hall darling meant for only a quick fling? He had told her that was all he could give her, hadn't he? That he couldn't stay? So, if she came to him now, it would be with the understanding that there was no tomorrow. There would only be the here and now of their loving. If she came to him, she'd understand that, wouldn't she?

No promises. No wedding rings or marches. Those weren't his to give.

What he had given her—the house—was more for his own stiff pride. The money, mostly poker winnings, was weighing down his saddlebags anyway and was only going to be discovered one day by an enterprising undertaker who had it in his head that a man of Tom Bolt's fame might be a rich man, too. Whatever the paid-up mortgage meant, though, it wasn't generosity. For all he knew, it was a way to salve his conscience for making love to her when he knew he shouldn't, or if—miracle of miracles—his loving left her with a child.

He smiled. She'd like that, his butterfly. A baby to love and care for, to fill each nook and cranny of her cocoon.

The door opened an inch then and Tom's heart rammed against his ribs. Slowly—so slowly he thought he'd scream or explode—it opened farther.

She stood there, looking like a little girl on Christmas morning. All joy and apprehension. All eagerness and bafflement, hesitating on the threshold, worrying her lower lip.

"I don't understand," she said.

Tom shifted over on the mattress, then thumbed his hat up, disclosing his grin. "I can't say I understand it all that well myself, darlin'." He patted the empty space beside him. "Come on over here and we'll try to figure it out."

She didn't understand—any of it. Zena perched on the edge of the bed, her feet on the floor, ready to spring up at a moment's notice. She felt breathless and winded, as if she had just run a race then crossed the finish line without a clue as to whether she'd won or lost.

The home she'd struggled for six years to keep was hers all of a sudden. Bought and paid for. But she couldn't quite grasp it. Worse, she wasn't sure she should. Dealing with Lemuel Porter had been unpleasant, but maybe it was preferable to bargaining with the devil.

That was surely what Tom Bolt resembled, lying there black as midnight on her white coverlet, all lazy grace and insolent charm. A great cat with his claws sheathed.

She stared at her folded hands. "Four hundred dollars is a lot of money." Idiot! she berated herself. The man knows full well just how much it is and what he expects in return.

"Ill-gotten, most of it, from too many hours at poker tables," he said. "I'm glad it's finally doing somebody some good."

A bubble of nervous laughter rose in her throat. "I can't say I'm not glad to be out from under the mayor's thumb. I am. But now I'm beholden to you."

"No, you're not. That wasn't my intention."

"Nevertheless . . ."

His butterfly was poised for flight so he surrounded her with his arms and drew her down beside him. "Don't talk, Zena," he breathed against her ear.

"We'll talk this to death later. Right now I just want to hold you. Just hold you. Nothing more."

It took her forever to relax. Tom could feel each stiff muscle give way and hear how her breathing evened out and fell into the rhythm of his own. He held her the longest time while the warm day dwindled to dusk. There was no urgency anymore. The heat that had ripped through him earlier in the kitchen burned like bedded coals now, spreading a warm glow throughout his body. Tom breathed in the scent of her hair, replete with roses. He let his fingertips drift lightly over her shimmering skin and kept his voice low and patient as he tried to explain in a hundred different, diplomatic ways that she wasn't beholden or obligated to him, that she owed him nothing. She wasn't a woman who traded her favors no matter what was at stake. He was convinced of that now, he told her.

He couldn't, after all, just come right out and tell her how tenuous his life was without casting a dark pall over their time together, could he, or tell her that the money he'd given the banker meant nothing to him ¬ince he couldn't imagine being around to spend it?

Finally, though, out of sheer frustration, he said, "Call it conscience money, then. Or an outright gift. Whatever you want to call it, I don't expect anything in return except what you want to give me. And if that turns out to be just a how-do and a handshake, then so be it."

She was quiet a long while before she replied. Over the course of the afternoon as Tom had gone on and on about his reasons for paying off her mortgage, Zena was listening to what he wasn't saying. The words *marriage* and *future* were conspicuously absent from his speech. He wasn't saying he loved her, even though the fact that he hadn't touched her yet spoke eloquently of his care.

Conscience money, he'd called it. When she had first met him, she would have said he didn't have a conscience, but after hearing his agony the night before, Zena knew better. And, she realized, no matter how many ways he said he wanted her, Tom felt he had purchased the right to leave her.

With his warm shoulder pillowing her head now, she turned to meet the gray intensity of his gaze.

"It's my choice, then?" she whispered.

"That's right."

"What would you do, Tom Bolt, if you were me?"

His answer came on a ragged sigh. "I'd tell me to go to hell, I guess. I'd lock all my windows and doors."

It was too late, she thought. And he was already in a hell of sorts, a private damnable place deep in his soul where she might never reach him.

She sat up slowly, easing out of his embrace, then walked to the window, closed it and turned the lock. As his hooded gaze followed her, she went to the door and gave the key a deliberate twist in the lock. Then she stood by the side of the bed. "I choose," she said softly, "to lock you in."

He lay unmoving, eyeing her as warily as a cat watches the approach of a stranger. His voice was thick, catching in his throat. "You can't."

"I can." A smile touched her lips as her fingers lifted to the buttons on her bodice, beginning to ease them through. "And I will. I promise you I will."

Chapter Eleven

He let her continue, watching while her trembling fingers worked the buttons on her dress, while her eyes darkened to the color of smoke as they sought his again and again. She was all butterfly now. There was nothing of the inchworm, the prim and cautious widow who had measured him and found him lacking. Rather, she wanted him now, perhaps with a desire as fierce as his own.

It seemed to give her pleasure, that slow disclosure of inch after inch of skin. The sun had sunk below the horizon, leaving the room hovering just on the brink of dark, leaving a bronze light to burnish the sleek column of her neck and the fine slope of her shoulders.

So hot was his desire for her, so piercing his arousal, Tom had to clench his teeth against the need to reach out and bring her slow undressing to a quick, ripping halt.

He could wait, he told himself. This was right, even if he couldn't promise her anything beyond his own desperate need. He had told her that in a million dif-

ferent ways. He knew she understood he had no tomorrow to give. And still she wanted him. If it helped
her to play the temptress, to believe she could seduce
him into staying here forever, he wasn't going to argue. No sane man would, unless he was one part fool
and nine parts saint.

Standing in a pool of calico now, her courage seemed
to be faltering somewhat. Her fingers flitted to the
shoulder straps of her thin white camisole, then hovered there, suddenly shy and indecisive.

"Don't stop now, darlin'." His voice sounded like his
vocal cords had been scruffed up with sandpaper.

Hers sounded wispy. "I'm no good at this. I
don't..."

"You're perfect." Tom held out his hand. "You just
need a little encouragement, is all."

His hand was warm and dry as it engulfed hers and
drew her toward the bed. He sat beside her and his encouragement consisted of a chain of kisses draped
around her neck and drifting over her shoulders, each
kiss linked to the next by the scrape of his whiskers and
deep-throated, husky murmurs, each kiss a little hotter, a little wetter, a bit more insistent than the last. His
fingers clenched on the straps of her camisole and
dragged them down her arms. With undisguised urgency, he jerked the soft white cotton down to her
waist.

Tom's breathing altered then. It seemed deeper,
rougher at the edges. "You *are* perfect," he whis-

pered, taking the weight of one breast in his hard palm, his thumbnail grazing its rigid peak.

Zena closed her eyes, giving herself up to the warm pleasure of his touch. She drew her lower lip between her teeth in a vain attempt to stifle the moan pressing at the back of her throat, but the urgent, almost animal sound broke forth despite her efforts and her hands drew into tight fists in her lap.

"It's all right," he murmured, uncurling her fingers and licking a hot path across her palm. "Don't hold back with me, butterfly. I want all of you. Every sigh. Every sweet, soft inch." His tongue traced over her wrist. It felt like fire along a fuse as it continued up the delicate and sensitive skin of her inner arm. His hot breath penetrated her skin and seemed to catch fire inside her—a liquid fire that coursed through her and made it difficult to breathe, impossible to think.

Then he was melting her—skin and bones and all—with that errant tongue of his and those searing lips. Wonderful. It was wonderful, yet wild and dangerous somehow. She'd never melted before. Ever. With Eldon, she had merely glowed. Her husband's kisses had made her feel safe and secure and warm as a kitten on a hearth. But this! It was all raging fire and rampant lightning. Instead of glowing, Zena thought she was going to be utterly consumed.

Tom was whispering against her skin now, not words so much as the sound and feel of fire, urgent tongues of flame. Zena's head lolled back in response, and she felt as if she were floating away, light as ashes in a hot wind. Her eyes fluttered open for a moment, seeking something, anything to anchor her before she burned up and blew away.

Her gaze lifted to the gun belt slung over the carved bedpost. Her eyes widened and fastened on the black holster and the smooth-worn wooden butt of the gun stowed there. That deadly instrument, its dark wood polished from the slick of a killer's hand. The same lethal hand that was giving her such intense pleasure now. A shiver spiked through her, and she didn't know if it came from fear or desire.

Zena fought the wild emotions rising in her as Tom's mouth fastened on her breast. His tongue swirled voraciously and then his teeth closed on its sensitive peak.

A strangled cry ached in her throat. Instinctively she pushed the flat of her hands against his hard shoulders and struggled to turn away, to deflect his fierce, consuming mouth.

"Zena," he groaned, his forehead pressed to the swell of her breast and his hands clenched about her waist.

"Oh, don't," she whimpered, aware of the small voice in a corner of her brain crying out for more. "I'm . . . I'm afraid. I'm so afraid."

His grip loosened immediately and Tom drew back as if she had slapped him. When he sucked in a rough breath and lifted his head, his struggle for control was evident in the molten gray of his eyes and the taut, nearly nailed down set of his mouth. A muscle tightened in his cheek.

Then a savage curse ripped from Tom's clenched teeth. He stood, unable to even look at the butterfly he'd just terrorized and probably bruised, and walked to the window where he gripped the frame with both hands and bent his forehead to the clean, cool glass. She was afraid of him! She was absolutely terrified! Shivering beneath his hands with fear rather than desire. Dear God, was violence such a part of him now that he didn't even know how to make love to a woman anymore? Had he lost whatever gentleness he'd ever possessed? Was death itself running in his blood now rather than warm, reaffirming life?

Unable to speak, Tom could only shake his head in self-disgust. He was surprised a heart so hardened could still be pounding like a damn drum, or that blood as cold as his apparently was could keep stoking a fire below his belt line.

What kind of an animal was he, inspiring fear instead of passion? What in the name of God had he become? Not daring to return and take Zena into his arms while his control was only barely in his grasp, Tom continued to stare out the window. It was night now. Close by, the street was dark and quiet, but down by Bird's a wash of yellow light spilled onto the sidewalk with every arc of the batwing doors. The place was busy, but then he remembered that it was a Saturday night, a good time for whiskey and women and for ridding oneself of a week's pay and all the pent-up wildness.

Maybe Bird's was the remedy for what ailed him, he thought bleakly. Maybe he should have taken Nettie upstairs weeks ago whether he felt like it or not. If anybody knew how to handle the flash fires and storms of male desire, it was the ardent redhead. If anything, the violence of his needs would inflame her rather than cause fright.

If nothing else, he figured he'd better get out of this house for a while, at least till he was cooled off and more in control. He wasn't all that sorry just then to see young Billy Dakin burst through the saloon doors and head down the street in a lope.

"You looking for me, Billy?" he called down, hoping to prevent the eager youth from rushing through Zena's front door, barreling up the stairs and discovering the disheveled butterfly who was still hovering on the edge of the bed.

The boy halted at the porch steps and looked up, squinting. "That you, Marshal?"

"Yup. What do you need?"

"You. There's trouble down at Bird's. Old Jimmy Two Hats is drunker than a skunk and nobody can get him to leave."

"Where's Clete?" Tom asked. "He can handle a soused half-breed. That's what Bird pays him for."

"Jimmy said if Clete laid so much as a finger on him, he'd put a Cherokee curse on him so bad he'd be blind and deaf by sunrise." The boy shrugged his shoulders helplessly. "Clete believed him, I reckon. Anyhow, he's keeping his distance."

Tom's mouth hooked into a beleaguered grin as he pictured Bird's three-hundred-pound bartender trying to make himself invisible from the sinewy little half-breed. He sighed. "I'll be right along. You go on back and tell Bird I'll take care of it." And tell her, he added to himself, I plan to take care of some other long overdue business, as well.

Walking back to the bed, he swiped his gun belt from the post and proceeded to buckle it on.

The brisk clip of Tom's boot heels on the hardwood floor cut into Zena's thoughts. She'd been sitting there, bewildered, feeling like a child who'd been playing eagerly with matches when all of a sudden the room had gone up in flames. Four years of marriage to Eldon Briggs had taught her the rudiments of making love, but nothing of the fiery passion Tom and his touch had instilled in her. She had panicked—there was no other word for it—when that fire storm of emotion had swept through her, threatening to sweep her away with it or else leave her burnt to a crisp in its hot wake.

She knew she couldn't have stopped him with all her strength, but with a single word from her, Tom had put on the brakes immediately. Her first reaction had been a rush of relief coupled with a befuddled gratitude. Her body, after all, was still burning for him. It had been her mind that had reacted with such icy fright.

Now, however, Zena bitterly regretted her childish reaction. It was clear—from Tom's stance with his back to her at the window and from his stony silence—that he was disgusted with her. Certainly he wasn't used to women who led him blissfully down a garden path only to push him away. Probably no woman had ever done that before. Until now. The man had made her choices clear. She had chosen to make love, and then she'd reneged. He had every right to be disgusted. She was disgusted herself.

And now he was strapping on his gun belt, getting ready to leave, and she didn't know what to say or do to explain or make amends. Her glance strayed from the black holster at his hip to the hard evidence that he had wanted her and that that desire remained unsatisfied thanks to her sudden schoolgirl fears. It was all she could do to lift her eyes to meet the gray and unforgiving gaze she fully expected and rightly deserved.

But before she could look up, Tom's hand cupped her chin with exquisite gentleness and his thumb grazed softly over her cheek. In contrast, his voice was a rough, deep-throated rumble when he spoke her name, then the rumble cracked and he patched it with a gruff curse. "Well, hell." Then his hands were gently threading her arms through the loose straps of her camisole.

She hadn't even realized she'd been sitting there so exposed until he drew the fabric up to cover her, adjusting it so carefully his fingertips never even brushed her skin.

"I swear to God I'll never hurt you again," he whispered.

Hurt her? What was he saying? Her eyes lifted to meet his, but instead of the impenetrable gunmetal gray she had expected, she saw a silvery sheen of tears. Zena's heart surged into her throat and she couldn't speak as Tom bent to kiss a stunned corner of her mouth.

"I'll be back," he said softly, then turned and walked out of the room.

Bird's wasn't quiet exactly, but as soon as he came through the doors, Tom recognized the hushed tones of impending violence. Dread and excitement were in the air, thick and acrid as tobacco smoke.

Jimmy Two Hats had all ten feet of Bird's carved walnut bar to himself. The half-breed stood with one moccasined foot on the brass rail, one hand clenched around a half-empty bottle. His black eyes flicked to Tom's in the long gilded mirror. "Come and get me," they seemed to say, "if you think you can."

At nearly the same moment, Nettie sidled out of the smoke to curl around him like a cat. Her sharp little teeth sank into his earlobe as she whispered, "You take care of him, honey, and then I'll take care of you."

Tom had to remind himself that what he wanted and what he needed were not necessarily the same thing, and with that dubious promise of physical delights and victorious spoils still ringing in his head, he started toward the bar and the drunkenly defiant half-breed.

"He ain't armed, Marshal," Billy Dakin rasped close to his ear. "I already checked."

Lord, he could almost smell the boy's excitement, nearly taste the blood that young Billy was so eager to see spilled. "Look again," he growled.

Billy squinted through the smoke and whined, "He's got no gun, nor any knife that I can see. All that injun's got is half a quart of rotgut and a damn nasty disposition."

"You listen to me, son," Tom hissed, "and you listen hard if you want to live to see eighteen. I once saw a man's throat cut so fast by a broken bottle that his life's blood had poured out of him before he could get his elbows off the bar. Now you tell me again. Is that half-breed armed or not?"

The eager expression crumpled. "Yessir," Billy answered quietly, his eyes downcast.

"All right, son." There was an almost gentle, soothing note in Tom's voice now. "You go sit down and let me take care of this." His mouth crooked in a rueful little grin then and he winked sidelong at the boy. "It's what they're paying me for, I reckon."

Certain now that young Billy would remain out of harm's way, Tom sauntered forward to the bar, nodded to Jimmy Two Hats as he hitched a boot up on the brass rail, and called for Clete to bring him his own bottle of whiskey.

"Damnation!" Zena wrenched her dress over her head and shot her arms through the sleeves. Tom had misunderstood her completely. He thought he had hurt her, and she had just sat there too stupefied, too stunned by his tears and the soft touch of his hand, to tell him otherwise.

She'd never witnessed such guilt, such self-loathing on a human face before. No, that wasn't quite true. Tom had worn a similar expression after the shooting the other night. Grief etched deeper than an epitaph.

Dear God! And she had just let him walk out of here not knowing the truth. She had let him go to meet whatever fate might be waiting for him in the menacing form of a drunken Jimmy Two Hats. It wasn't the first time Jimmy had caused a ruckus at Bird's. Usually they just let him do whatever he wanted until he passed out. But now, of course, there was the new marshal to call on for help.

Doing her buttons up without even looking, she walked briskly to her room. "Fool," she berated herself in the mirror while dragging a brush through her hair. What if something happened to Tom? What if he died believing that she feared him, never knowing he was loved?

Did she love him? The face staring back at her from the looking glass was flushed and frantic. Was that the look of a woman in love or merely the residue of the heat that Tom's touch had generated in her?

She slapped the hairbrush down on the dresser. She'd decide that later. But tonight—right now—it was crucial that she let him know he hadn't hurt her, that she wasn't afraid.

Well, not of him anyway.

* * *

The first swallow of rye went down so smoothly Tom had to remind himself that he wasn't standing here drowning his troubles in drink, but rather keeping a cool and constant eye on Jimmy Two Hats. The second the half-breed let go of that bottle, Tom was going to make sure Jimmy didn't get his hand on it again. After that it would only be a matter of hustling him across the street to the jail and letting him sleep it off.

As much of a threat as that damn bottle was, Tom was thankful the man wasn't wearing a gun. Hell, he was half surprised somebody hadn't strapped one on Jimmy just to spice things up, considering the blood lust in this town. Through the haze of smoke, he could just make out the bespectacled Marcus Hale, licking the tip of a pencil, already making up tomorrow's headline for the *Gazette*. But it damn well wasn't going to be Tom Bolt Kills Again.

He downed another jolt of rye in the grim knowledge that his blood was so thick tonight after touching Zena that even half a bottle of booze wouldn't affect him. Maybe a more appropriate headline for the morning paper would be Marshal Bruises and Batters Butterfly.

Keep thinking about that, he cautioned himself, and pretty soon you'll be standing here with your throat cut, tracing hearts on the bar top in your own warm blood.

The half-breed's hand moved, but only to clench the bottle tighter. Out of the corner of his eye just then

Tom saw the saloon doors swing open like a pair of butterfly wings. Zena! At the sight of her, his heart rammed like a fist against his ribs, and then the bottle shattered and he felt the jagged glass like lightning through his sleeve.

Chapter Twelve

By the time Zena had been able to choke out a scream, Tom already had Jimmy Two Hats facedown on the bar with his arms wrenched behind his back. And by the time she had gotten her quaking knees under enough control to go to him, Tom had the halfbreed by one arm and both braids and was muscling him through the crowd toward the door.

Even in the saloon's blue and smoky light, she could see that the gash in Tom's black sleeve was already soaked with blood. She hadn't been sure if the expression on his face signaled anger or pain, but there had been no mistaking the molten fury in his eyes. And they had been aimed right at her.

He had paused just long enough to say something to Billy Dakin, then had hauled his hapless prisoner past her without so much as a glance, leaving a bloody handprint on one of the swinging doors.

Zena had been picking up her skirts to run after him when Billy latched on to her elbow.

"I'm s'posed to see you home, Miz Zena, then see that you stay put. Marshal's orders, ma'am."

Rather than stand there and argue, Zena had allowed Billy to walk her home. But now she was stalking from one side of her front porch to the other, pausing at the top of the steps each time to cast Billy Dakin what she ardently hoped was her most scathing if not lethal look. But either the glare wasn't hot enough or young Billy was too dim-witted and thick-skinned to wither beneath it, because he just kept flashing her that silly gap-toothed grin of his while blocking her every effort to escape.

"I'm only doing what the marshal told me to do, Miz Zena," he said, "so don't go getting all riled at me. He said to see you home and keep you here, and that's exactly what I'm doing."

She halted directly above him, aiming a .44 caliber glare right between his eyes. "Well, that's just fine, Billy. You're here lollygagging on my porch steps while the marshal's bleeding to death down at the jail house." Her hands clamped on her hips. "When everybody blames you for his pitiful and preventable death, you can tell them you were just doing your damn job."

The boy blinked in confusion and threaded all ten fingers through his wheat-colored hair. "Yeah, but—"

"On the other hand—" Tom stepped out of the darkness on the far side of the porch "—if I don't bleed to death quite so pitifully, I'll be obliged to you,

Billy, for following my orders." His dark gaze cut to Zena. "And for suffering the tongue-lashing."

Her breath left her in a long sigh of relief as she stood still, looking at Tom, taking a quick inventory of his condition. A blood-soaked bandanna circled his upper arm. In the sallow porch light his face was pale beneath a day's growth of dark whiskers. But he was alive! Thank God. Alive and scowling at her! Never, Zena marveled, had such a harsh look felt so good.

She hugged her arms about herself to keep from reaching out to him, telling herself there would be time to touch him later. "You need to come in and let me tend to that," she said, pointing at his left arm. "I'll go heat up some water and get a needle and thread." She turned and walked into the house.

"You all right, Marshal?"

Tom had misjudged the top porch step, and the boy had gripped his elbow, then snatched his hand back when Tom swore.

"I'll be fine," he said through clenched teeth as he held on to the roof post. The wound itself wasn't all that serious, but he'd had a hell of a time getting the drunk half-breed up the stairs to the jail. By the time he'd locked Jimmy up, Tom's sleeve was soaked to the cuff and the loss of blood had started to make his head feel light as a tumbleweed in a stiff wind. Even now he had to make an effort to bring Billy's anxious face into focus.

"You go on home now, son."

"You sure?"

Tom put his hand on the boy's shoulder. "Much obliged for your help. You can do me one more favor. If you want to, that is."

The gap-toothed grin flared as Billy nodded enthusiastically. "Just name it."

"Keep your eye on the jail house tomorrow, will you? Maybe see that Jimmy gets something to eat when he comes around."

Billy stood taller, hooking his thumbs through his gun belt. "Sorta like your deputy?"

Tom sighed as he let his gaze drift to the boy's holster. His arm was throbbing so badly now, it was all he could do to sound more threatening than a tomcat with its back up. "No gunplay, Billy," he warned. "If I hear that you've done anything more than wear that weapon, I'll melt it down for horseshoes. You got that?"

The kid had nearly snapped a salute before taking his leave. Tom leaned his forehead against the screen door for a moment, hoping to hell he'd done the right thing with the overly eager, itchy-fingered youth, by trusting him with some responsibility. If anything happened . . .

Something cold and wet pressed into his palm, and when Tom's eyes jerked open, he was sitting at the kitchen table and his dog was looking up at him expectantly, almost quizzically. He slid a reassuring hand over the animal's silky head and tried to muster a smile.

It emerged as a grimace, but the dog wagged his tail gladly in reply.

"I must have blacked out." His own voice sounded as though it were coming from the depths of a well. And then he felt as if he had pitched headlong into that dark well. Damned if he wasn't drowning. He dragged in a lungful of air and came up coughing.

"Oh, no, you don't," Zena said firmly, grabbing a fistful of his hair to keep him upright when he began to slump over the table. "You're going to drink every drop of this beef tea or else, Tom Bolt. And I'm frying you up a steak and you're going to eat every bite of that, too, if we have to sit here all night. Do you hear me?"

She was relieved to see him nod, but when he started to reply she pressed the cup of warm broth to his lips again and tipped it up. This time he swallowed it. And kept swallowing. She made him drain the cup.

"That's better," she said. "Think you can sit here now without falling over while I go turn the steak?" She loosened the grip she had on his hair, and when she was satisfied that the broth had revived him a bit and that he wasn't going to pitch over onto the floor, she went to the stove.

"What the hell was that?" he grumbled almost coherently. "Sheep dip?"

"Beef tea." Zena kept her back to him as she stabbed the good-sized cut of sizzling meat with a fork and flipped it over in the skillet. "That and this red meat will help restore some of the blood you've lost."

He swore softly. "I'd rather have a slug of that tonic you nip at now and then."

Zena frowned into the hot skillet. She wondered if the loss of blood was affecting his brain. "I have no idea what you're talking about," she said, glancing over her shoulder to make certain he was still vertical.

"Never mind," he grunted.

When the steak was seared and still bloodred inside, she slapped it on a plate, cut it into manageable pieces and carried it to the table. "Here." She stabbed a small morsel with a fork and put it in his right hand, then planted her hands on her hips. "Eat every bite," she commanded.

"Yes, ma'am." Tom raised his chin with obvious effort and was summoning a smile when his half-mast gaze fastened on the front of her dress. The fork clattered onto the tabletop.

Zena looked down at the bloodstained calico then back to Tom's stricken expression full of the same guilt and self-loathing she had witnessed earlier tonight. Dear Lord! Somehow, in his confused state, he seemed to believe that she was the one who was hurt and he was the one responsible.

Tears welled in her eyes as she took his face in her hands. "Oh, Tom. I'm not hurt. It's your blood, love. I got covered with it when I helped you in from the porch. You remember that, don't you?"

For a second all he could remember was tearing at her clothes and sinking his teeth into her warm and vibrant flesh, terrifying her and making her cry.

"Tom! Listen to me." She shook his shoulders. Pain sliced down his left arm. "You were at Bird's, standing at the bar. Jimmy Two Hats cut you."

The pain snapped his mind to sudden attention. He heard the whiskey bottle shatter again, but what he more clearly recalled was the pretty butterfly coming through the doors, shattering his concentration. "I remember," he said dully, dragging his eyes back to the plate and the bloody meat that almost turned his stomach now.

Zena's hands fluttered from his shoulders to his sleeve. "You go to work on that steak," she said with quiet determination, "while I go to work on you."

Tom woke to church bells. And when he felt the warmth of a woman beside him in bed, he thought he had died—a happy though unrecollected death—and gone to heaven. The fact that it was Sunday dawned on him slowly. The other fact—Zena, all warmth and riffling breath beside him—remained a mystery shrouded in a tangle of dark hair and a drift of snow-white linens.

Easing up on one elbow, he decided that he felt a hell of a lot better than he probably should have under the circumstances, a few of which were still hazy and vague. His gun belt was slung over the bedpost as if he had done it himself. His boots were neatly aligned beside the bed and his pants were . . .

Hell and damnation! He hauled himself out from under the covers. At least his drawers were still on. And buttoned, he noticed before casting one grateful glance heavenward and another more quizzical one at the still-sleeping beauty.

The dog greeted him happily outside the kitchen door and ran circles around him on the path to the privy and back to the pump, where Tom stuck his head under the bracing water. When he was done, he kept pumping while the animal lapped at the cool stream. While the dog drank, Tom studied the tiny black stitches that slanted across his upper arm thanks to the Widow Briggs. Of course, it never would have happened if she hadn't followed him to Bird's and played havoc with his concentration. By God, he hoped that half-breed's head was pounding like a tom-tom this morning.

He brought the remains of the undercooked steak out onto the back porch and sat, watching the dog tear into the meat with tail-wagging gusto. It was a little after eight o'clock, judging from the church bells and the slant of the sun. Tom was briefly tempted to walk down to the jail, but when he recalled the shine on Billy's face and the pride in the boy's eyes last night, he decided not to. You didn't give a boy a chance to do a man's job—however unimportant—and then renege on it. He sighed and reached out to absently scratch the dog's ears. Billy would be fine. It was Zena he ought to be worrying about now. And maybe give a moment's thought to his own vulnerable hide.

For a gunfighter, he'd had a pretty good run. He'd lasted as long as he had primarily because of his ability to focus on danger, to hone his concentration to a sharp and lethal edge. But the butterfly hadn't just shattered that concentration last night; she'd shot it to hell and back.

He didn't even have to wonder why. Tom knew it was because he cared for her too much for his own good. She'd come through the doors at Bird's and promptly decimated his instincts for self-preservation because he put her safety above his.

"Love," he muttered as if it were a bitter curse. The dog pricked up its ears, and Tom patted his knee, urging the animal to rest its silky head there. His hand drifted back and forth over the soft fur.

"We ought to get while the getting's good, fella," he said. Only, Tom knew the getting hadn't been good or even possible since he'd first laid eyes on Zena Briggs.

Funny, he thought now. He'd always figured it would be a bullet that brought the legendary Tom Bolt down. Who'd ever have dreamed it would be a butterfly instead?

Zena was awake. She had even raced to a rear window and peeked out just to make certain Tom was all right. Reassured by the length and strength of his stride as he crossed the backyard, she had climbed back into his bed. But now she kept her eyes closed as the mattress canted beneath his weight, pressing her against bare skin and sleek muscle and soft chest hair. He sighed—with contentment, she decided, rather than pain—as he slipped his arms around her and drew her closer, burrowing his face into the hollow of her neck.

"You're better," she whispered. "I'm glad. I was so worried, Tom. That's why I stayed close last night. Just in case you needed me."

His lips moved softly over the column of her neck, sending tiny shivers along her spine. His breath was warm and his voice deep and rich as it thrummed at her ear. "I need you now."

Zena opened her eyes—wide. The summer sun was shining through the window, bright as footlights on a stage. The rose-patterned wallpaper was distinct. Every pink petal and thorn. "It's daylight," she said, trying to subdue the panic that was leaping into her throat and thinning her vocal chords.

The response she got was a husky "mmm" and a warm tongue tracing the shell of her ear. She tried to ignore the rush of desire it sent throughout her body, but when Tom shifted his hips against her backside, there was no ignoring the fact that he did indeed need her. Now.

In four years of marriage she had never made love with anything but moonlight coming through the window, and even then Eldon had drawn the drapes before undressing her under the covers. She remembered the one time early in their marriage when she had turned to him suggestively at dawn. The man had practically shot out of bed. "Only whores do that, Zena," he had told her brusquely. "You're not a whore anymore." She had never heard him utter that word again. Neither had she ever reached for him in the daylight.

"It's daylight," she repeated, her voice more of a gasp now than a whisper.

"Uh-huh." Tom's big warm hand curved down her flank, found the hem of her gown and slipped up beneath it.

"*Broad* daylight," she croaked.

The heat of his palm settled over her breast. The hand held still as he spoke, his lips at her ear. "Don't be afraid of me, Zena. What happened yesterday..." He dragged in a rough breath, letting it out in a measured and obvious effort at control. "Let me love you, darlin'," he whispered. "Slowly. Gently. The way you deserve."

A wild little bubble of laughter rose in her throat. Right now she was afraid to even guess what a former whore might deserve, but she wasn't afraid of Tom and she was determined to make him believe that. "What happened yesterday wasn't your fault, Tom. It wasn't you I was afraid of. It was me. It was the way I was feeling, as if a hot wind were blowing through me, right through my soul. Kind of wild and... and..."

"Uncivilized?" he offered with a low chuckle as his hand moved on her breast, a lazy thumb circling its center.

"Quite," she said breathlessly. "That's why I went running after you last night. To tell you how wrong you were blaming yourself. It was my fault for behaving like a skittish schoolgirl."

His deep sigh of relief trembled at her ear. "I thought—"

"Hush," she whispered. "I know what you thought. You were wrong."

Now his tongue blazed another hot trail on her ear. Flames licked up from the pit of her stomach. Heat pooled in her womb.

"Tell me you're not afraid of me now," he rasped.

"I'm not." Her voice quaked now not from fear of Tom but from her own desires, her own deep-seated apprehensions. "I'm not afraid of you. Not you. Only..."

"What?"

Again his hand stilled. His patience, Zena thought, was almost palpable. As strong as the beating of his heart against her shoulder blade.

She squeezed her eyes closed now. "Only it's daylight!" she blurted. "What will you think of me?"

Slowly then, with the ease of a cat, he lifted on his elbow, and with one smooth motion turned her so he was looming over her. His chest covered hers like a dark, warm blanket. His eyes were dark despite the brilliance of the morning sun. Then his taut mouth flared at the corners.

"I think you're beautiful." Tom dipped his head and scorched her lips with the tip of his tongue. "And now I'm all done thinking," he added huskily just before his mouth settled over hers.

If Zena had meant to protest, that deep, claiming kiss and the hot surge of his tongue dissuaded her. It only took a moment before the daylight that had worried her had paled before the wildfires sweeping through her.

The butterfly went up in flames beneath him. Her kisses were fearless now, and her hands were as bold as his own—touching, teasing, tempting him until Tom thought he'd explode. He drew back a moment, letting his eyes rove over her flushed skin, drinking her in to cool himself momentarily. She was all cream, he thought, and rain-drenched roses. Her breasts were slick with his sweat and her lips glistened with his kisses. She was his, by God, as no other woman had ever been.

A slow smile spread across his mouth as he watched her blue eyes deepen to midnight and felt her long legs slide around his hips. She dragged in her wet lower lip then and raised her passion-laden lids.

"Please," she breathed.

He entered her slowly, like a hanged man finding himself at the gates of heaven by mistake. Slowly, gauging each flicker of her lips, each infinitesimal quickening in her eyes. Afraid. In the depths of his soul—dear God!—so afraid he'd wake where he truly belonged. In hell.

Her arms wound around his neck then and her hips surged up like a sweet, warm, all-encompassing tide, claiming him as surely and as irrevocably as any angel ever claimed a lost soul. She pulled him down to her mouth, and with a lingering kiss she put out the hellfire in his gut and lit a candle in his heart.

Gently. He took her gently, with whispers of love and with every shred of constraint in his grasp until the last thread snapped. Then, as he drove into her, she wrapped him tight in her warm, warm wings and—in brilliant daylight—brought him home.

Chapter Thirteen

It was, Zena decided, the best Sunday of her life. And quite aptly named, to boot. *Sun*day. If she had any lingering doubts about the propriety of making love while sunlight streamed brazenly through the window, Tom obliterated those doubts with every kiss and every touch. Each time he took her, Zena felt sunshine streaming through her and lighting up every corner of her heart. Or, as just moments before, when sunset went glittering through her like topaz and amethyst jewels.

Had her heart been so sunless before? she wondered as Tom's dark head rested in the crook of her shoulder and his warm breath feathered over her breast. Perhaps it had, she thought. She had never doubted that her childhood had been one long and hard-frozen winter. By comparison, she had imagined her marriage to Eldon as warm as springtime, as bright as moonlit nights. Maybe it had been. But now! Now she knew what it was like to dive headlong and gloriously naked into golden summer sunshine. And she knew there was no going back now that she had shared that with Tom. Now that she loved him with her whole and suddenly sunlit heart.

"I love you, Tom Bolt." The whisper crossed her lips before she knew she was going to speak.

He smiled. Zena couldn't see it, but she could feel his mouth curve against her skin, and when he spoke—a drowsy, deep-throated rumble at her bosom—she felt the vibration of his words as well as heard them.

"I love you, too, Zena Briggs."

They lay there quietly in each other's arms. Having spoken what was in their hearts, Zena thought, there was nothing else to say. Not now anyway. Whatever was going on in their heads was best saved for another time.

She welcomed the muscular weight of the leg Tom shifted over hers.

"You weren't always Zena Briggs," he murmured. "What was it before?"

"My name?"

"Uh-huh." He shifted an arm to draw her more closely against his chest. "I'll bet you were a pretty little girl." He chuckled softly. "Prissy, though."

"I was not," she sniffed.

"Who were you before you were the beautiful Mrs. Briggs?"

"My name was Grayson," she answered quietly and truthfully before she added, less than truthfully, "of the Virginia Graysons," thus elevating her dirt-poor, ne'er-do-well clan to the status of the Randolphs or the

Lees, and hoping Tom would let the whole sorry subject drop right there.

But he didn't. Nestling more firmly against her, he said, "Tell me about it. About Virginia, and the Graysons. About all those years of your life that I missed."

"There's nothing to tell." Nothing she wanted to tell was more like it.

"There's everything," Tom urged. "What did your father do?"

Zena sighed. "He was a planter." Well, it wasn't all that much of a lie, she told herself. Whoever her sire had been, he had planted at least one seed. "But he died when I was very young."

"I'm sorry," he murmured. "Did your mama remarry?"

"No." Her reply was clipped, almost curt. Lying about her dismal youth had never bothered her before. In fact, she had rather enjoyed inventing a family far different from her own. But there was no enjoyment in lying to Tom. It hurt, emotionally and very nearly physically. Zena drew in a long breath and willed herself to smile as she turned to him.

"I don't want to talk about the past right now, or even think about it."

"All right." He raised his hand to brush a stray lock of hair from her cheek, the better to see her blue eyes. A blue as clear as a summer sky, he thought. Cloudless. Innocent. He knew why he chose not to talk about his own misguided past, but he wasn't sure why the butterfly was reluctant to discuss hers. Her first cocoon had undoubtedly been a substantial one if her father had been a planter in Virginia. The love of home and all its comforts had probably been deeply in-grained in her early on.

But if both of them shied away from talking about their pasts, he thought almost glumly now, then that left only the present. A small voice inside him prayed that Zena would shun any discussion of the future. He had, after all, confessed that he loved her. He meant it, too. But declarations of love didn't just hang for pure sparkle in the air a minute like fireworks against a night sky. Love begged commitment. That was how it went. A man said, "I love you," and a woman replied, "Well?"

He'd learned that at the ripe young age of nineteen when Hannah had jerked that particular line and set the hook firmly in his mouth. Not that he regretted it. But he'd had a future then. And now he didn't.

She sighed, curling against him like a kitten. "Let's not talk at all," she purred. She slid her hand along his arm, skimming over the stitches. "How's your poor arm? Are you sure you're up to all this?"

Tom grinned. Grateful for the here and now, re-lieved to postpone the future, he took Zena's hand and guided it beneath the covers. "My arm's got nothing to do with it, darlin'."

Zena stretched languidly, achingly, reveling in each love-induced tremor and twinge in her body. She felt used up and brand-new all at once. Exhausted, yet, at the same time, vital and humming with life. Her gaze strayed to the window, anticipating sunshine, but the morning light struck her as lackluster now. Sunday's gold was gone, replaced by the flat light from an overcast sky.

Monday, she realized with a sinking feeling in her heart. She hadn't wanted their special Sunday to end. Ever. Somewhere deep inside her she wished she knew some magical incantation to bring back yesterday, to make it last longer, to set it apart—an island of a day where she and Tom could be stranded. Forever.

She heard the clatter of Zeb Harmon's milk wagon, the ring of the anvil down at the smithy's. Both signaled a day of work after a day of rest. Then came the brisk whistle of the Monday morning train. Lord only knew what that signaled or who was coming to Glory now.

Tom was buckling his gun belt. That sight—Tom in black against her pale rose wallpaper—put an end to her stay-abed musings. Their glorious island had disappeared. They were back in Glory once more, home of the fastest gun in the West.

"It's early," he told her quietly as he bent to strap his holster down. "Go back to sleep, love."

She shook her head against the pillow, momentarily coveting its soft warmth as she contrasted it with the firm set of Tom's jaw and the cool gray of his eyes. A Monday expression if ever she had seen one, full of resignation and wistfulness. It was time to strap his gun on and go back to work.

"I'm going down to the jail house," he told her as if reading her thoughts.

Zena wanted to grab his hand and pull him back into bed. She ached to rip those devil-colored garments off him. The gun, too. Especially the gun. Sitting up with the sheet bunched around her, she patted the mattress beside her. "Come sit a minute."

All he did was lift a suspicious eyebrow.

"Sit," she repeated. "I want to take a closer look at your shirt. I'm going to make you a new one to replace the one Jimmy cut."

He sat on the edge of the bed warily, as if it might collapse, while Zena ran her hands over the width of his shoulders.

"I'm developing a distinct dislike of black," she said with a sniff. "Why do you always—"

"It's what I wear," he said, cutting her off.

"But why?"

He shook his head. "Habit. Laziness."

Her hands stilled on his shoulders. "I think it's more," she murmured. "I expect it's because it makes you look dangerous."

"That, too, maybe." He shrugged. "Maybe this dark getup has made one or two young hotheads think twice."

Her voice wavered. "Tom . . ."

Here it came, he thought, hearing the ache in her voice when she spoke his name. Her plangent tone said it all. Stay, it said. Stay. Here. With me.

And damned if he hadn't lain awake half the night trying to figure out how he could. But he didn't have an answer for her. He wasn't sure he ever would. "I have to get going, sweetheart," he said softly as he drew her bed-warm body into his arms, doing his best to sound like any man heading off for a day's work. A banker off to count money. A barber off to cut hair. A man who left for work with every intention of returning. "Supper's at six?" he asked, knowing full well it was always at six. Sharp.

"Sharp," she said, leaning back and capturing his face in her hands, bringing a smile up from her worried depths. "But first there's breakfast."

About to tell her no, Tom stopped himself. And a while later, as he was sitting at the kitchen table, he was glad to have her fussing over him. It made him feel ... civilized. He relished the sight of Zena in her crisp white apron. He loved the sound of eggs cracking on the lip of a bowl, the whisk of a fork and the sizzle of butter in a skillet.

There had been a time when a morning like this in Hannah's cozy kitchen had been just another day, and he found himself wishing he had appreciated it more, wondering if he had ever really told his young wife how much he had loved her.

A pang of guilt stitched through his heart. But Hannah was dead and his love for the butterfly didn't diminish what he had felt for his wife, whether he had expressed it or not.

Hell, it was just that he'd been so young. So young and damn near immortal. All he'd been was a poor farmer, a nobody just starting out, but—by God—back then everything had been possible. And now he wasn't young anymore, and he was aware of his mortality with every breath, waking as well as sleeping. He wasn't a nobody, either, but a somebody with a reputation that he couldn't shake. It was a pretty grim irony, he thought, that now, when everything was impossible, he felt capable of truly appreciating it. This woman. This sweet Monday morning in a clean little kitchen where he'd gladly spend the rest of his life if he only could.

"Zena," he said quietly, shifting sideways in the chair and patting his knee.

Her smile was quick and bright, like the sun suddenly coming from behind a cloud, and she rushed to him, filling his arms with her warmth and his senses with her fragrance, filling his heart with more love than he'd ever hoped to feel again. Even filling his eyes with tears.

There had to be something he could do, Tom thought as he held her tightly against his chest. The only solution he had come up with so far—asking her to pack up and leave town with him, to lay low with him in the mountains until everybody forgot that a shootist named Tom Bolt had ever existed—was out of the question. Even assuming that Zena would consider it, he wouldn't dream of taking her away from her secure home to live always looking over her shoulder the way he had all these years. Anyway, there was no guarantee that he could hide from his damn reputation even on a remote mountaintop. The town fathers of Glory had found him, hadn't they?

He kissed her then, capturing her mouth not with heat but with warmth. "This is good," he whispered. "Just being here with you. Honey, I wish . . ."

Tom stopped. He pulled back slightly, taking in her wide, expectant eyes and the hopeful tilt of her mouth. She made him forget he wasn't in the wishing business anymore. He lived by his wits and his instincts alone. Wishes, sweet as they were, would only get him killed.

After planting a quick kiss on the tip of her nose, he said, "I wish those eggs were done. I'm starving."

She sat there smiling at him, making no effort to return to the stove.

"Did you hear me, woman?" he demanded with mock gruffness as he jounced her on his knee.

"I heard you."

"Well?" he growled.

"Well, let me go."

"What?" Tom followed the drift of Zena's gaze to where his arms were still wrapped tightly around her waist. He smiled mournfully as she pressed her forehead to his.

"Make up your mind, Marshal," she whispered seductively. "Me or the eggs?"

"Tough choice."

Her fingers threaded through his hair as her blue eyes locked on his. Blue eyes deepening from morning to midnight once more. "Is it?" she asked huskily.

"I wish." Tom shook his head now as he rose to his feet with Zena in his arms, then strode across the kitchen to take the skillet from the burner before carrying her back up the stairs.

With a luxurious sigh, Zena opened her eyes and gazed at the ceiling above the bed. The rhythm of her heart was settling back to normal. Tom's, too, although she couldn't tell the difference anymore between their heartbeats or their urgent cries. They seemed to be one. This way. With his body still so deep within hers. With her legs and arms twined around his solid warmth. She never wanted to let go.

Not when his stomach rumbled against hers. Not even when she heard the knock on the front door.

"Oh, Lord! That'll be Billy with the first of this week's laundry." She sighed with resignation. "I almost forgot there's a world outside this bedroom door."

When she unwound her legs and began to slide out from under him, Tom dug his elbows into the mattress.

"Let him wait."

There was an urgent quality in his voice that put an immediate end to Zena's efforts to wriggle away. She held still, imprisoned between his arms, beneath his weight. She held her breath after seeing the hard set of his jaw and the muscle that jerked in his cheek. Whatever urgency he felt was not from the heat of passion now, but from the cool realm of decision. The icy press of cold hard facts she was sure she didn't want to hear. Not yet, she prayed silently. Oh, please, not yet.

As if in answer to her prayer, all hell broke loose on the front porch. Tom's dog set up an ear-splitting howling, broken only by vicious growls. The raps on the door downstairs became more persistent, then quite panicky as knuckles gave way to fists. There was a good deal of shouting, but with the dog barking it was impossible to identify or understand.

Now, above her, Tom was growling, too, and yelling through the window at the wild dog. While he was distracted, Zena took the opportunity to scramble out from beneath him and into her dress. Then, before he could stop her, she was doing up her buttons and finger-combing her hair while trotting down the stairs.

She frowned at the latched screen door, not recognizing the large man silhouetted there. Pausing at the foot of the stairs, she called to him. "What can I do for you?"

"Madam, please," he gasped, angling his bowler-hatted head toward the raucous dog now nipping at his pant leg.

When she unlatched the door, the big man very nearly trampled her in his rush to get inside. Zena pushed the door closed before the agitated animal could follow. "Behave yourself, Lucifer," she snapped at him through the screen. When he continued to bark and growl, she slammed the inside door.

The stranger was slumped against the vestibule wall, mopping his damp brow with a red silk hankie. "I am forever in your debt, madam," he said a little breathlessly.

Zena crossed her arms. "That's all right." Ordinarily she didn't let uninvited strangers into her house. But how dangerous could it be, she figured, with Tom upstairs and the hound from hell just on the other side of the door? And this particular stranger had *city* written all over him, from the top of his bowler hat to the pointed tips of his high-button shoes. She lifted a curious eyebrow. "What's your business, mister?"

He stuffed the wilted hankie into the breast pocket of his brown checkered coat, then cleared his throat. "I do apologize. That odious beast made me quite forget my manners." The big man bowed ever so slightly, a gesture that creased his green brocade waistcoat and made his ornate gold watch chain disappear in the folds. "Allow me to introduce myself. My name is Philo Gordon. I'm—"

"The biggest, blood-suckingest son of a bitch east or west of the Mississippi." Tom's voice thundered from the top of the stairs.

Chapter Fourteen

The big man merely laughed, casually lifting a wrist to readjust a gold cuff link. "Ah, Thomas. They told me I might find you here."

Tom came down the stairs, black and coiled tight. Like a tornado, Zena thought. A dark storm bent on destruction. He crossed the hall and grabbed the portly man by his checkered lapels.

"You found me."

For a split second then, Tom smiled. Sort of. It was more like a glinting saber slash than any grin Zena had ever seen. A dangerous display of lightning across a dark sky.

"I guess you're real happy now."

Philo Gordon blinked. "Actually, I—"

Tom yanked him away from the wall, spun him around and shot a hard fist firmly into his face.

Gasping, Zena watched in stunned horror as three hundred pounds of loose flesh went wobbling backward across her parlor, crashed into the whatnot in the far corner, then slumped insensibly to the floor amid the porcelain shards and sprung works of her music box collection.

A wretched little sob broke in her throat as she looked from the wreckage to Tom. His fists were clenched like rocks and the expression on his face was one of barely controlled fury. He seemed to be willing himself to stand still, to stave off the fierce anger that was driving him.

When she took a step toward him, he held up his hands.

"Don't." His gray gaze flicked toward the havoc in the parlor then returned to her face. "I'm sorry," he growled from between clenched teeth. "I'm so goddamn sorry."

He stalked past her, nearly ripped the front door from its hinges and slammed it at his back. The walls of the little vestibule reverberated from the hard jolt, and in the parlor one of her shattered music boxes lofted a few tinny notes of "Beautiful Dreamer" and then fell still.

Tom took the stairs outside the jail house two at a time. Inside he ripped the badge from his vest, glared at it a minute in the palm of his hand, then with a rough curse threw it clear across the room. The tin star hit the floor and skidded under the iron bars of the cell.

He launched a booted foot at the swivel chair behind his desk and sent it spinning. When it stopped, he dropped onto its worn wooden seat, leaned his head back and closed his eyes.

"Bad as all that, is it, Marshal?"

Tom lifted his head and opened his eyes just wide enough to discover Jimmy Two Hats grinning at him through the bars of the cell. Dragging in a long breath, Tom let it out with a soft groan. "How're you doing, Jimmy?"

The half-breed shrugged. "Been worse. Wouldn't mind getting out of here though."

Why not? Tom thought. He opened the desk drawer, reached for the keys, then hauled himself out of the chair.

"Did Billy see that you got something to eat?" he asked as he turned the key in the lock.

After the man nodded, Tom opened the door and swung it wide. "Stay away from Bird's for a while, Jimmy," he muttered. "Lay off the sauce, too, you hear?"

Jimmy paused on the threshold of the cell, his dark gaze directed at Tom's left arm. "Hope I didn't cut you too bad," he mumbled.

"I've had worse," Tom said. "Go on home now."

"Here." The Indian held out the tin star.

Tom shook his head.

"Don't blame you," Jimmy grunted as he closed his tobacco-stained fingers over the badge. "Me, I'd just as soon shovel horse apples for a living as wear one of these."

He dropped the badge into the trash can on his way to the door, then turned back, eyeing Tom as he lifted his shoulders in a shrug. "You were good at it, though. Better'n most. See you around, Marshal."

After Jimmy left, Tom sagged back into his chair. Hell, he thought, right this minute a career as a manure shoveler didn't sound half-bad. It sounded pretty good, in fact, compared to what his life was going to be now that his "good friend" Philo Gordon had turned up.

Just when he'd thought he could do it, too. He opened the center drawer now for the pure pleasure of slamming it shut, then swiveled around toward the window. This morning, after taking Zena back to bed and after their urgent loving, Tom had lain there—still hard inside her and wanting her again—again and always. The foreboding that usually lodged in his gut had disappeared. Maybe, he thought now as he stared out at the gray sky, love had turned him into a hopeful fool. Love was certainly what he'd been feeling then. And hope.

Life had suddenly seemed full of possibilities. He had felt twenty again. Immortal as a god and innocent as a babe. He had wanted to tell Zena that and so much more. "Marry me," he'd been about to say. "I'll find a way to stay here. Alive."

His gaze skimmed the overcast sky. It figured, he thought morosely, that Philo Gordon could drive the blue right out of heaven just the way the journalist had ripped the hope out of Tom's heart. Damn him. Damn him to hell and beyond.

While he was relegating people to hellfire, Tom decided, he might just as well include himself in the curse for the way he'd lost control in the butterfly's tidy sanctuary this morning. He grimaced as he pictured the big-bellied Gordon lying in the wreckage of Zena's precious music boxes. But even as he regretted the violence of his temper, Tom was wishing he had put a bullet through that scribbler's greedy heart a dozen years ago.

His mouth quirked sideways at the notion that Philo Gordon's heart, assuming the man even had one, was probably too small a target—even for the great and probably soon to be the late Tom Bolt.

Zena swept the last sliver of porcelain into the dustpan, then carried it into the kitchen where she dumped it into the trash can with a sigh.

"A regrettable collision," Philo Gordon murmured from his seat at the table.

"It wasn't your fault," she said stiffly as she wiped her hands on her skirt. The man made her nervous with his citified clothes and his half-dollar words. At least his nose had stopped bleeding now and he'd soon be on his way. "You probably ought to get a piece of raw meat for that eye, Mr. Gordon. I expect you'll have quite a shiner."

He lifted a finely manicured hand, testing the bruised flesh with his fingertips. "A badge of honor, I assure you. I shall wear my...what did you call it?"

"A shiner."

"Indeed. I shall wear my shiner with pride, Mrs. Briggs."

Zena's mouth thinned and she crossed her arms. "That's a fool thing to say."

"Not at all. I suspect there are hundreds of men in this country who would be only too happy to sport a black eye if it had been delivered by our Thomas."

She clucked her tongue now. "Such silliness."

The journalist dabbed at his nose again, peered at the hankie, then poked it into his pocket with satisfied finality. "Dear lady, there's nothing silly about fifty thousand readers, all of them eager to participate in the adventures of Tom Bolt."

"Fifty thousand?" she echoed.

"At last count." Gordon gave a little wave of his hand. "Of course that doesn't include the English or the Dutch. Nor, for that matter, the novels that are passed along from one reader to another. A hundred thousand is probably a more accurate estimate, I should think."

Zena shook her head in frank amazement. She had envisioned a few dozen young and gawky boys like Billy reading those dime novels, but never half a planet of them.

"You're surprised." It wasn't a question, but a comment as the journalist leaned back, coolly observing her expression. In fact, he seemed to be regarding her quite closely now from the top of her head to the tips of her toes. A curious smile was spreading across his lips.

Her hand flitted to her hair, still tangled from the passage of Tom's fingers when they'd made love. She sucked in her lower lip as if to hide the fact that she had so recently been kissed. And more. Suddenly, under Philo Gordon's scrutiny, Zena felt transparent. Except for the color that burned across her face.

"That's quite all right, Mrs. Briggs," he said even as his smile increased. "It's delightful. Absolutely charming, in fact. I can't tell you how long it's been since I've witnessed a blush."

Zena's face burned all the more. She was grateful that Philo Gordon was now occupied in a thorough search of his coat pockets rather than an examination of her blazing cheeks.

"Eureka!" he exclaimed as he produced a stub of pencil and a small notebook. "I must say I had grown rather weary of describing Thomas's dalliances with dance hall dollies and soiled doves. You're a refreshing change, my dear. An inspired choice." He snapped the notebook open. "Tell me about yourself."

She swallowed, audibly.

Tom was still staring out the jail house window. His feet were up on the desk now, his arms were crossed, and in his mind's eye Philo Gordon was drowning in an inkwell the size of a galvanized washtub. The vision made Tom's mouth draw up at the corners. Vaguely he wondered what it might take to get the journalist to draw on him. Hell, if he was going to have to keep on using his gun, he might just as well use it on the man who was responsible for the whole sorry mess his life had turned out to be.

When he decided he'd spent just about enough time feeling sorry for himself, he dragged his boots off the desk and stood up. Retrieving the tin star from the trash can, Tom held it a moment, feeling the metal grow warm from the heat of his hand, thinking the damn thing ought to be heavier for all the grief and responsibility that came with it. But of all the jobs he'd ever had—farming, then soldiering, then trying to ride herd when his reputation didn't interfere—this one fit him best.

And Zena. Of all the women he'd ever known— *Forgive me, darlin' Hannah*—the butterfly fit him best. He hadn't expected any of this to happen when he rode into Glory. Now that he was about to ride out, he wished he'd never come. It hurt too damn much to have to let it all go.

"Bolt! Thank God, you're here!" Lemuel Porter— beet-faced and bug-eyed—burst through the door. "They're robbing my bank!" he gasped, holding his hand over his heart.

Tom closed his fist over the badge and with his free hand he led the agitated Porter to a chair. "You best sit before you bust something, Lemuel," he told him, pushing him down with a firm hand on his shoulder.

"But they're robbing me. Two of them. I . . . was in the back room when I heard them." He struggled for a breath. "I got out through a window. Came here. Up . . . up all those damn stairs."

Tom scowled. What difference had stairs and inaccessibility made when all the mayor had wanted was a tourist attraction? Those two bastards could loot his vault and strip the bank down to bare wood for all Tom cared.

He was about to tell the man just that when Porter crumpled onto the desk top. "My wife...Mrs. Porter's in the bank. She has a delicate heart."

In Tom's clenched fist, the tin star bit into his palm. "I guess this has turned into a bigger sideshow than you ever figured, hasn't it, Lemuel?" he muttered as he stabbed the badge through his vest, then took his gun from its holster and eyed the cylinders. "Two of them, you said?"

As the mayor was nodding, Billy Dakin stumbled—breathlessly and big eyed—through the door.

"Marshal, they're robbing the bank!"

Tom shoved the Colt back in his holster, wondering if—between Mrs. Porter's delicate ticker and Billy's itchy fingers—anybody was going to come out of this alive.

"So I hear," he told the boy calmly.

Billy straightened up, his hand hovering near the butt of his gun while one foot scuffed nervously. "What do you want me to do? How 'bout if I..."

"See that the mayor stays put."

"Yeah, but I—"

"Not this time, Billy," he growled, skewering the boy with his eyes. "You got that?"

Billy's lips stiffened and his eyes smoldered with defiance. "What makes you think you're so goddamned great?"

In the flash of his hands, Tom had the belligerent Billy pinned to the door frame. "Because I'm alive, kid," he snarled, "which is a whole lot more than you're going to be if I see you within a hundred feet of that bank. Understand?"

Billy's gaze canted sideways.

Tom shook him, hard. "I mean it, Bill."

Maybe it was the name that did it. Tom wasn't sure. But the boy nodded and mumbled "yessir" as if he meant it, so Tom eased his grip and angled his head toward the distraught banker. "Lemuel's in bad shape. I'd be much obliged if you'd see to him so Mrs. Porter isn't a widow after this is all over with."

"Yessir."

Tom walked out the door. Halfway down the stairs, he called over his shoulder, "If anything happens to me, Bill, you keep an eye out for Mrs. Briggs, you hear? I'm depending on you now, son."

The "yessir" that Billy called back had a touch more pride than the one before it.

The boy would be all right, Tom decided. And if that was his own final accomplishment, maybe it was enough. He felt his lips twisting in a grin and thought maybe they could put that on his tombstone. *Here Lies Tom Bolt. Enough.*

* * *

While Zena cranked a sheet through the wringer, she glanced once more at the sky, ready at the first drop of rain to pluck her wash from the line and run it into the kitchen. Of course she'd have to squeeze past Philo Gordon, who seemed to have installed himself as a permanent fixture just inside the back door.

She smiled a bit mischievously, recalling how he'd tried to follow her out into the backyard only to scuttle back inside when Tom's dog went after him again. She could have tied the animal up, she supposed, but then she'd have to contend with the man's confounded curiosity. This way—with Gordon trapped in the kitchen and the black-and-white dog growling on the porch—it was easy for Zena to pretend she couldn't quite hear all those pesky questions of his. The man was persistent. Worse than a gnat.

She had to admit, grudgingly, that she was impressed with his high-toned vocabulary and his city manners. After all, it wasn't every day a famous writer came to Glory. World famous, no less. She had to keep reminding herself, though, that it was Philo Gordon who had turned Tom into little more than a target, a magnet for all the wild young guns west of the Mississippi.

"How'd you settle on Tom to write about?" she called to him over her shoulder while she pinned the sheet to the taut rope line.

"Serendipity, my dear. A pure, albeit fortuitous, accident," he replied. "My editor at *The Syracuse Sun* sent me to Texas, of all places, and told me not to come back without a good story." He chuckled. "I must say, I not only stumbled upon a good story but an entire new career, as well."

Zena brushed a strand of hair from her eyes, then angled another sheet through the wringer. "You still haven't answered my question, Mr. Gordon. Why Tom?"

"Isn't that obvious? A wronged widower seeking vengeance for the deaths of his wife and son. The story simply begged to be told. Then, of course, I met him and realized he was perfect." His voice took on an excited trill as he continued. "Tall. Strong as an oak. Handsome in a rugged sort of way. An aura of danger about him that was attractive to the ladies and challenging to the gents." He lifted an eyebrow in her direction. "Surely you haven't failed to notice those enchanting qualities in our Thomas, Mrs. Briggs?"

She cranked the wringer harder, barely able to speak for clenching her teeth so hard. "Actually, Mr. Gordon, I've noticed other, deeper qualities. Tom's a fine man. Have you failed to notice that, sir?"

He snorted. "*Fine* doesn't sell books."

"Maybe it should." Zena snapped the damp sheet like a whip. "Maybe you could—"

Gunfire cut her words and made her heart skip a perilous beat. Before she even knew it, she had dropped the sheet, hiked up her skirts and was running in the direction of the shots with the dog and the portly journalist in hot pursuit.

Front Street was empty, or so it seemed as Zena halted on the sidewalk in front of the office of *The Glory Gazette* directly across from the bank. She could see window curtains rippling all along the street and scores of watchful eyes. Down at Bird's, the girls were perched on the balcony rail like a flock of bright-colored finches, all of them looking toward the bank.

Zena did, too, just as gunfire cracked again and the bank's big plate glass window was shattered by a black-clad body that pitched backward and then lay still in the broken glass.

Her heart squeezed tight as a fist and all she could see was black. She thought she was going to faint when a voice close to her ear crowed, "Well done, Thomas. Well done, indeed. The scoundrel is dead."

It wasn't Tom! She could see that clearly now. The fallen man wore black, but it was a black duster and his boots were tan. The dog sat suddenly, heavily, letting out a wet sigh and leaning against Zena's leg as if he, too, had just realized it wasn't his master lying there.

For a moment then everything was quiet inside the bank and on the street. Beside her, Philo Gordon was scribbling furiously in his notebook. Behind her, a door squeaked open and the editor of *The Glory Gazette* crept out onto the sidewalk, his head dug deep into his shoulders like a turtle under siege.

Marcus Hale extended a shaking hand. "Mr. Gordon, sir. This is quite an honor. My name is Hale, sir. Marcus Hale."

Philo Gordon scribbled one last word then snapped his notebook closed and took the editor's hand, pumping it heartily. "Hale! Yes, indeed. It was your letter that brought me here. I'm inordinately grateful to you, I must say."

The bespectacled editor raised his head an inch from his collar and managed an edgy smile. "Thank you. Thank you ever so much, Mr. Gordon. This is such an honor."

"Nonsense." The big-bellied journalist clapped the smaller man on the shoulder. "As brothers in the esteemed fourth estate, I consider us no less than equals. I expect you to join me for dinner some evening this week. We'll—"

"Stop it," Zena hissed. "Tom's in trouble and you two are going on like it's the Fourth of July and you're just standing here waiting for the parade to begin."

Marcus Hale blinked. "Well, Zena, I—"

"Don't you well, Zena me, Marcus. You and your wild ideas about putting Glory on the map by hiring Tom." Her voice broke as she stabbed a finger toward the bank. "Just look what you've done."

There was another quick exchange of gunfire and sudden, violent movement as a man in a long black duster dragged Eustacia Porter through the bank door and out into the deserted street.

"A hostage!" Philo Gordon cried gleefully, reaching for his pencil once again. "This is marvelous!"

The editor gulped and ducked back into his office at the same moment that Tom appeared in the bank door.

"Let her go," he called to the robber, who was now in the middle of Front Street, looking a little wild-eyed and desperate as he tried to handle the swooning Eustacia in addition to his pistol and a canvas sack.

At the sound of Tom's voice, the dog gave a happy little bark and stood up. Zena grabbed a fistful of his fur, holding him back.

"Don't be a fool," Tom called now, his voice as level as his gun. "Your partner's already dead, fella. I don't want to have to kill you, too."

The desperado hauled his hostage closer to his chest and waved his gun. "You shoot at me, Marshal, and you're liable to kill this here innocent female."

"No, I won't," Tom said slowly and distinctly. "Now let her go."

"I ain't letting her go nowhere. She's my—"

Tom fired a single shot.

Zena gasped. Beside her, Philo Gordon chuckled softly then murmured, "Shield? Do you suppose that's what he was going to say?"

Chapter Fifteen

Billy Dakin was the first one out in the street, waving his hat, then exclaiming "Hot damn!" again and again while he tried to untangle the dazed Eustacia Porter from the dead robber's grasp.

In a matter of minutes Front Street was swarming with people. Even Bird, still in her satin wrapper and hair papers, followed her girls down the street to get a look at the two dead men.

Philo Gordon crooked his arm and angled his head toward the crowd. "Shall we, my dear?" he asked Zena.

She shook her head, barely able to speak. "You go on."

"Very well." About to step forward, his gaze dropped to the dog still caught by the scruff of the neck in Zena's tight fist. "I'd be grateful if you'd restrain the beast a while longer," the journalist muttered.

His words barely registered on her though as she watched Tom crossing the street toward them, refusing to shake any of the hands that were thrust his way, looking as if each and every pat on his back or tug on his sleeve were painful. He looked just plain wrung out, she thought. When he gave a whistle and gestured to the dog, the animal tore out of Zena's grasp. She continued to watch as the two of them headed away from town, the dog nearly dancing around the man who seemed to be carrying the weight of the world on his broad shoulders.

They were both drinking out of Royal Creek when Zena caught up with them. The dog glanced at her over his shaggy shoulder, gave his tail a wag and went back to lapping up water. Tom didn't turn, but Zena had the distinct feeling he knew she was there and that he was aware of her every move even though his back was turned.

She didn't blame him, if he didn't feel like company. On the other hand, recalling the muted grief she'd heard through his bedroom door, she didn't want him to be alone. She folded her legs and sat—but not too close. Hardly as close as she wanted.

Tom shifted on his haunches, scooping another handful of water from the creek, swallowing it greedily, like a man who had just walked out of a desert. When he finally spoke, though, his voice sounded rough and parched, as if he hadn't drunk at all. "Fear," he said, not looking at Zena but past her, into the brambles on the other side of the creek. "It tastes like blood. Coppery and bitter." He dipped both hands into the water and scrubbed his face while she moved slowly and quietly beside him.

Done quenching his own thirst, the black-and-white dog trotted west along the creek bed. Zena and Tom watched until he was out of sight, then Tom tipped his hat back and looked up at the sky.

"Looks like rain," he said in a flat tone. "You ought to get back to the house before—"

"I'm not afraid of a little rain," she interrupted, moving closer now, leaning against his arm. "And I'm not afraid of you, Tom Bolt."

He shook his head. "Maybe you should be."

Zena sighed and tilted her head onto his shoulder. "Maybe. And maybe, considering my feelings about guns and all, I should love a carpenter or a tinsmith. But I don't. I love you."

Drawing in a deep breath, he encircled her with his arm and tipped his head against hers. "I love you, too."

"You make it sound like a fate worse than death," she responded, a trace of laughter in her voice to disguise the apprehension in her heart.

"There's not much future in loving a man like me, Zena. I thought for a while…oh, hell, it doesn't make any difference what I thought. Nothing's going to change. Not now. Not with that damn, ink-swilling vulture here to stir things up."

"You could make him leave town. Being the marshal and all, you could—"

"It wouldn't make much difference. He's going to write his garbage no matter where he is. I'm his career, his whole damn life. He's not about to quit.'' He sucked in a breath and let it out with a soft, almost helpless curse. "He'll quit when I take that last bullet, of course, but I'm not ready to trade my life for Philo Gordon's early retirement.''

His words chilled her, rippling along her spine like icy fingers. It was one thing to sense the dangers he continually faced, but to hear Tom voice such bitter resignation about "that last bullet'' was almost more than she could bear. *Leave*, she wanted to tell him at the same moment that her arms were winding around him, hugging him close as her own life.

"It's all right,'' he said softly, angling his head and feathering his lips over her hair. "Who knows, darlin'? With a little luck, I'll probably still be doing this when I'm ninety years old.'' He chuckled deep in his throat, drawing her closer against him. "I can just picture it, can't you? Then that bloodsucking scribbler will be having to write about 'The Oldest Gun in the West.' ''

Zena sniffed and swallowed the lump in her throat. "It isn't funny.''

"I guess not, but when you've done what I've had to do for so many years—'' his voice snagged and roughened ''—you have to laugh some or you'd go around crying all the time.''

"Today was different, Tom,'' she offered. "You saved Eustacia Porter's life.''

"Maybe." He didn't seem convinced or as if he took any pride in rescuing the banker's wife. "It just feels like killing to me."

"Next time, don't shoot to kill."

He laughed sharply, almost savagely. It wasn't the reaction Zena had expected.

"Well, why not?" she demanded, pulling back to study his face. "Why not just shoot somebody in the leg or the arm?"

His eyes darkened perceptibly and his jaw stiffened. "Because I still like living, that's why. The minute I start winging people, you can start digging right over there." He jerked his head toward the cemetery. "You can plant me six feet under and come tend to me on Sundays like you do to your husband and your baby girl."

"I'd rather have you in my bed," she whispered.

"Then you'll have to accept what I am, Zena. That's not going to change. Not as long as I stay in Glory. Not as long as I have to keep killing in order to keep breathing."

Her voice was little more than a flutter of breath as she whispered, "You shouldn't have come here."

His expression softened and he took her chin in the vee of his hand. "I wouldn't have missed loving you for the world, butterfly." Tom leaned forward then to kiss each corner of her mouth. "I wouldn't change that or trade a single, precious minute of it."

Nor would she, Zena thought, though she wasn't sure that their loving—wonderful as it was—was worth what Tom seemed willing to risk or the high, perhaps fatal, price he might be forced to pay.

They had kissed awhile on the hidden banks of the creek, a little like two errant but happy schoolchildren. When they emerged from the thicket, Zena cast a worried glance in the direction of the cemetery she had failed to visit yesterday. It gnawed at her conscience now, not that she regretted having spent an entire Sunday in Tom's warm arms, but that she had so easily forgotten her other loved ones.

Even though Eldon and the baby were dead, their presence in the graveyard was very real to Zena. Very dependable. For six years it had provided her with a kind of stability and a peacefulness that she treasured. The need to visit the graves now, right this minute, was as sudden as it was overwhelming.

"I need to pay my respects," she said, easing her hand from Tom's and heading briskly for the small fenced-in plot. "I won't be but a minute."

He opened the little wrought-iron gate for her, then stood there, hat in hand. "I'll wait."

The weeds had gotten out of hand since her last visit. She got down on her knees, muttering as she yanked up half a dozen dandelions along with the sticktights that were putting down roots near the baby's headstone. She sighed and sat with her hands folded in her lap.

"I apologize for the weeds, Eldon. You can be sure I won't let that happen again. The town's getting along pretty well. There was a bank robbery today, but it

turned out all right. Well, not for the robbers, but..."
Her voice drifted off as she tried to frame what she wanted, needed to say.

"You'll be glad to hear the mortgage is all paid up. It was a worry to you, I know. Nobody can take the house away from me now. Guess I ought to be feeling more comfortable about things, but..."

Her gaze strayed over her shoulder to where Tom stood, looking patient as a preacher in his black clothes. She looked back at the headstone.

"That's Tom Bolt, if you're wondering. He's a good man, Eldon. All those stories about him aren't worth the paper they're printed on."

She reached out and tugged another dandelion from the plot, then dragged the dog-toothed leaves through her fingers, wondering just how much honesty the dead required. As much as the living? she wondered. Her eyes narrowed on the granite stone. A stitch of resentment pulled tight in her heart.

"That wasn't right, Eldon," she whispered. "What you told me about daylight and making love. I know different now. I wasn't truly a whore—even Bird says that—but somehow, in a million little ways, you made me feel like one."

Tears welled up in Zena's eyes. One trickled down her cheek and she swiped at it with the back of her hand. "I won't hold it against you, Eldon, but I had to say it. That's all."

She continued, in whispered tones to make sure that Tom couldn't hear, and speaking not so much to her dead husband now as simply pouring out her heart. "What'll I do if he leaves? What'll I do if he leaves Glory and doesn't ask me to go with him?" She dragged in a wet, shaky breath. "Or worse—what'll I do if he asks?"

At the cemetery gate Tom's knuckles whitened on the brim of his hat. Being jealous of a dead man didn't make much sense to him, yet he couldn't ignore the bitter feelings that were twisting inside him as he stood there watching Zena shed tears over the grave. He tried to tamp down on his ill feelings toward the dead barber. Hell, he and Eldon Briggs might wind up with more than a woman in common. If things went the way Tom expected, he and Zena's late husband would be lying shoulder to shoulder for all eternity.

You shouldn't have come here. Her words rolled through his head now. There was no going back, though. Nobody knew that better than Tom Bolt. There was no going forward, either. They'd just have to take it day by day. Moment by moment.

"I'm ready." Zena came through the gate and reached up on tiptoe to kiss him. "We better hurry. It's starting to rain."

He'd been so deep in thought he hadn't even noticed the fat raindrops that were splashing on the backs of his hands. The next thing he knew he and Zena were running away from the cemetery, hand in hand, more like two people trying to outdistance death rather than merely racing to get out of the rain.

His dog—being faster and probably smarter, Tom thought—was already on the back porch and keeping dry under the little roof. The animal preceded them into the kitchen where he circled and settled immediately beside the stove.

Zena pulled cotton towels from a drawer, laughing brightly as she tossed one to Tom. "Dry off," she commanded. "I don't want you catching your death from pneumonia."

"Maybe that's not such a bad idea," he said, rubbing his hair with the towel. "It would serve my good friend, Philo Gordon, right if I expired from a few raindrops."

Zena's smile turned to a frown. "If I never hear that man's name again, it'll be too soon," she muttered, applying a brisk towel to her own wet tresses. "And if he comes snooping around me again..." She stood still. The journalist didn't have to snoop around her to learn the truth about her past. He could ask just about anybody in Glory. Anybody, that was, except Tom. Zena gazed at him now, wondering whether or not he knew about her less-than-respectable past, whether or not he was simply being polite when she had mentioned the high-toned Virginia Graysons.

"It doesn't matter much what you tell him," Tom said as he straddled a chair and began meticulously applying the towel to his gun. "He'll write what suits him whether it's true or false." Lifting his head, he gave her a quizzical look. "You worried he'll write about you, butterfly?"

"I suppose," she murmured as she combed her fingers through her damp hair, finding it difficult to meet those intense gray eyes, wondering what knowledge lay behind them.

"Well, I wouldn't worry too much if I were you." He spoke softly, his head bent over his gun once more as he methodically dried each cylinder.

"Why? What are you going to do? Break every finger on his writing hand?" She spoke in jest, but the minute Tom glanced up from his gun, she knew it wasn't a joke. Not to him. His expression was deadly serious.

"If I have to," he said. "You're a lady, Zena. A woman of quality. I intend to see that Philo Gordon knows that and behaves accordingly. I don't want your family back in Virginia to suffer any indignities because of your association with me."

They'd love it, her wretched uncles and aunts, she thought, seeing little Zena in the pages of a dime novel. Far from a disgrace, they'd think she'd moved up a notch or two in the world. Of course only one or two of them would even be able to read the confounded books.

"I appreciate that, Tom," she said, forcing a certain primness in her voice, the cool tone of a lady reassured of the good name of her fine family. "Thank you." And, please, she prayed, don't hate me when you find out otherwise, or treat me like trash when you discover that's what I come from.

Flustered, she glanced at the clock and then began pulling pans from the cabinet by the stove. "It's nearly supper time. You must be famished."

"I am."

There was an unexpected depth in his voice, a surprising, almost sultry timbre that caused Zena to turn. Tom was standing now, gun belt slung over his shoulder, his damp black shirt molded to his chest.

"For you."

Her heart caught fire, and desire rushed through her. Every bone in her body began to melt. Having just reestablished her credentials as a lady, Zena felt distinctly unladylike now beneath Tom's hot gaze. Her own eyes flitted to the clock again and she found herself babbling something altogether unintelligible about daylight and the deleterious effects of skipping meals.

He closed the distance between them more like a vandal than a lover. Even the dog whimpered and scuttled farther back into a corner. But Tom couldn't stop. When she'd looked at the clock, this little creature of habit and domestic comfort, something had ripped inside him. They didn't have time, dammit. Didn't she know that?

He needed her suddenly with a ferocity he could barely control. He needed to bury himself in her generous warmth, to lose himself in her deep, secret core, to forget that time even existed and, most of all, to forget death in a wild and skyrocketing explosion of life.

His hands were trembling so badly he could hardly take hold of the tiny button on the collar of her dress, much less unfasten it. Desperate in his desire, Tom clenched the damp fabric in both hands and was about to rip it when Zena's fingers fluttered over his.

"Let me," she whispered, beginning to work the little buttons through, sensing his desperation as clearly as she felt her own powerful urges.

Tom dropped his hands to her hips and his fingertips bit into the folds of the fabric. His voice was a hoarse plea as he pressed his forehead to hers. "I don't know how to take it slow anymore, darlin'. Help me. Please."

She led him up the stairs, putting away her notions of what a lady did or didn't do, in daylight or moonlight or the dark. All Zena knew was that Tom needed her—now, completely, with a desire so fierce it made his strong body tremble.

At the top of the stairs, she turned toward her room rather than his. Once inside, she closed the door softly, then took the gun belt that was still draped over his shoulder and hooked it over the post of her white-ruffled, pillow-laden bed.

It was, Tom thought, an incongruous sight at best— his weathered black gun belt and scuffed holster swaying above the prim white bed. At worst, it seemed to symbolize their differences. His world was dark with the devil and death at every turn while hers was light, innocent and white as the wings of angels.

If this was her tactic in slowing him down—inviting him into her prim and snow-white bower—Tom discovered just the opposite effect in the face of these delicate, feminine frills. If anything, he wanted her more. And more violently, as if he could beat back time by driving his body into hers. He shook his head and walked to the window to stare out into the rain, not even daring to touch her now for fear of injuring her slight body with the sheer force of his desire.

He stood there then listening to the distinct sounds of a woman undressing—to the swish of fabric gliding over itself then sliding over skin, to the soft whisper of long hair tangling and untangling, to the feathery sound of fragile garments falling onto the floor. Sounds that would have set him ablaze once. But how could a man burn any hotter than he was burning now? He'd damn well walk out, he thought, if it came to that. If he couldn't get a better grip on himself. If—

"Tom."

He turned toward the sound of her voice with grim reluctance, steeling his body, as well as his mind, against a renewed onslaught of hot blood and hard desire. She lay in the bed looking so damn small and defenseless, as pale and delicate as a doll with her bare shoulders just peeking from the sheets and her rich dark hair spread over the pillows. So pure. So breathtakingly sweet. He found himself making a conscious effort to take air into his lungs, and instead of fire ripping through him, Tom suddenly felt his body absorbing a warm and surprising peacefulness.

The smile that played about her lips was meant to be seductive, but it struck him more as the innocent and unintentional beckoning of an angel. In spite of her marriage and their own lovemaking, she still possessed a virginal quality that was tempting and daunting at once. Lying before him in the white, white bed, Zena Briggs looked just like a beautiful bride on her wedding night.

And *that* was what slowed him. His heartbeat even seemed to slow as violent passion gave way to a flood of tenderness, a world of patience. Suddenly there was time. Time was his, as surely as Zena was his. As surely as he was hers. For all time.

A moment later, Tom slid into bed beside her, skin to skin, gathering her warmth in his arms and letting her sweetness fill his senses. The sheets smelled like sunshine. Her hair was fragrant as wild roses wet with rain. All of her so soft. So willing and warm.

"Butterfly," he whispered, when what he yearned to say was *Marry me.* Now. Here. We'll have the Reverend Mr. Bedpost for our preacher. Every raindrop on the window will be our witness. He yearned to make all those sacred promises. To love and to honor. For better or for worse. Till death do us part. That last grim promise, he figured, was the only one he could keep.

No, that was wrong, he thought as his hands moved over the warm satin of her skin with luxurious possessiveness. There was one other promise, one other sacred pledge that he could make and keep. With my body I thee worship. Here and now in this white wedding bed. And as he made slow, sweet love to her, those words drifted through his head— *With my body I thee worship*—silent and sacred as a hymn.

Chapter Sixteen

Zena felt married. No other word could quite describe the state of domestic bliss in which she had been reveling—practically wallowing—for the past week. Ever since the bank robbery, Tom had seemed calm and strangely content. She didn't know why.

She thought perhaps killing those two desperadoes for a good purpose may have had something to do with his new mood. Maybe using his gun to save Eustacia Porter's life rather than simply to administer death had purged some kind of poison from Tom's system. She didn't know. She didn't care. All Zena knew was that Tom seemed content, and that she was blissfully happy—glad as a pig in pokeweed, or as Tom might have described her, as a butterfly in a bright cocoon.

And how she loved having him around, sharing that cocoon with him. He no longer spent his evenings at Bird's under the pretext of making rounds. If he made rounds at all, he returned quickly, taking off his gun and settling in for the evening with a contented sigh. Like a husband.

They kept to themselves, making love each night like honeymooners. Slow, delicious, honeyed love after which they both slept peacefully, wrapped in each other's arms.

Glory, too, had been peaceful since the robbery. The townsfolk seemed to have a deeper appreciation of the man they'd hired solely to be a gunslinger. The *Gazette* had been singing the marshal's praises all week, and the mayor had even started talking about building a brand new jail house. One without stairs.

Her life was close to perfect, Zena thought now as she sat in the parlor with Tom. Consciously resisting the notion that it was much too good to be true and far too perfect to last, she lifted her gaze from her sewing and regarded the man she loved across the room. He was gluing the last finial atop the whatnot.

"All done?" she asked.

He nodded. "Doesn't look half bad, does it? All I have to do now is hold this piece in place until the glue takes hold."

She smiled at the touch of pride in his voice, the satisfied slope of his mouth. "Hard telling it was just so much broken wood a week ago after meeting up with three hundred pounds of flying journalist. I wonder if he's still sporting that shiner?"

Tom shrugged, his hand still clamped on the finial. "I haven't seen him up close. I've managed pretty well to be where Philo Gordon isn't all week."

"I haven't seen him, either." Zena frowned suddenly, not knowing if that was good or not. She was aware that Gordon had taken a room at Bird's and that the girls had welcomed the famous writer with open arms. But if the man hadn't come back to pester her with questions, perhaps it meant he'd already gotten his answers elsewhere. She pushed that notion aside, though, not wanting anything to spoil this lovely evening.

She rose from the sofa, holding up her handiwork. While Tom had spent the week repairing the whatnot, Zena had been working on a new shirt for him, a replacement for the one Jimmy Two Hats had slashed. Like their time together, she wanted the shirt to be perfect, too.

"I believe while you're just standing there, I'll take one last little measurement before I set to work on the cuffs." Fitting the fabric across his broad shoulders, Zena gloried in the feel of solid flesh and sleek muscle beneath the soft chambray. Lord, she loved touching him. It was hard remembering her purpose.

Tom stood there, absorbing her touch, trying to decide whether to let the whatnot go. He was better with a gun than a hammer, that was for certain, and he'd had a devil of a time getting the broken shelves back together, but he was determined to make amends for losing his temper with the dime novelist. Just as he had been determined to make amends for losing his control with Zena, though she kept doing her level best to shatter that resolve.

"Are you measuring me, butterfly," he murmured, "or making love to me?"

She moved in front of him now and held the shirt to his chest, tipping him a fetching grin as she smoothed the fabric out. "A little of both, I suspect."

"I suspect," he echoed, loving the delicate drift of her fingers over his sleeve as she fit the pale blue chambray to his arm.

"Do you like the color?" she asked. "I thought you might be getting just a mite tired of black after all these years." Her eyes flitted up to his, a hint of worry in their lovely depths.

He laughed softly. "I like it. I doubt if anybody will even recognize me in it."

"What's so bad about that?" she asked, fussing with a pin at his wrist.

"Nothing."

Nothing at all, Tom thought suddenly. By God, maybe it was time he altered his colors. A small change, but maybe with enough small changes he could put a whole new life together. He looked down at Zena's lush mouth, thinking how he hadn't witnessed even a touch of her former, thin-lipped primness this past week. If the inchworm could turn into a full-blown butterfly, then maybe there was hope for him, too.

Maybe it was time to stop waiting for miracles to simply happen. Maybe it was time, he thought, to start doing a little something to hurry those miracles along.

Tom knew good and well that Philo Gordon wasn't in the miracle business, but that's where he decided to begin. All week he'd watched from the jail house window as the journalist waited for the noon train. Every day the man stood like a fixture on the platform, juggling his ever-present pencil in order to check and recheck his watch, craning his thick neck to search the eastern horizon time and again for the telltale plume of smoke. And every day, after the train arrived and spilled its passengers, Philo Gordon walked back to Bird's. Alone. Tom didn't even want to think about what the journalist might be waiting for. Or who.

The big man was there again—alone now on the platform—when Tom sauntered over from the jail.

"This some new Eastern pastime, Gordon? Waiting for trains?" Tom put a boot up on a wooden bench, then leaned his forearms on his knee. "Doesn't seem like much of a sport to me."

"Quite the contrary, I assure you." Philo Gordon smiled as he thumbed his watch back into his brocade vest and gave his pronounced belly a hearty pat. "I perambulate the several thousand yards from the brothel and back, all the while breathing in this wonderful, midcontinental Kansas air." As if to demonstrate, he expanded his chest, which strained the buttons on his waistcoat and pulled his watch chain taut.

Tom grinned. "Not to mention all that exercise you get consulting your watch and craning your neck down the track," he drawled.

The journalist proceeded to do just that as he replied, "One needs to find a few amusements, however small, in such a quiet town." Once his watch was tucked back in his vest, he arched a quizzical eyebrow in Tom's direction. "It has been rather quiet, don't you agree? Ever since the attempt to rob the bank."

Tom straightened up now, hooking his thumbs through his gun belt. "Well, now, that's not altogether true. I'm surprised at you, Philo. I thought you had keener powers of observation. Just yesterday Amos Cleary's mule got his head wedged in a barrel of molasses. Then there was Sunday when the Reverend Hazlitt came up a half dollar short in his collection plate." Tom's mouth slid into a grin meant solely to irritate the big man. "Hell, Glory's been downright lively."

He was gratified to see that Gordon was indeed irritated. The man's neck reddened under his tight collar and his lips stiffened perceptibly.

"Very amusing, Bolt," he said with a distinct sniff. "You know what I mean."

"Yeah, I do." Tom paused for a moment, tilting his head slightly. "I like it quiet like this."

"Humph." The man pulled out his watch once more, clicked it open and stared intently at its ornate face, ignoring Tom as he did.

"I've been thinking," Tom said as he crossed his arms and leaned a shoulder against a post. "I've been wondering, when all is said and done, which one's more powerful. The pen or the gun? What's your opinion? Which one of us is stronger, Gordon? Me with my .44 or you with that little bit of sharpened lead?"

The watch clicked closed. Tom saw the quick and unmistakable glimmer of curiosity in the man's eyes. The cat was suddenly wondering what the mouse was up to.

"No pun intended, Thomas," he said with a wry twist to his lips, "but what exactly is your point?"

"Simple." Tom raised both hands palm out in a gesture of surrender. "I give up. You're stronger than I am. All I can do is kill. Take a man's life. Period." His eyes narrowed on the journalist now as he continued. "You, on the other hand, can take a man's life and then turn it inside out, upside down and all backwards."

"Backwards, indeed," the man huffed. "I made you a legend, Bolt. You'd be nobody if it weren't for me."

The oath Tom ground out now was low and lethal, but Gordon didn't even blink.

"What were you but a man—a nobody—with a sad story, a fast hand and an instinct for survival? I turned you into a star of magnificent proportions. Good Lord, Thomas, give me at least a modicum of credit. Don't you realize my novels have made you the envy of thousands of young men? Why, they'd give anything—"

"They do," Tom bellowed. "They give their lives!"

Gordon's body stiffened as his mouth sputtered. "I'm not responsible for that."

"The hell you're not."

Tom's fists clenched and his knuckles whitened. He fought the urge to slug the man again and turn his other eye black-and-blue. At the very least, he wanted to wipe that smug, self-satisfied expression off that meaty face. The violent emotions churning in his gut were nearly painful, and he realized he had Gordon to thank for those, too. He barely knew how to reason anymore. Only explode. It had to stop. He had to stop.

"I don't want to go on like this anymore," he said as quietly as he could, aware of the pain and the bone weariness in his own voice. "I'm tired of it. Dead tired." He paused for a moment—to swallow the bile in his throat, to make sure the journalist was still listening. "It's not just me anymore, Gordon. There's a woman in my life now."

The curious glint rekindled. "You're referring to the lovely Widow Briggs, I assume?"

Tom merely nodded.

"An extraordinary creature," Gordon murmured. "I commend you, Thomas."

"It's not your commendation I need, Gordon. It's your help." He let his hand fall to the gun at his hip. "I don't want to use this anymore. I can't stomach any more killing. No more. It's killing *me*. I want to marry Zena Briggs. I want to have children and watch them grow up. I want to live to see their children. Hell, I just plain want to live. Can you understand that?"

Gordon's expression was sober and thoughtful. His reply was quiet. "Yes, I believe I do understand."

"Then help me, for God's sake," Tom said, his voice a raw plea he didn't even bother to disguise now while his eyes searched Gordon's face. "You made me. Now, dammit, unmake me."

For a moment, the light in the big man's eyes seemed to warm with sympathy. For a hopeful second, Tom believed that his impassioned plea had struck home.

Then the train whistle blasted three long, harsh notes and the platform began to tremble with the approach of the big black locomotive. The brakes squealed and the wheels shot sparks as the massive engine ground to a halt. Steam hissed from the stack overhead. For a moment the entire platform was shrouded in a gray, swirling mist.

A door swung open then, and a man in black stepped down with a slow, almost chilling grace. The sun cut through the mist suddenly and settled on the pearl handle of the gun he wore.

"My dear Thomas." Philo Gordon let out a ponderous sigh. "I'm afraid it's too late."

But already Tom could see that for himself.

Chapter Seventeen

The dime novelist's chest swelled up like a randy prairie chicken's as he prepared to make the introduction. "Tom Bolt, meet Dev Mecklin. Dev is short for—"

"Devil," Tom snarled. "We've met."

But never tangled, Tom thought grimly, until now. The lean, gray-haired gunfighter was fast and accurate with that pearl-handled Colt he carried. In short, Dev Mecklin was deadly. The man was as experienced as Tom. He was just as good. Probably better.

The newcomer's dark, cautious eyes lingered for a moment on the star on Tom's vest, then he extended his hand. "Looks like you're fighting other people's battles these days, Bolt."

"It's a job," Tom drawled, shaking Mecklin's hand.

"Quite a job!" the journalist exclaimed. "I'd call it a brilliant endeavor in law and order, myself." Philo Gordon sidled closer to the newcomer, barely able to contain the gleeful edge to his voice. "I know of two bank robbers who would gladly testify that Thomas is doing a magnificent job as marshal if, alas, they could only speak."

"Two of 'em, huh?" The sneer on Mecklin's face said quite clearly that he was unimpressed.

"Two," repeated Gordon, holding up the appropriate number of fingers for emphasis. "Armed and dangerous to boot."

"Armed, maybe." Dev Mecklin shot a wolfish grin in Tom's direction. "But not all that dangerous."

The two gunfighters exchanged cold stares then— clear statements of icy purpose. With a single look, Mecklin was communicating his sole reason for coming to Glory and revealing just how dangerous he was.

Tom had seen that look before, on Mecklin and on a score of other men. It didn't surprise him much. It frightened him even less. He'd probably even used it himself a time or two. In the past, such a blatant challenge would have spurred him to action, wanting to get it done—one way or the other. But not now. God, not now.

He felt the savage curve of his mouth slacken, then twist into a grin. "Welcome to Glory, Devil," Tom said, then turned his back on both men and returned to the jail.

When she heard the train whistle, Zena frowned at the clock on her kitchen wall. Billy, blast his young hide, was getting worse every day about being on time to pick up the laundry. If he wasn't out by Royal Creek wasting bullets on bottles, then he was hanging around the jail house, bothering Tom with his big-eyed, colt-ish idol worship. Bird was just going to have to clamp down harder on that boy, and Zena had every intention of telling her so after she lugged the big laundry basket down the street.

"Come on, Domino," she said to the dog who was lazing on the back porch.

He lifted his head and blinked, but made no effort to rise.

"All right, you lazy, nameless critter." Zena shrugged as she got a better purchase on the heavy basket. "Stay there. See if I care. One of these days, though, I'll latch on to the right name. You just wait and see."

The dog yawned and lay his head back down on the sun-warmed porch boards. With a sigh more of resignation than defeat, Zena clutched her basket and headed for the saloon.

She stuck her head in the back door, expecting to see Bird or one of the girls, if anyone. Certainly not Philo Gordon. And certainly not hunkered over a table with his face stuffed with pie and his fingers slathered with whipped cream.

He smiled at her rather sheepishly, as much as that full mouth could manage, then licked his fingers with gusto before he rose to greet her.

"My dear Mrs. Briggs. I'm afraid you've caught me partaking of one of Bird's finer pleasures."

Entering the room almost warily, not knowing just how much the journalist knew about her past and dreading finding out, Zena placed the laundry basket on a table. "I'll bet that's one of Fat Alice's pies," she said. "She's a fine cook."

"Indeed." Gordon shook out a silk handkerchief and proceeded to wipe his fingers with laborious, almost loving care.

"How are you, Mr. Gordon?" It was all Zena could do not to blurt out an additional *and just how much do you know?* "I expected you'd come around to visit me again."

He raised an eyebrow as he continued to tend to his fingers, concentrating his efforts on the nails. "Did you? Now why, I wonder, was that?"

"Curiosity, I guess. I...I don't know." She could feel the color rising in her face and the flutter of panic in her chest. Why in the world was she standing here like a fool, quizzing this man, when she should have said a quick hello and an even quicker goodbye?

"My curiosity or yours, Mrs. Briggs?" He folded the hankie into a neat square and put it back into his breast pocket. His eyes danced merrily as he regarded her. "Another blush goes stealing o'er her delicate cheeks! How enchanting."

Zena gritted her teeth. Tom had been right, she thought. This man would write what he wanted independent of the truth. What he knew or didn't know wouldn't make much difference when it came time to put it all down on the lurid page. She was about to bid him goodbye when Nettie Fisk sashayed through the door that led from the saloon.

"My, my! Look who's slumming!" the redhead exclaimed when she saw Zena. Her hands went to her hips and she took a stance that more closely resembled a schoolmarm than a prostitute. "You're sure at the wrong end of town."

Zena's jaw loosened in surprise. She'd never said an unkind word to Nettie. She barely knew her, yet the woman was glaring at her now as if Zena had done her a thousand wrongs. And then it dawned on her. It was Tom.

"Hello, Nettie," she said in as level a tone as possible, hoping not to make matters worse. Lord, the last thing she wanted to do was find herself in a cat fight right under the snoopy nose of Philo Gordon.

Nettie sniffed and gave her hennaed curls a toss. "Hello, yourself. The marshal's not here if that's who you're looking for. He's probably hiding out somewhere now that Dev Mecklin's in town."

The name meant nothing to Zena, but the little twitch she spied on the journalist's mouth and the gleam in his eyes told her just about all she needed to know.

"More killing," she breathed.

"Well, don't get yourself all twisted up, Mrs. Briggs," Nettie said. "They're taking bets out front, and the smart money's on Tom. Actually, that's why I came back here. Bird needs another jar to hold the wagers."

While Nettie started rummaging through cabinets in search of a jar, Philo Gordon began rummaging through his pockets.

"I wouldn't mind making a small wager myself," he murmured while his chin was buried in the lapels of his coat. "What are the odds, my dear?"

Nettie turned, an empty pickle crock in her hands. "Even," she said. "Bet ten, get ten. But the pool's up to a couple hundred now. Whoever's closest to the right time is going to win a big, fat bundle."

"Really?" The big man's eyes sparkled as he reached into his pocket once more.

Zena thought she was going to be sick. Tom's life, not to mention his soul, was in jeopardy, and people were making bets as if this were nothing more than a horse race.

"Put me down for four o'clock, will you? No. Make that four-fifteen." Gordon tossed a gold coin to the redhead, who caught it in the jar, jingled it, then aimed the mouth of the jar in Zena's direction.

"You want some action, honey?"

All Zena could do was stare at the leering Nettie. If she spoke, she thought, her voice would be little more than a screech. If she moved, even so much as an inch, it would be to rip the ruby grin off the whore's face and the crockery out of her hands.

"Nettie, dammit, where's that jar?" Bird called from the doorway. She drew in a quick chuff of a breath when she saw Zena, and just as quickly her face settled into a polite, inscrutable mask. "Oh! How do, Mrs. Briggs."

"Hello, Bird," Zena said softly.

The madam's gaze went to the basket on the table and she clucked her tongue. "Well, I see you had to bring the laundry back yourself today. That Billy! I won't let it happen again, Mrs. Briggs. You can count on that. It isn't fitting for a lady like yourself to have to do all that hauling. A pleasure to see you again, though."

Bird turned back into the saloon then and called over her shoulder, "Let's go, Nettie. Quit dawdling. You bring that jar and then you're wanted. Upstairs."

Nettie rolled her eyes as she replied, "Yes, ma'am," then she waited until Bird's ample silhouette had disappeared from the doorway before she swished past Zena, her pert little nose in the air.

"How do, Mrs. High-and-Mighty Briggs," she taunted. "It beats me how Bird believes people don't know about you." She halted, tossing her head toward Gordon. "He knows. Everybody in Glory knows you used to be a whore. And I'll tell you what else. You still are as far as I'm concerned."

Nettie's red lips curled viciously and her eyes narrowed to kohl-rimmed slits as she moved closer to Zena. "Only now, Zena Briggs, you're a fool as well as a whore, 'cause you're not getting paid for it."

After the redhead had disappeared back into the saloon, Zena found herself wishing she could disappear, as well. She wanted the earth to open up and swallow her whole. She wanted to run from the saloon's back room, only her feet wouldn't move.

Philo Gordon's voice seemed to come from a long distance away. "It's quite all right, my dear. I'm afraid our little Nettie is just the victim of that green-eyed monster known as jealousy. I'm sure she didn't mean—"

"Yes, she did," Zena hissed as she leaned against a table, crumpling like a balloon leaking air. "Everybody knows. Even you." Her eyes flicked to his, accusingly. "But it's just more grist for your mill, I suppose. My wicked past probably doesn't mean any more to you than Tom's terrible future."

He laughed softly. "In all honesty, Mrs. Briggs, your wicked past, as you call it, doesn't interest me in the least." He folded his hands over an ample swatch of brocade vest. "You needn't be concerned. I believe I told you I was weary of writing about prostitutes and saloon girls. I have absolutely no intention of portraying Tom Bolt's newest fancy as anything but a lady, born and bred."

The pledge that might have held a certain comfort earlier sounded like so much hot air now. Her reputation didn't matter anymore. She didn't care if the whole town knew. It didn't even matter if the whole country or half the planet or one particular black-clad marshal found out about Zena Grayson Briggs. What mattered was that they were out in the saloon now, taking bets on whether Tom would live or die, making wagers and standing by to profit on the exact time "that last bullet" would rip through his heart.

And she didn't know how to stop it. It was as if a tornado were bearing down on the town and there was nowhere to run to escape it. There was nothing to do but flatten herself in the dirt and let the violence blow over her.

"Don't torture yourself, my dear," the journalist said now as if reading her thoughts. "It's unfortunate, but there's nothing you can do."

Zena drew herself up. Her eyes were wet with unshed tears, and Gordon's beefy face was a mere blur in her vision as she walked to the door. "I wouldn't bet on that if I were you, Mr. Gordon. Not one bloodred cent."

Outside, she could practically feel the man's beady little eyes burning two holes through the door as he stood there wondering just what she'd meant with that parting shot. God Almighty, she wondered, too. Other than begging Tom to leave, what was there to do?

Tom came home at six o'clock for supper as if it were a normal day. Or was it, Zena wondered, just an average day in the life of a gunfighter? Had he lived so long with the specter of death hovering at his shoulder that he wasn't even aware of it now?

Well, she certainly was. She'd spent all afternoon wrestling with that grim specter—on her hands and knees scrubbing the kitchen floor, on tiptoe going after spiderwebs, and in between, cleaning everything in sight and in reach with a vengeance. If dirt were death, by God, she'd all but banished it from this house.

For all the good it had done, she thought now, so exhausted she could barely remain upright at her end of the table. She had no more idea how to help Tom now than she had had earlier. Less, perhaps, because she realized she was too much of a coward to tell him to leave for fear that he would. Without her.

Unable to eat, she prodded a lima bean across her plate, noting that the prospect of an imminent gunfight had done nothing to diminish Tom's appetite. He was putting away roast pork and potatoes as if he'd never eat again.

Dear Lord, that wasn't what he was thinking, was it? Her fork fell from her listless hand, clattering onto her plate.

"Something wrong, butterfly?" Tom asked as if he didn't know, as if he hadn't noticed her drawn expression or her coloring as pale as death. Her blue eyes were brimming with tears and her lush mouth was thin with worry.

"Everything's wrong," she answered. "And I don't know how to make it right."

Putting his own fork down, Tom pushed his chair back from the table. No sooner had he patted his knee and murmured for her to come to him than Zena was nestled on his lap, her wet face buried in his neck.

"I'm afraid for you, Tom," she sobbed. "I'm scared to death I'll lose you."

"Zena, darlin'," he whispered, rocking her like a child. "You're not going to lose me. I'm stuck to you, honey, like a burr on a blanket."

"I heard about that gunfighter who's come to town." Her voice became urgent as she pulled back to seek his gaze. "Tom, they're taking bets in the saloon."

"Shh." He pressed her head back onto his shoulder. "That's my problem. Not yours."

Fine words, he told himself. And he meant them, but Tom didn't think for a minute that Zena would accept the notion that their troubles were independent of each other. Hell, he wouldn't. Her troubles were his. That's what loving somebody meant.

Predictably, she muttered into his collar, "The hell it's not."

He wrapped his arms more tightly around her, resisting the urge to rise and carry her out the door and just keep going—just the two of them—west, southwest, wherever. Just away. But the sad fact was that it wouldn't be the two of them. It would be Zena and Tom and Tom's reputation. Not two, but three. An unholy trinity if ever there was one. There was no escaping that. No escape, that was, other than dying. And that, Tom thought, was exactly what he had decided to do.

Chapter Eighteen

If she could have sat there forever—feeling the comfort of Tom's arms and his warm breath riffling her hair—Zena would have. Forever, though, was something Tom didn't have. At least not as long as he stayed in Glory.

She straightened up, wiping a last tear away before leveling her eyes on his. "You can't stay here with that Mecklin person gunning for you and the whole town making bets on the exact second when he's going to shoot you dead. I want you to leave, Tom. Tonight. Right now."

His mouth slanted in a grin. "That's quite a vote of confidence, butterfly. Last I heard, half of the money was on me."

"How can you even joke about something like this?"

"I told you, if I don't laugh..."

Zena rolled her eyes in exasperation. "I know. I know. If you don't laugh, you'll cry. Well, I think I'd rather have you cry, Tom, as long as you did it while we were riding out of town."

His eyes narrowed to gray slits as Tom tilted his head. His voice rumbled deep in his throat. "We?"

Damn, she thought. Why not just kneel down on the floor and lick his boots, Zena Briggs? But as long as you're begging, you might as well go through all the pitiful motions. That way, at least he'll feel worse when he finally works up enough grit to tell you no. Which was what he was going to do. She could see that from the way his mouth tightened suddenly and from the muscle clenching in his cheek. His face could just as well have been a signboard with a single word painted on it. No.

"I'd go," she said softly, searching his face for a glimmer of assent, for the tiniest crack in that stern exterior. But all she saw was a hardening of resolve that made her all the more desperate. "Leave," she begged him. "Take me with you."

"No."

Not tonight anyway, Tom thought, only he couldn't tell her that. Nor could he tell her that right that second his heart was turning wild and dizzy cartwheels because she had said she would go. Dear God, he hadn't been sure. He hadn't been sure that, despite her love for him, when forced to choose, his butterfly would not have preferred her safe cocoon. Relief and joy were rushing through him, but he dared not let those emotions show. His plan, if it were going to work at all, required Zena's complete and unconditional grief. Otherwise . . .

"I can't do that, Zena."

"Can't," she snapped, "or won't?" She shot out of his arms and stalked to the far side of the table, desperate now to find a way to make him leave, to keep him alive. If he didn't love her enough to take her with him, fine. But she loved him enough—dammit—to make him go. To make him glad if not downright eager to go. Alone.

Her trembling fingers strayed along the polished tabletop a moment, then gripped the edge. "Well, I hope you're not staying on my account, because, if you are, then you're nothing but a fool, Tom Bolt." She swallowed hard, trying to keep her voice from breaking, then plunged ahead for fear if she stopped, her voice would desert her entirely. Her voice along with her courage.

"Only a fool would stick around a town for the sake of a whore." Tears burned her eyes, but she blinked them back. "That's what I am, Tom. Not some fine lady from a fine family in Virginia, but a full-fledged, dyed-in-the-wool whore. I used to work at Bird's, just like Nettie and Fat Alice, before I married Eldon. Everybody in town knows that."

Oh, God! Except you, Zena thought suddenly as she watched the effect her words had on him. He winced, then his chest rose and fell as if he couldn't quite get enough air. His hands came up to the tabletop, long fingers flattening to brace himself. He didn't know! If he hadn't asked her to leave Glory with him, it wasn't because of her reputation. He didn't know! Until now....

She'd started, though, and it was too late to take her words back, no matter how much she wished she could. Tom looked as if she had stuck a knife in his ribs. Still, she meant to get him out of town and the only way she knew how to do that now was by giving that knife a twist.

In a voice as cool and sharp as a blade, she said, "I'm surprised, considering all the loose tongues in this town, that nobody told you."

"Nobody told me." His gaze lifted from the table-top. Pain flickered for a brief moment like candlelight in his eyes, then he seemed to snuff it out. "What suicidal idiot did you think was going to tell Tom Bolt his woman was...?"

Watching his mouth tauten in silence, Zena finished for him. "A whore? Nobody would tell you, I guess." She shrugged. "At least nobody in his right mind."

Those taut lips barely moved when Tom asked, "Why tell me now?"

"Because if you're staying in Glory on my account, then you ought to know the truth. The whole, damn, ugly truth." Zena dragged in a breath, trying to keep her tone level. "Because, now that you know it, I don't expect you to stay. Only a fool would—"

"I'm not a fool," he thundered, rising with such force his chair tipped over, his eyes burning like wild-fire as he strode to her end of the table. "I'm not a fool, Zena Briggs, and you're not a goddamned whore. Do you hear me?''

Tom grabbed her by the shoulders. "You gave yourself to me with love. Gave—not sold—me your body and your heart. You asked nothing in return.'' Now his hot gaze swept around the room. "Hell, if it's the mortgage that's bothering you, I'll sell the damn thing back. I swear. Do you understand that?''

She couldn't answer, couldn't even nod, for he was shaking the daylights out of her, not to mention shaking out the tears she had managed to hold back until now. Tom's face was dark with fury. His fingers dug harshly into her upper arms and he was bringing most of his strength to bear, literally rattling Zena's teeth within her head.

"You... are... not... a... whore.''

Beneath his molten gaze and caught in the full force of his rage, Zena wasn't sure whether he meant to addle her brain and make her forget the truth, or to reduce her to rubble and just have done with her, present as well as past.

"Say it, Zena,'' he roared. "You're not a whore. Say it, and believe it!''

"I...'' She could barely make use of what little air remained in her lungs. "I... Tom, you're... you're hurting me.''

Grinding a curse through his clenched teeth, Tom pulled her against him, wrapping his arms tight as iron bands around her. "I'm sorry,'' he breathed. "God! I'm sorry.''

He held her as she wept—stroking her hair, whispering softly and wordlessly. Cradling her in his arms, Tom wanted to shape his arms into a cocoon more strong and more secure than any four walls Zena could ever imagine. Along with her tears now, she began to pour out her heart—all the shame and disgrace and loneliness of a young and brutal life. The father she had never known. The mother who abandoned her to the mistreatment of shiftless uncles and coldhearted aunts. The privations of the war followed by the harrowing trek west to the Mississippi River. Then Bird O'Brien.

Though his warmth for Zena was boundless, at the mention of the madam's name, a cold rage whipped through Tom's whole body. Zena raised her tear-streaked face to his. Her eyes gleamed like candles that burned despite wind and rain.

"Bird was a better mother to me than my own, Tom. You mustn't hold it against her that the only thing she had to offer me was working in the saloon. She did her best."

"Don't count on my thanking her," he growled at the same instant he was inwardly thanking God or the devil or whoever had led both of them through separate hells, then guided them here to Glory and to each other. Silently Tom blessed every curse and burden, every hurt, every tear and every drop of blood that had been shed along the way. Because those terrible tear- and bloodstained paths had led them here.

His voice softened as he cradled Zena's face in his hands. Tears welled in his eyes while he spoke. "My darlin' butterfly, I wish I could have been there all those years to keep you safe from harm."

"Oh, so do I," she whispered.

"I'm here now," he crooned. "I'm here with you, and I promise you nothing bad will ever happen to you again. Never again."

It was a lie. Tom closed his eyes, letting his lips drift over Zena's wet cheeks and sodden lashes. It may have been the worst, most unconscionable lie he had ever spoken, he thought grimly. Of all his sins, it may have been the worst, and perhaps the one that would damn his soul to hell for all eternity if things didn't work out the way he planned.

But, after tomorrow—if all went well—he'd start reclaiming that soul. After tomorrow, neither he nor Zena would have a past to worry about. All they'd have would be a future. Together.

Before they could have a future, however, Tom had to deal with the present, so he left Zena with a lingering kiss and the excuse that he had to make his evening rounds. He walked down Front Street, feeling her worried, anguished gaze on his back. There hadn't been time to tell her that her past didn't matter to him. There hadn't been time to take her upstairs to the big white bed. Later, he told himself. Later there would be time to give her all those gentle reassurances and to love her like a bride. But not now.

Right now there was only time to survive. And right this minute, love—as much as he felt it—was a distraction, so Tom drove it ruthlessly from his mind as he pushed through the doors at Bird's.

Dev Mecklin was right where Tom expected him—in the rear of the saloon with his back to the wall and his eyes on the door. Nettie Fisk was trailing her fingers up his right arm, but at the sight of Tom, the gray-haired gunfighter brushed her hand aside and shifted slightly in his chair. Ready. Eager. Hungry as a wolf in winter.

Not yet, thought Tom as his gaze cut toward the bar and the ample figure of Bird O'Brien.

"Care for a drink, Marshal?" she asked him, smiling and tilting her head to fiddle with an ear bob as he approached. "On the house, as always."

Tom leaned his elbows on the bar and propped a boot up on the brass rail. He was so close to the madam that he could feel the swell of her hip against his leg. He could feel his anger, as well, like a red-hot brand on his heart, and not all of that heat was for Bird. A few hot sparks of it, he realized suddenly, were for the butterfly. Damn her. Damn her for telling him what he never wanted to know. Damn her for selling what ought to have been his. His alone.

"Just one question," he said in a rough whisper, looking down at the bar top instead of at Bird. "About Zena Briggs."

The madam laughed as she, too, leaned forward in imitation of Tom's pose. "What did the little fool do, Marshal? Confess?"

"You might say that."

"And you," Bird told him, laughter still trilling in her voice, "believed her." She clucked her tongue now. "Guess that makes fools of you both."

That made the second time in a single evening that a woman had called him a fool, and this time the word didn't go down as easily as it had earlier. It struck him now like a match flaring down a length of sandpaper.

"Then you tell me different," he snarled. His eyes flicked up to the mirror over the bar, quickly assessed Mecklin, then returned to Bird. "And tell me fast, Bird. I need to know the truth. Now."

The madam looked at him as if she were seeing him for the very first time. Her eyes narrowed and her red mouth crimped slightly. "You love her."

It wasn't a question, but still Tom nodded in reply.

"I was hoping for better for her," Bird said with a sigh. "Somebody a little more...permanent."

He let out a short, almost brutal laugh. "You and me both, lady."

"Oh, well." She shrugged her plump bare shoulders. "You want to know one thing, I guess, so I'll tell you flat out. Zena's got some funny, unshakable notion that walking up those stairs one time with the intention of doing the deed has marked her for life." Bird's mouth tightened at the corners and her gaze narrowed on Tom's face as she continued. "But I'm here to tell you that the girl was a virgin on her wedding night. That's gospel, Marshal, whether you want to believe it or not. Of course, if you love her, I don't know why the hell it makes any difference anyway."

"It doesn't," Tom growled. Then his lips tilted in a sudden grin. "Makes a damn big difference in how I feel about you, though."

The madam smiled, not so much with warmth as with understanding. "Yeah. I guess it would." She studied his face a moment before arching a dark sliver of an eyebrow. "You're all right, Bolt. For somebody not so permanent. My Zena could have done a whole lot worse."

His eyes flicked back into the mirror, seeking out the gray-haired gunslinger in the depths of the smoky room. "She still might, Bird."

Zena's past didn't make any difference, Tom told himself as he climbed the stairs in the saloon. He'd meant that. Lady or whore, he loved her just the same. Still he had to admit to a fleeting and somewhat shameful sense of relief when Bird had testified to Zena's good character. Silently he cursed her husband, the barber, for not driving those doubts from her mind and heart years ago. Tom was going to have his work cut out for him in the future, he decided, making the butterfly truly believe in her goodness. But he'd do it, he vowed, if it took a hundred years.

With a sense of renewed purpose now, he walked down the dimly lit brothel hall and knocked on Philo Gordon's door. He heard a quick rustling of papers and then the heavy shuffling of feet.

"Yes? Who is it?" Gordon inquired through the closed door.

"It's your dime novel darling, Gordon," Tom growled. "Let me in."

The door opened a crack, enough to reveal the journalist's quilted velvet smoking jacket and a single leg that ended in a velvet slipper. The look on the man's face was wary but tinged with curiosity.

"Why?" he asked with the merest hint of a whine. "If you intend to pummel me again, Thomas, I'd prefer a witness or two."

"No witnesses." Tom shouldered his way into the paper-strewn room. "Close the door," he ordered the startled and now wide-eyed journalist. When Gordon failed to comply, Tom slammed the door himself. "We need to talk."

"Talk?" The man uttered the word with a little gust of relief. "Very well."

He shuffled across the room, careful to keep his distance from the black-clad gunslinger, and lowered his own velvet-garbed bulk into a chair. "Talk," he said, cocking his head slightly. "I am, as they say, all ears."

"I need your help."

Gordon's eyebrows arched attentively. He crossed his legs and readjusted the folds of his jacket as he leaned back. "I'm listening, Thomas."

Tom's gaze cut to a stack of books on the bedside table. He picked up the top one and muttered the title, *"Death in the Dust."* Then he shook his head. "Maybe

I should autograph this for you, Philo. What do you think?''

The other man gestured to the table. "By all means. There's a pencil right there, I believe."

Pencil in hand, Tom put a boot up on the wooden bed frame, balanced the novel on his knee and stared at it thoughtfully for a moment before he proceeded to write. When he was done, he tossed it to Gordon. "There you go."

The original title had been obliterated and replaced with a new one in Tom's bold hand. The journalist held it at arm's length as he read aloud. *"Gone to Glory— The Last Adventure of Tom Bolt—*Testified to by his Good Friend, Philo Gordon, Journalist."

He blinked, then read it once more, silently, before lifting his eyes to Tom. "I'm afraid I don't understand this."

"With your agile mind and your unlimited grasp of the language, Philo?" Tom laughed softly. "That's the title of your next book. What exactly don't you understand?"

Gordon rapped his knuckles on the cover. "This is absurd. 'Gone to glory' is an expression for...for...it means..."

"Dying." Tom's mouth twisted in a grin. "Dying, Philo, my good friend. And that's exactly what I intend to do. Tomorrow."

"You can't." The big man shot out of his chair with surprising agility, but Tom's quick hand on his shoulder immediately forced him back down.

"I can," Tom snarled, "and I will. With a little help from you."

For a moment, Philo Gordon looked as if he were going to cry. His lips trembled and his eyes blinked rapidly. But then he drew in a deep breath, and when he finally spoke his voice had recovered much if not all of its former brash resonance. "Why in the name of God," he muttered as he glared up at Tom, "would I want to assist you in ruining my career?"

Tom leaned against the bedpost, draping a casual hand over his gun. "Well, let's put it this way, friend. Your career, not to mention your life, are at stake if you don't help me. Does that make the situation a little more clear?"

"Are you threatening me?" Gordon sat forward in his chair now as if he were preparing to lunge for the door.

"Yeah." Tom grinned. "And it feels damn good. I should have done this ten years ago."

Gordon snorted. "You have an amazing sense of humor, Thomas, for a man who seems to be contemplating suicide." He steepled his fingers, tapping his fleshy chin. "That is what you're doing, isn't it ?"

"Sort of." Tom crossed his arms and shifted his stance. "Let me tell you my plan."

"It's sheer folly," Gordon exclaimed when Tom concluded. The man sniffed and waved a brusque, dismissive hand. "It's quite insane, Thomas. I won't be any part of it. Nor, I suspect, will Mecklin."

"The hell he won't," Tom snapped. "Dev'll be getting just what he came to Glory for. My reputation, along with a guarantee of being the new dime novel darling. As for you, Gordon, you'll be getting yourself a more willing subject and a couple years' worth of fresh material. You'll both profit."

The journalist's eyebrows drew together and his gaze traveled from Tom to the altered copy of his novel. He picked it up, then stared at it a long moment, his mouth thin with contemplation.

Watching the man, Tom felt his breath snag in his chest. Every nerve in his body was strung tighter than wire right then, while his future—his and Zena's—was hanging fire. Everything—everything!—depended on this.

"It'll work, Philo," he said quietly, not quite disguising the catch in his throat. "And you owe me, goddammit. You owe me. A death if not a life."

Philo Gordon's fingers slowly and methodically traced the penciled letters on the cover of the book, and when he finally lifted his gaze, the journalist's eyes were moist. Tom wasn't sure whether that glistening came from sympathy or greed, but regardless of its origin, he knew where it would lead.

"Gone to Glory," the journalist murmured almost distractedly. "It has a definite ring, Thomas."

There was one person left to see. Tom stood at the foot of the saloon stairs, peering over Billy Dakin's shoulder and squinting through the smoke toward the empty table in the rear of the room.

"Where's Mecklin?"

"I been keeping my eye on him for you, Marshal," Billy said, drawing his shoulders back and expanding his chest. "I figured you wouldn't want him too far out of your sights."

The boy was unfinished work, Tom thought, and there wouldn't be time now to guide him properly. He could only hope Billy's enthusiasm and that damn gun wouldn't lead him into too much trouble. Sighing inwardly, he noticed that at least the boy's holster was properly anchored on his leg now. For what that was worth.

"I appreciate that, son. Where'd you last see him?"

"Out back." Billy angled his head toward the rear door. "He went out to the privy, but Miz Zena caught him on his way back and she was giving him what for."

Chapter Nineteen

The words were barely out of Billy's mouth before Tom was slapping the batwing doors out of his way and heading around the building. But whatever the butterfly thought she was doing, she had already done it and disappeared by the time he reached the alleyway behind Bird's. Zena was gone, and Dev Mecklin stood alone, licking the edge of a smoke then striking a match with his thumbnail.

By the time he had dropped the match in the dirt, the barrel of Tom's gun was digging into his ribs.

"Evening, Devil."

The gray-haired gunfighter blew out a hard stream of smoke. "Bolt," he growled, acknowledging the man who had come up soundlessly behind him. "You got the drop on me. Now what?"

"Now we talk." Tom holstered his gun. "Why don't you start by telling me what Mrs. Briggs wanted?"

Mecklin snorted. "Hell of a woman you got yourself tangled up with. It'll be a shame to—"

Just then the back door opened a crack, sending a banner of yellow light into the alley. "Everything all right out there, Marshal?" Billy called.

"Yup," Tom drawled over his shoulder. "We're just talking. You go on back inside now, son."

Beside him, Dev Mecklin muttered through clenched teeth, "You ought to keep that kid on a shorter leash, *Marshal*. He's been dogging my heels ever since I got to town."

Tom waited until he heard the door click closed before he continued. "What did Zena Briggs want, Mecklin?"

The gunfighter turned slowly, his hands raised slightly to demonstrate his peaceful intent. There was just enough light in the alley now to reveal his tight-lipped smirk. "She wanted me to spare your life."

Laughter ripped from Tom's throat. "She wanted *you* to spare *my* life?"

"Apparently the little lady doesn't have too much confidence in your skills, Bolt. She was prepared to do just about anything to save your hide." One gray eyebrow arched. "Including offering me one fine frame house—free and clear of debt."

Tom shook his head, muttering a soft curse.

Mecklin shrugged. "Women have offered me plenty of enticements over the years," he said with a chuckle. "Their warm little bodies mostly, in exchange for their men's lives. But I'll be damned if any of them has ever tried to buy me off with a piece of real estate. She's something else, Bolt."

Something else, indeed, Tom thought. And if nothing else now at least he knew for certain where he stood with Zena Briggs. He had replaced her cocoon. And, by God, he meant to keep it that way.

So it was with quiet desperation and more than a few implied threats that he outlined his scheme to Dev Mecklin, who stood in the dim alley listening, regarding Tom as if he were several cards short of a deck.

"You're joking," the gunfighter said when Tom had finally concluded.

"I've never been more serious in my life. Can you do it, Mecklin? Or are all those stories about you just a lot of hot wind?"

Dev Mecklin took a last drag from his cigarette, dropped it in the dirt and ground it out with the toe of his boot. "Oh, I can do it, all right." He slanted his gaze—cold as a snake—toward Tom. "I can make you a new belt hole at thirty paces if that's what you want. You just show me where."

"Right here." Tom touched his side, just above his belt line. Then he gave his black leather vest a tug. "I'll be wearing this. That might make it harder."

The other man shook his head. "You moving is what'll make it harder." He grinned. "If you really want to pull this off, Bolt, then you better not even blink or breathe."

Tom didn't reply, but he doubted if he would be able to breathe. Considering what he had just asked the gunfighter to do, he figured his heart would be pounding so badly when the time came that there wouldn't be room in his chest for any air.

Zena sat on her top porch step—her knees drawn up and her arms draped around them—waiting and watching. She didn't know what else to do after trying to buy off Dev Mecklin earlier. She had offered him her house—a fortune as far as she was concerned—and he'd turned her down. Cold. The gunfighter was set on murdering Tom, and short of killing the man herself, Zena didn't know how else to protect Tom.

"A fine thing, Zena Briggs," she grumbled to the dog who lay beside her with his muzzle resting on his paws. "The way you feel about violence and all, and here you sit, contemplating murder."

But she'd do it, she said to herself. If it meant saving Tom's life, then, dear Lord, she'd do it a million times over. For a minute she nearly wished she'd been practicing the way Billy had all summer. Considering her knowledge of guns, she'd probably only wind up killing Tom or herself instead.

When she sighed, a long and mournful sound, the dog lifted his head. Zena mustered a halfhearted smile and reached out to stroke him. "What are we going to do, puppy?" She sighed again, still frustrated by her failure to come up with a name for the animal, but too distraught over his owner this evening to be able to consider anything else.

The dog gave a little bark then and his tail thumped on the porch boards as Tom came out of the darkness. Zena sat up straight.

"You scared me half to death, Tom," she exclaimed, pressing her hand to her heart. "My Lord! There's nothing sneakier than a man dressed like midnight."

He chuckled softly as he lowered himself onto the step beside her. "Better get to work on that blue shirt, then."

Zena leaned against him, loving the hard heat of his body and the way it seemed to flow into hers at the merest contact. "I wasn't sure you planned to wear it." She eyed him sideways. "It'll make you look half-civilized, you know."

Grinning, he looped an arm around her shoulders and pulled her closer. "As long as it's just the top half, darlin'."

In spite of her grim mood, Zena laughed.

"That's better," Tom murmured. "I hate to see you sitting out here looking so sad." He nodded toward the dog. "Both of you. I could make out those hangdog expressions all the way down the street from Bird's."

"We're trying to figure out how to keep you alive," she said, "only we don't know what else to do." Zena gritted her teeth. She was sure word of her attempt to bribe Dev Mecklin had circulated through town by now, and she was prepared for Tom to tell her it was none of her business.

"I think you've done enough for one night, butterfly." He clasped her even closer, turning slightly and tipping her chin up for his gaze. "Well, almost enough. You still need to answer one question for me."

She closed her eyes a moment, dreading the question that she knew was coming. It wasn't the present that weighed heavily on Tom's mind, but the past. Her past. But since she had told him the truth, it was only human for him to be curious about the life she had tried so hard to forget. And it was only fair that she give him honest answers now. She had, after all, deceived him from the start.

Her lips trembled as she met his dark, unwavering gaze. "You want to know why I did what I did. Why I worked for Bird."

He shook his head. "No, honey," he said softly, "I already have a pretty good idea why. You didn't have a choice. But that wasn't what I had in mind to ask you."

She blinked. "Then, what?"

Tom traced his thumb along her cheek. A tiny smile touched his mouth. His voice was thick, slow and sweet as honey pouring from a jar. "I was going to ask you if you'd consider sharing your cocoon permanently with a broken-down old gunfighter. I'm asking you to marry me, Zena. Soon. Tomorrow."

It wasn't at all what Zena had expected, and her jaw loosened as she sat there, speechless. Stupefied.

Tom cupped that slack chin in the palm of his hand. "Say yes, butterfly. Please," he whispered. Worry etched his brow and drew down the corners of his mouth. "Tell me you'll marry me tomorrow."

She slipped her arms around him, holding him as if she feared he might vanish any moment into the darkness beyond the little porch. Tom could feel the surge of her heartbeat against his chest. The heart that abhorred violence drumming now in concert with his own. Why she loved him he wasn't sure. Her willingness to give up everything for his sake seemed more miracle than anything else. A pure miracle he wasn't certain he deserved, even as he knew he was willing to risk his life to preserve it. And he would. Tomorrow. But first there would be tonight.

"Tomorrow," he said as his lips brushed her soft, fragrant hair. "You finish that shirt in the morning, and I'll wear it for our wedding. Would that make you happy, love?"

A shiver coursed through her. "With Dev Mecklin for our best man? As sure as you stand up before a preacher, that awful man will be standing behind you somewhere, looking down the barrel of his gun." Her arms tightened around him. "My answer's yes, but I want to be your wife, Tom. Not your widow."

Tom dragged in a long, slow breath. A hot breath, tinged with hellfire for the lie he was about to tell. Zena wasn't going to get a chance to be his widow, for the wedding would never take place. Not tomorrow, anyway.

"You don't have to worry about Mecklin. I talked to him a while ago, and we came to an agreement." He forced a laugh, one that felt as hard and tough as a scrap of jerky lodged in his throat. "Not exactly what you'd call a gentlemen's agreement, I guess, but we swore to leave each other alone."

Zena blinked up at him. "Do you trust him?"

He nodded somberly. "I trust him." Hell, he thought grimly, he had to trust him now that he was betting with his very life on Devil's skill and ambition.

"Then I do, too," she said softly. "But, more importantly, I trust you."

Don't, he wanted to tell her. Don't trust me, because I'm planning to make tomorrow one of the blackest days of your young life. But not tonight. Not tonight.

"You can trust me, darlin'," he whispered, curving his lips into what he hoped was a fair imitation of a smile. "And you can trust that tonight I'm going to love you well enough to last a lifetime. Both our lifetimes." He slid one arm beneath her knees and the other around her back, rising in one fluid motion to hold her against him.

The dog scrambled upright, wagging his entire backside while craning his neck upward expectantly.

"Sorry, fella," Tom drawled as he opened the screen door and angled Zena through it. "You go on and find a lady of your own tonight. We'll be seeing you in the morning."

With a disappointed little woof, the animal plopped back down onto the porch boards.

"Good night, Midnight," Zena called to him over Tom's shoulder.

The dog merely sighed as he planted his chin on his paws.

Upstairs, as low lamplight flickered across the cabbage roses on her wall and washed a golden glow over the white bed, Tom undressed Zena with slow, exquisite, nearly agonizing care. Each loosened button was accompanied by a gentle, lingering kiss. Each discarded garment brought another whisper of love from his lips, while each pin from her hair was plucked with tantalizing promises and warm endearments.

"Butterfly," he whispered. "My beautiful bride."

When she stood before him, naked, her skin burnished by the lamplight, he kissed her for long, delirious moments while his fingers threaded through her unbound hair and skimmed over each sensitive inch of her flesh. Kissed her as if kissing were an end in itself. As if they had a hundred years for just that. Until her knees weakened and her eyes began to lose their focus and she swayed dizzily in his arms.

Tom lifted her onto the bed then set about his own undressing with deft speed. Zena didn't fail to notice that, after he unbuckled his gun belt, he let it drop to the floor and didn't bother to pick it up and drape it over the bedpost within easy reach.

If she hadn't quite believed him before, that single act convinced her that Tom had been telling her the truth about his agreement with Dev Mecklin. There would be no trouble between the two of them. No death in the dust. Not tomorrow, at least.

Relief flowed through her, mingling with the warm tide of desire that was already thrumming in her blood. Relief and sweet, sweet hope. They would marry. Tomorrow.

She couldn't recall ever having felt so complete, as if all her fears had suddenly turned to hope, and as if everything bad in her life had become good. Out of her tarnished past, she had emerged a glittering silver. Her fears and her frailties seemed to be welding now into a wonderful, newfound strength.

All because of the man who stood before her now, his lean form looking all the more masculine against the roses on the wallpaper, his angles sharper and darker in contrast with the pallid blooms. At that moment Zena imagined him as a pagan bridegroom with gold lamplight glistening on the hard curve of his chest and weaving through his dark hair like golden thread.

When he sat on the edge of the bed to take off his boots and trousers, she let her fingers drift along the warm, ropy muscles of his arm.

"We can't stay here, can we?" she asked quietly. "After we're married, I mean?"

"Not without being hounded by more glory seekers." Tom yanked off a boot and let it drop onto the floor. "I know it'll be hard for you, Zena, giving up all of this."

"Not so hard," she said with a sigh as her gaze took in the room she had created, the wallpaper she had chosen with such care, the polished surfaces she had touched hundreds, probably thousands, of times. "I always felt so safe here. But you're my safety now, Tom."

"Your cocoon," he murmured as he whisked off the last of his clothes. Then he slid under the covers and drew her into his arms, nuzzling his face into the warm hollow of her neck. "I'll take good care of you, butterfly. I swear to you."

"And I'll take good care of you." Zena laughed softly while her fingertips skimmed the solid muscles of his shoulder. "Who knows? I might even civilize you, Tom Bolt."

She could feel his lips curve in a smile against her skin. His tongue left a cool trail on her neck that was instantly warmed by his breath. His hand moved over her rib cage, then burned an even hotter trail along her flank as it sought the part of her that felt anything but civilized right then.

Her hips arched for his touch.

"Then, again," she whispered as waves of heat shimmered through her, "I might not."

Chapter Twenty

It was barely dawn when Tom slipped soundlessly from the bed and fumbled on the floor for his clothes. In the pale light coming from the window, he could just make out the shape of the roses on the wall, but their color remained indistinct. He'd always remember those roses, he thought, as he shrugged an arm into his shirt. No matter how long he lived, he'd forever see his butterfly surrounded by lush, lamplit flowers.

He'd left the bedside lamp burning low the night before, the better to see her, the better to memorize the delicate shape of her face and the soft contours of her body. He had loved her long into the night until the oil lamp had given one last frail flicker and had finally sputtered out.

He had made a study of loving her. Again and again, he had held back his own release until Zena had gone over and beyond the brink of passion. Again and again, she had lain quivering and spent in his embrace only to be urged toward further, more breathless heights. Only to call out his name—again and again— begging him to follow.

And follow he had, Tom thought now as he buckled his gun belt and bent to tie it to his leg. If things didn't go right today; if Dev Mecklin's aim was off; if Tom Bolt wound up standing at the gates of hell, then at least he'd know he'd been to heaven the night before. He and Zena both.

He bent to kiss her, brushing aside a tangled strand of her dark hair. When he placed his lips on the warm flicker of pulse at her temple, her lips curved in sleepy delight and she murmured his name.

He longed to remind her that it was her wedding day, but he couldn't manage another lie. Not now. Not when this might be the last time he would ever lay eyes on her. Instead he whispered, almost to himself, "Goodbye, my love." Then he turned and walked quietly from the room, pausing in the doorway for one last glimpse of the butterfly fast asleep in a roomful of roses.

It was her wedding day! That notion kept twinkling in Zena's brain and setting off little fireworks in the pit of her stomach all morning as she worked furiously to set her house in order in preparation for leaving Glory. Tom hadn't said just when they'd be going, but she figured it would be soon. The sooner the better, she thought. Before another shootist hungry for a bite of Tom's reputation showed up in town.

She stripped the linens from her bed, hugging them to her for a moment, remembering the night before when Tom had made her feel like his bride already. A bride to be worshiped and adored as he had postponed his pleasure again and again in order to send her to dizzying and undreamed of heights of her own pleasure. She thought it ought to have bothered her more when he had insisted on leaving the lamp burning beside the bed, but it hadn't. The light had allowed her to witness the loving warmth in Tom's eyes and the ecstasy that made his handsome face all the more beautiful.

Grinning now, with an armful of sheets, Zena glanced at the carved wood that Tom had christened the Reverend Mr. Bedpost. She felt married already in her heart and soul. More married than she'd ever felt during the four years that she was Mrs. Eldon Briggs.

Eldon! With all she had to get done today, not the least of which was finish Tom's shirt, Zena suddenly felt compelled to pay a visit to the cemetery, to say her last farewell and to give the grave site one final, thorough weeding before she left.

And, though she'd awakened with no second thoughts about marrying Tom, by the time she had walked to the cemetery, Zena was wondering if she hadn't been a bit too impetuous and more than a little rash in agreeing to leave Glory so soon. She knelt by the gravestones, her head bowed and her eyes closed. Glory had been her home—the only one she'd really ever had—for ten years. Before that, she had remained with abusive relatives too long in the childlike hope that indifference would turn to love, that whippings would turn to embraces. They hadn't, and when she had finally run away, she remained briefly with Bird O'Brien, preferring life among friends in a whorehouse to facing her fate alone and homeless. Then along had come Eldon Briggs and a true home of her own.

"Home," she murmured now, clasping her hands in her lap. Even here in the cemetery, these cold, hard stones had served her as a kind of anchor. But suddenly her future seemed like a vast, uncharted sea where she might very well find herself adrift and alone.

Panic fluttered in her chest. Tom called her a butterfly, but she wasn't like that winged creature at all. She wasn't light and free, gaily skimming the currents of a summer breeze, flitting from bloom to bloom. She wasn't a butterfly in any way. Just the opposite. As if to prove it, her limbs began to feel heavy and cumbersome, and her whole body seemed incapable of motion, as if she were rooted to the spot in which she sat.

"What am I going to do, Eldon?" she whispered, staring at the epitaph etched deeply into the stone as if the letters might magically rearrange themselves, offering her an answer.

But they didn't. Eldon wasn't listening to her any more now than he had listened to her during the four years of their marriage. It was Tom who truly listened to her. It was Tom who made her feel—with every word and every touch—not only safe, but beautiful and good.

She reached out to yank a dandelion from the ground, then shook the loose dirt from its long taproot. Tom might better call her a dandelion, she thought, for she was closer in spirit to an earthbound weed than to a winged creature. And she was afraid. Afraid that if she ripped herself up by the roots, she would wither and die. Afraid that Tom was wrong, that she wasn't anything like a butterfly and that if she broke out of her cocoon, she would plummet to the ground rather than soar by his side.

Lifting her wet gaze from the granite headstone, Zena whispered heavenward, "Help me fly. Please turn my roots to wings."

It was an hour later when Zena stood, clamping her hands on her aching back, rolling her neck to smooth out the kinks. She had weeded the grave site as never before, wrenching dandelions from the soil and pulling up stalks of panicum as if she were searching for a buried trove of courage instead of just cleaning up a few square feet of ground. About all she'd managed to do, however, was work her hands raw and break her nails.

Exhausted now and damp with perspiration, she still didn't have an answer. Could she go and survive? She stared down at the two graves for a long while, hopefully, sadly, and finally with the realization that she'd find no courage here among the dead. If she found it at all, it would be among the living. So, with a ragged sigh and a last goodbye to Eldon and the baby, she began the walk back to town.

She hadn't gone far when Tom's dog bounded from the bushes along the creek. His black-and-white coat was soaking wet, and Zena waited until he had shaken himself before she knelt down to pet him.

"Poor old nameless," she muttered, picking burrs from his wet fur while trying her best to avoid his friendly, persistent tongue. "How in the world am I going to marry Tom and name his babies when I can't even come up with a decent name for you?"

Astonished by her own words, Zena sat back on her heels. Babies! Hers and Tom's. The notion hit her with the force of a stiff wind off the prairie, blowing through her and taking her breath away. Not that the possibility of children hadn't occurred to her before, but it had always seemed more dream than real. A sweet fantasy rather than a solid fact. Now, as she sat there only vaguely aware of the dog as he lapped at her cheeks and hands, she could truly picture those dark-haired, gray-eyed babes, the sons and daughters born of her love for Tom.

The future, she thought as she drew in one frayed breath after another, might have arrived already, taking hold inside her like a tiny seed. Their future. Hers and Tom's. She'd been so mired in the past, so bogged down in the present that she hadn't given the future much credence. But it could be here already, as solid and warm and real as the grip of a baby's fist or the tug of a tiny mouth on her breast. More safe and sure than anything she had ever known before. How she longed for that future now, wherever it was meant to be. For wherever it was, it would be home. How she yearned to share that home with Tom.

She pictured a house not so different from the one she lived in now. The rooms would be sunny and bright, especially the nursery. A little smile flitted across her lips as she wondered if she'd be able to find the same cabbage rose paper for the bedroom. If nothing else, it was a lovely way to decorate a cocoon and the perfect background for a butterfly.

The next thing Zena knew, she had scrambled to her feet and was running toward Glory with the dog barking at her heels and bounding in circles around her. Running for all she was worth toward her future while her skirts billowed and skimmed over the ground as lithe and graceful as wings.

Closer to town, she could see her house with its fresh white paint nearly glowing in the bright sunshine. The windows, spotless as always, glinted almost gaily, as if they were winking in her direction. Such a pretty little house, Zena thought. But only that. A house. From this day forward—this day, her wedding day—Tom Bolt would be her home.

Then, as if her thoughts had suddenly conjured him up, Zena saw Tom on Front Street. Hard to miss that tall, broad-shouldered, black-clad form, she thought, and the tin badge on his vest that twinkled like a star on a midnight sky. Hard, too, as she got closer, to miss the other black-clad figure or the pearl-handled pistol glowing on his hip.

Only then did she finally notice that half the town's population was out on the sidewalk, gathered in cautious little groups, and the other half was leaning from windows or peeking around doors. At the far end of the street, Bird's balcony was brimming with men waving their hats and girls flaunting hankies. And right in the middle of it all, Philo Gordon sat in a straight chair in front of the bank, looking self-satisfied and pleased, for all the world like an expectant judge at a beauty contest rather than a witness to murder.

Tom heard Zena's scream as if it came from miles away. He saw the butterfly running toward him—dark hair flying and white petticoats whipping around her legs—as if in slow, slow motion.

All morning time had crawled. Minutes had taken hours, it seemed, and he wondered now if he were really going to die today and this was just the Good Lord's way of letting him savor his final hours by making each moment seem particular and precise.

If that was the case, there hadn't been much to savor ever since he'd kissed his butterfly goodbye and left her in her bed of roses. Nothing savory in skulking around town, stealing sausage casings from Mueller the butcher, then filling them with the blood of the chicken he had filched from Lemuel Porter's coop, and finally securing the slippery, smelly cases in the lining of his vest to serve as his fatal wound. How he'd ever come up with such a stupid notion, Tom wasn't exactly sure now. Desperate men did desperate things. But this! It was pure insanity. He probably ought to be shot for this foolishness alone.

Maybe all the years of losing sleep and living on the edge of his reflexes had finally caught up with him. Maybe it was a good thing he didn't need to depend on those reflexes today, because his mind felt slow and hobbled. Every second seemed to lumber past like a box turtle, trying to get from here to a faraway there. He was even sweating slowly, Tom realized, feeling each trickle slide separate and distinct down his side.

Thirty feet in front of him, under the noon sun, Dev Mecklin didn't cast a shadow. Probably wasn't sweating, either. Well, hell, why would he? Devil was about to realize his greatest ambition by bringing down Tom Bolt. It would be his face on the dime novels from now on. The face that wore just the hint of a smirk right now beneath eyes slitted in fierce concentration.

That was how it was supposed to be. But Tom hadn't counted on Zena winging out of nowhere. She was supposed to be home, safe in her cocoon, not rushing toward him with fear in her eyes and her pretty face as pale as death. She was supposed to hear of his death, not see it. One way or another, his butterfly was going to get hurt, and there was nothing Tom could do, because if he moved now—a fatal fraction, a twitch—Mecklin stood ready to respond with a flash of that pearl-handled gun. Somebody ought to stop her.

Then suddenly somebody did. Billy Dakin's long arms snatched her back to the sidewalk in a swirl of petticoats and curses and flying little fists and feet. A feisty blur at the edge of Tom's vision.

Only that was wrong, too, Tom thought, because he had sent the brash kid on an errand only a while ago to make sure that Billy and his itchy fingers were nowhere near. Only now he was here, dammit.

But it was all too late. Mecklin was going for his gun.

God Almighty! He wasn't dead, Tom thought. At least he didn't think so, although he was on his knees in the dust, with a pain in his side as hot as a branding iron and not all of the blood there from the mayor's missing chicken.

He tried to clear his head, to remember what came next. There had been the simultaneous roar of two pistols. He had put his own bullet dead center in the hoofprint just to the left of Mecklin's heel—precisely where he planned it. Then a stunned gasp had gone up from the crowd, followed by one piercing, agonized scream.

What came next, dammit? He hadn't counted on the pain—his own or Zena's painful scream—or on his head being a slime-dark swamp that he had to slog through in order to recall the sequence of events. He was down. He knew that was right. Hell, he couldn't do anything else.

"Psst! Lie down, for God's sake, Thomas. I can't very well disguise a kneeling corpse."

Philo Gordon's face—pink as ham, panicky—appeared before him. That was it! Gordon, the man who'd ruined his life, was going to salvage what was left. Tom slumped the rest of the way to the ground, which wasn't hard to do considering that he could barely keep upright.

Darkness covered him then. A musty, stifling darkness that made him wonder again if he was dead, until he realized it was the blanket Gordon had covered him with. Dead men didn't feel pain, after all, and since Tom hurt like hell he concluded he was still most assuredly alive.

And dead men didn't hear, did they? His ears were ringing, but just above him he could hear Philo Gordon's grim, dramatic pronouncement. "Tom Bolt's dead." Then somewhere above his dark shroud, he heard the unmistakable wail of the butterfly, a forlorn keening that made him hurt all the more. He hadn't meant to hurt her, he thought. The hell he hadn't.

There was muttering then, and murmuring, and the muted clucking of tongues. "Dead." "He's dead."

And then, at the very last—the dark of the blanket somehow seeping inside his head—Tom heard the kid. Oh, God! The damn, dumb, eager, loyal kid—who was drawing on Dev Mecklin to avenge Tom Bolt's death.

Chapter Twenty-One

It was a little after sunset when Zena finally rose from her corner of the settee to light the lamp. Her hand was steady as she touched the match to the wick. All afternoon her hand had been steady and her mind had been focused on a single task. She was finishing Tom's shirt. Every time she felt the tears rising in her throat to choke her, she would bite down on her lip. Whenever her hand threatened to waver, she would prick herself with the needle and continue to sew.

Tomorrow she would cry. Tomorrow her tight heart would explode in a million irretrievable pieces. And tomorrow she would give herself up to grief for a lifetime, floating away on a sea of grief as vast and vacant as the prairie. But tonight she was going to finish the shirt that Tom had planned to wear for their wedding.

"I'll be damned if they'll bury him in black," she muttered now as she stepped over the dog who lay curled in a black-and-white ball on the rug. She had said those same words so often and each time with such fierce conviction that the animal didn't even react when she uttered them once more.

Settling in her corner of the settee once again, Zena picked up the nearly finished garment along with her needle and thread. For a moment she allowed her fingertips to caress the finely woven chambray. For a second she pictured Tom's steel gray eyes softened by its delicate hue. Then, with pain surging in her throat and her lips twisting with grief, she announced to the dog and the empty chairs and the four walls, "I'll be damned if they'll bury him in black."

They seemed to be the only words she could manage in the aftermath of the terrible events on Front Street. She had spoken them first to Philo Gordon—after she had stopped screaming and after he had ordered Bird to drag her away from Tom's poor blanket-covered body.

She didn't even remember walking home. As Bird ushered her along, Zena kept looking back over her shoulder at the two gunfighters lying in the street. Her Tom, lying in the dust.

It had happened so fast that she could barely comprehend it. She'd been running and then somebody— Billy, she thought—had yanked her back onto the sidewalk. After that, gunfire ripped through the summer air. She had wanted to close her eyes, but she couldn't, so she had stood there watching in wide-eyed, wild-eyed horror as blood sprayed in a red mist from Tom's vest just before he dropped to his knees.

She remembered looking at Mecklin then, at the smug twist of his mouth as he holstered the pearl-handled gun. She remembered Philo Gordon rushing past her, waving a blanket like a matador, hissing "Shoo!" and "Scat!" to the curious folks who were crowding up to get a closer look at Tom.

She'd been trying to get to him, using her fists and elbows and all her might to make her way through the crowd when she heard Philo Gordon say that Tom was dead. Dead! Then all of a sudden Billy was yelling that nobody could shoot Glory's marshal and get away with it.

Foolish Billy. Foolish and fast. Lightning fast, for Billy shot Dev Mecklin before the deadly pearl-handled gun cleared leather, before the crowd could even run for cover. Then everybody was cheering, and Billy was being lifted shoulder high and passed from hand to hand. Zena remembered seeing a kind of stupefied smile on the boy's face as the crowd swept him up and away. She remembered the dust that their feet stirred up and how it settled on the two bodies left lying in the street.

And now, as she worked the needle through the soft edge of a buttonhole, she remembered feeling dead herself, wanting to lie down beside Tom, to take him in her arms, close her eyes and let the dust sift over both of them until the end of time.

But first she had to finish his shirt. She'd be damned if she'd let them bury him in black.

* * *

The dog lifted his head from the carpet just as the knock sounded on the front door. Zena broke the thread from her last knotted stitch.

"There," she said, rising to answer the door.

Billy stood there, hat in hand, his eyes bright despite the darkness, almost feverishly so.

"I came to tell you how sorry I am, Miz Zena." He scuffed a toe along a porch board. "There wasn't time before," he mumbled, "what with all the shouting and fussing."

"Thank you, Billy." Zena opened the screen door for the boy to step inside. Down the street she could hear the raucous music at Bird's. Not funeral dirges, but happy, toe-tapping tunes. Well, why not? she thought disgustedly. Tom Bolt's death had put Glory on the map. The double killing would undoubtedly put the town in the history books, and now one of their very own wore the title of "Fastest Gun in the West."

Tears glistened in the boy's eyes as he stood in her vestibule. Zena's immediate instinct was to comfort him, but she had no comfort to give. Her heart was empty. And her head, too, as she searched for a few words of wisdom for this boy who had just entered manhood with the speed of a bullet.

"I'm sorry, too, Billy," she finally said. Even those few words came painfully.

But he nodded solemnly, as if taking comfort from them anyway. Then he reached into his back pocket, managing the merest quirk of a grin as he handed her

a bottle. "I figured you'd be feeling down, Miz Zena.
A few nips of ol' Dr. Stillwell's cure-all might just
help." He pointed to the label. "Right here it says it
eases heartaches, too."

Zena accepted it reluctantly, unwilling to tell Billy
that her heart was so empty it couldn't even ache.

"Well, I guess everybody's expecting me back at
Bird's," he drawled as he moved toward the door.
Then he paused on the threshold, gazing back at her.
There was a trace of wistfulness in his voice, along with
a hesitant note of pride, when he said, "I don't sup-
pose I'll be fetching laundry no more, Miz Zena."

"No. I don't suppose you will. You take care, Billy."

Take care, she thought, watching him amble back
toward the saloon where his hand would be shaken and
his back would be slapped and his whole future
wrenched out of his control.

Long after Billy had disappeared through the batwing doors at Bird's, Zena stood there, staring at the
street, one hand drifting over the silky head of the dog
who had come to sit beside her, the other hand hoist-
ing the bottle of cure-all, toasting young Billy Dakin in
all his terrible glory.

In the dim back room of Beeson's Funeral Parlor, in
a clutter of empty vases and silk lilies and vacant cas-
kets, Philo Gordon was humming. Off-key. One beat
behind the string band at the saloon two doors down
the street. He lifted the corner of one drawn curtain,
peered outside a moment—still humming—and then

intoned, "Darkness, that bosom companion to deceit, has at last descended upon us."

The journalist turned, brandishing the hammer he held in his hand. "Time to nail you in, Thomas."

A groan, more of disgust than pain, rose from the depths of the long pine box. The sawhorses beneath it rocked slightly. "That's real good thinking, Philo. What do you plan to do then? Levitate a couple hundred pounds of corpse and casket out to the wagon?"

"Oh, dear," Gordon murmured. "I'm afraid I failed to consider that."

Tom lugged himself to a sitting position, draping his arms over the edges of the pine box, more like a man in a bathtub than a body in a casket. He almost laughed at the journalist's distraught expression. Almost.

"How about considering this?" he asked wearily. "You go get the wagon. Then, after I haul the box outside and climb back in, you can wield that hammer to your heart's content."

"A capital idea, Thomas."

Gordon unlatched the back door, then poked his head out to make certain the alley was empty. Before exiting, he saluted Tom with the hammer. "You're quite intelligent . . . for a dead man." His lips twitched upward in his beefy face. "I'm going to miss you, my friend."

"Good," Tom muttered as the door closed. With a sigh, he glanced down at his bandaged side, glad to discover that the cotton strips were white, not bloodstained like the last ones. His wound had turned out to be less serious than he'd first feared. Dev Mecklin's lead had plowed a neat little furrow in his side at the same time it was ripping his vest and releasing the gory mess sewn in its lining. Poor Devil. He'd done it perfectly, only to get a bullet in his heart as a reward.

The undertakers had done the gray-haired gunfighter up real handsome, according to Philo, then had put him in a pine box and tilted it toward the window for all the world to see. For all of Glory to see, at least. Tom tried to console himself by thinking that Devil might have enjoyed the attention and that if he hadn't met that last bullet here, it would just as likely have been in the next town down the line.

Gritting his teeth against the remnants of pain, Tom eased his shoulders back down in his own pine box. He was glad to be alive. Hell, he was glad to be officially dead even though it had meant spending a long afternoon locked in the back room of the undertaker's, listening to Philo Gordon stall the eager mortician and then having to endure the journalist's incessant review of the day's events. From the sound of him, Philo had at least a nickel's worth of his dime novel written already.

On the other hand, he thought glumly, maybe he was just as dead as Devil and this was his personal hell—sharing a coffin-cluttered room with a chattering, nattering Gordon, all the while worrying about Zena, wondering how she was getting through this day that should have been her wedding day, willing her to hang on for a little while longer while she made his death all the more believable by her grief.

Worrying about the kid, too. Kid, hell! He'd have to be a man now. The man who shot the man who shot Tom Bolt. With a single bullet, Billy had bought himself a big, bad reputation. To do anything about that now, though, Tom would have to jeopardize his own official demise.

A hell of a thing for a man to have to do—die in order to live. Tom wondered if, given a second chance, he'd do it again. He grunted softly, shifting his large frame in the pine box, crooking his knees a bit more so the top of his head didn't keep scraping the wood. Yeah, he probably would do it all over, but next time he'd get a better fitting coffin. This one was too damn short.

Course they said that old folks' bones had a tendency to settle, so maybe he'd be a little shorter when his real time came. He'd have to remember to caution his butterfly about that a couple decades down the road. Maybe in half a century or so. Because Tom planned to be a very old man before he ever saw the inside of one of these boxes again.

Zena smoothed the pale chambray over the ironing board. She had sprinkled the finished shirt with water only moments ago, but now she was sprinkling it with tears. Once more she cursed Dr. Stillwell's Amazing Vegetable Cure-All. It hadn't done anything to ease her heart; it had simply loosened her tears, allowing them to fall on the fabric where they sizzled and steamed now beneath the hot iron.

She was trying not to think at all, to make her mind a painless blank while she worked the tip of the iron into the gathers at the cuff. Then she heard a wagon creak as it pulled up near the back door. A moment later she recognized Philo Gordon's ample shadow moving past the kitchen window.

What did he want? To interview the grieving Widow Briggs? To get a firsthand impression of her broken heart and a glimpse of her tears? Or perhaps to apologize for having her dragged away from Tom's lifeless body? Or to say he was sorry for the whole catastrophe that had been Tom Bolt's life and the tragedy of his death?

Zena wrenched the back door open, greeting the journalist with a scowl on her face and a hot iron in her upraised hand. Beside her, the dog growled menacingly for a moment. But then, instead of standing his ground or lunging for Gordon's throat, the animal let out an almost happy bark before he scuttled out the door and disappeared into the darkness.

It was no surprise, though, when Gordon doffed his bowler hat and graced her with an oily smile.

Zena waved the iron in his face. "You're not welcome here, you ink-spotted, bloodstained, death-peddling demon. Go away."

She started to close the door on him, but Gordon's foot slid out to block it. "I understand your sentiments, Mrs. Briggs," he replied in a raspy whisper.

"But, please, if you'll listen to me for a moment, I assure you that you won't regret it."

Zena's response was a stiffening of her spine and an upward ratchet of her chin. "Well?"

The big man moved sideways, maintaining his foot in the door while he shifted his bulk just enough to afford her a clear view of the back of the wagon where the dog, his white fur silver in the moonlight, sat patiently with his muzzle resting on a simple wooden casket. Zena's knees gave way and she dropped the iron in order to hang on to the door frame.

"No!" The word left her with the last of her breath. Tom was dead. No amount of busywork could fend off that stark realization anymore. All the stitching and ironing in creation would never bring him back. All the cure-all in the world would never ease her heartsickness or her desolation.

Philo Gordon's hand was clutching her elbow now. He wasn't smiling anymore, but wearing a look of urgency as he led her toward the wagon.

"We really must hurry, my dear," he said, propelling her along.

"Hurry?" Zena echoed numbly. Nothing was making sense except the long pine box in the back of the wagon. She couldn't tear her gaze away from it.

"To the cemetery." Gordon's voice was as brisk as his strides. "It's all arranged. You'll see."

Cemetery. That sole word filtered into her consciousness. It was time to lay her love to rest. Time to bury Tom. But not in black. She'd be damned if he'd go to glory wearing black.

Jerking her arm from the journalist's grasp, Zena ran back into the house, where she snatched the shirt from the ironing board and took one more—well, two more—bracing, heartache dispelling, mind-numbing swigs of cure-all.

Philo Gordon had informed her that he intended to lay Tom to rest with dignity rather than allow the townsfolk to make a circus out of his burial. She sat beside him, clutching Tom's shirt to her bosom, while Gordon drove the wagon uneasily, holding the reins as if they were snakes about to writhe out of his grasp. The road was dark despite the bright moon, but there was enough light to make out the grin that seemed to have settled permanently on the journalist's lips. Zena had thought her heart was numb and that she couldn't feel anything, but that self-congratulatory grin riled her no end. And there was enough cure-all humming in her bloodstream now that she didn't hesitate to let him know.

"I suppose you're mighty pleased with yourself, Mr. Gordon," she said tartly. "I suppose you're planning to get rich selling a million books telling people how Tom Bolt met up with his last bullet."

He gave her a sidelong glance as he contended with the horses at the end of the wriggling reins. "The thought had crossed my mind, dear lady." His grin widened.

"Tom was right. You've got ink running in your veins instead of blood, and a wallet where your heart ought to be." Zena sniffed, then angled her shoulders once again to look in the back of the wagon where the dog rode contentedly beside the casket, nestled among piles of bulging burlap sacks. Poor thing, she thought. He didn't realize his master was gone. On the other hand, perhaps the animal was blessed in his ignorance.

Moonlight glinted on the granite headstones in the little cemetery as Gordon tugged back on the reins.

"We have arrived," the journalist intoned as he surveyed the scene, "and it would appear that we are alone and unobserved." He wrapped the leather reins around the brake, then said once more, louder this time. "We have reached the cemetery, and the coast, as they say, is clear."

Zena looked at the man as if he were a lunatic. She was about to tell him she wasn't deaf nor was she blind. She knew very well where they were. And why. Just because her head was buzzing a little bit with cure-all didn't mean she couldn't grasp the situation, for heaven's sake. But just as she opened her mouth to speak, the dog began barking wildly while he scratched frantically at the coffin.

Maybe Tom's death had made them all a little crazy, she was thinking. Her head was swimming. The journalist was talking as if he had an audience, and the dog was making such a ruckus now she could hardly hear herself think.

Then there was the sound of muffled cursing from inside the pine box.

Inside! Oh, dear Lord! A thousand visions—wonderful, terrible, incomprehensible—tumbled through her brain while a thousand emotions went cartwheeling through her heart. Her hand shot out to clutch Philo Gordon's sleeve.

"He's alive!"

"Well, yes and no," the journalist replied calmly as his eyes continued to scan the road behind them.

Zena's fingers dug perilously into the man's arm now. "What do you mean yes and no? I hear something back there. It has to be him. Tom's alive."

"In a manner of speaking," Gordon murmured.

"In a manner of..." Zena's voice dropped off to a shocked intake of breath when, suddenly, the air was rent by a loud thump, more muffled curses and the sound of nails ripping from wood as the lid of the coffin flew off. A second later the dog, in a flurry of fur, leapt into the pine box.

There was low, rumbling laughter then from the depths of the coffin. "All right, fella. All right. It's good to see you, too, but there's really not room in here for the both of us."

Zena's head was spinning. She wasn't sure right now if what she was hearing and seeing was real, or merely some wild and hopeful figment of her imagination. Philo Gordon had already climbed down from the wagon, so she scrambled after him. But when her feet touched the ground, her knees wouldn't support her and she crumpled in a heap. She sat there, staring at the chambray shirt she still clutched in her hands.

"It's that blasted cure-all," she mumbled forlornly, not even sure if she had spoken out loud or not. "I'm hallu...hallu...I must be losing my mind."

"No, you're not hallucinating, butterfly."

Strong hands locked on her elbows and lifted her to her feet. Warm lips grazed over her face, then settled possessively over her mouth. God! If she was kissing a ghost, she didn't care. How she loved the sweet glide of that tongue and the scrape of whiskers against her cheeks.

It wasn't easy, but Tom pulled back from that eager, tipsy mouth that had beguiled him so when he first arrived in Glory. Being dead might be the best idea he'd ever had, he thought. But he wasn't dead and *buried* yet, nor was he home free.

"You're real," Zena breathed, clinging to him, her arms circling his waist. "Oh, Tom. Are you alive? What in the world is happening?"

"I'm alive, butterfly, but my reputation's dead. I'll tell you all about it later, but right now we have to move fast before anybody sees us. Just answer one question for me." He stepped back, tipping her face up. "Will you come with me? Away from here? Forever?"

Even though she nodded happily, Tom wasn't sure she understood. He grasped her shoulders now. "You can't go back, Zena. It means leaving everything—" he angled his head toward the graves "—and everyone behind. Now. Tonight. Philo's already made up a story about you going back east. There's not a person in town who won't believe it. But it means you can't go— you can't go home ever again. You need to understand that."

Her smile was just slightly askew. "My head may be a little bit fuzzy right now, and I may not understand everything that's going on, but I do understand that you're my home, wherever you are," she said with absolute certainty. "I love you, Tom Bolt, and I'd go with you to the very edge of the earth if I had to."

Tom hadn't realized it, but he'd been holding his breath in anticipation of her reply. Now he let it out with a joyous gust of laughter as he pulled her close. "Well, not quite to the edge of the earth, darlin'. You'd probably teeter right over in this condition."

Philo Gordon came up beside Tom, angling his watch into the moonlight. "Time is of the essence, Thomas. Need I remind you?"

Zena watched then, idly petting the dog, while the two men lugged the empty coffin to an open grave. Once they had lowered the pine box into the hole, Tom took off his black shirt and tossed it into the grave. After he had convinced Zena that the bandage on his side didn't need fussing over, he unbuckled his gun belt and, without a second's hesitation, dropped that in, too.

Philo Gordon sighed dramatically. He held a shovel in one hand and with the other he pressed his bowler hat over his heart. "A few words might be appropriate at this time."

Tom rolled his eyes as Zena guided his arms into the chambray shirt.

"Here lies Tom Bolt," the journalist intoned.

"May he rest in peace," Zena whispered.

Even the dog gave a somber little woof.

Tom squatted down to pick up a handful of dirt and sprinkled it into the grave, then brushed his palms together briskly as he stood.

"You're looking at a free man," he said, grinning while he buttoned the pale blue shirt.

"A wealthy man, too." Philo Gordon planted his hat back on his head and reached into the pocket of his coat, producing a slip of paper that he handed across the grave to Tom. "That's a bank draft made out to the bearer. It should be enough to start over, wherever you go." He cleared his throat, seemingly at a loss for words then. The paper, still in his proffered hand, riffled in the cool evening breeze.

Tom's mouth tightened at the corners as he stared at it. Zena broke the silence.

"You old goat," she exclaimed, wrapping her arms around the journalist. "You do have a conscience after all. And more than just black ink in your heart."

Gordon's gaze remained fastened on the man standing across the open grave. "Take it, Thomas," he insisted. "Please. If it helps, you might consider it a bequest from the late Tom Bolt."

Something flickered in Tom's eyes then. Zena wasn't sure if it was pride or fury, but before she could identify it, the flare had disappeared. She breathed a little sigh of relief as Tom took the paper and tucked it into his back pocket.

He leveled his steely eyes on the journalist. "Much obliged, Philo," he said. "And I'll be grateful if you'll keep that other promise you made me."

"I promised to give him a choice, Thomas, and I shall. The rest is up to the lad."

"Are you talking about Billy?" Zena asked.

Tom nodded.

Even in the dark, she could read the concern etched deeply in his face. "He's a man now, Tom," she offered quietly. "Billy's got to make his own choices, whether they're good or bad."

"He'll be fine," Gordon said, picking up the shovel and beginning to toss dirt into the grave. "You two, on the other hand, will not be fine until you're several miles down the road. Off with you now. I have work to do here."

Tom's frown edged into a grin. "Not too different from your other occupation, is it, Philo? Shoveling dirt, I mean." He reached for Zena's hand. "Let's go, butterfly."

"You're going to require a new name, Thomas," Gordon called after them. "Perhaps you'd consider—"

"Thanks anyway," Tom shouted back from the wagon seat. "Zena's real good at names." Tom winked down at her. "Aren't you, darlin'?"

Ten miles west, Zena raised her head from Tom's shoulder.

"You fell asleep," he said softly.

She stretched, glanced at the dog who was dozing in the back of the wagon, then curled her arms around Tom's waist, careful of the bandages on his side. She had thought earlier that she might be sad leaving Glory. Not the house so much as the cemetery where her loved ones lay. But she realized now that she wasn't really leaving Eldon and the baby behind. Wherever she went, she would carry them in her heart.

Zena smiled. "You said we weren't going to the edge of the earth, but you didn't say exactly where we were going, Tom."

He looped an arm around her shoulders. "I've been thinking about that," he drawled. "I was out in California once. There are some pretty little valleys there. I wouldn't mind trying my hand at farming again."

"All right," she said decisively. "California it is."

In the back of the wagon, the dog jerked his head up, then lurched to his feet. He barked. Once. Twice.

Tom slowed the horses. He and Zena both looked back into the wagon bed.

"What's the matter, fella?" Tom asked. "Don't you want to go to California?"

The dog's tail started slashing back and forth. He barked again, this time insistently.

Zena's mouth dropped open. "Oh, my Lord! That's it!" she exclaimed. "Oh, Tom. That's it!"

"That's what?"

"His name!" She slid around in the seat so she was facing the animal. "Come here, California. Come on, California."

Obediently, and with great gusto, the black-and-white dog bounded toward her, whimpering while his tongue slathered her face.

"I'll be damned," Tom murmured. "How'd you do that?"

She laughed, eluding the affectionate animal to turn back to the man at her side. "You said it yourself. I'm good at names."

Tom pulled her close against him. "Well, it's my turn now. And you best come up with a good one, butterfly, 'cause it's going to be your name, too. We're going to be married for a long, long time."

* * * * *

Harlequin® Historical

MORE ROMANCE, MORE PASSION,
MORE ADVENTURE...MORE PAGES!

Bigger books from Harlequin Historicals. Pick one up today and see the difference a Harlequin Historical can make.

White Gold by Curtiss Ann Matlock—January 1995—A young widow partners up with a sheep rancher in this exciting Western.

Sweet Surrender by Julie Tetel—February 1995—An unlikely couple discover hidden treasure in the next *Northpoint* book.

All That Matters by Elizabeth Mayne—March 1995—A medieval about the magic between a young woman and her Highland rescuer.

The Heart's Wager by Gayle Wilson—April 1995—An ex-soldier and a member of the demi-monde unite to rescue an abducted duke.

Longer stories by some of your favorite authors. Watch for them in 1995 wherever Harlequin Historicals are sold.

HHBB95-1

HARLEQUIN®

Deceit, betrayal, murder

Join Harlequin's intrepid heroines, India Leigh
and Mary Hadfield, as they ferret out the truth
behind the mysterious goings-on in their
neighborhood. These two women are no milk-
and-water misses. In fact, they thrive on

MISCHIEF
& MAYHEM

Watch for their incredible adventures in this
special two-book collection. Available in March,
wherever Harlequin books are sold.

Harlequin® Historical

Why is March the best time to try Harlequin Historicals for the first time? We've got four reasons:

All That Matters by Elizabeth Mayne—A medieval woman is freed from her ivory tower by a Highlander's impetuous proposal.

Embrace the Dawn by Jackie Summers—Striking a scandalous bargain, a highwayman joins forces with a meddlesome young woman.

Fearless Hearts by Linda Castle—A grouchy deputy puts up a fight when his Eastern-bred tutor tries to teach him a lesson.

Love's Wild Wager by Taylor Ryan—A young woman becomes the talk of London when she wagers her hand on the outcome of a horse race.

It's that time of year again—that March Madness time of year— when Harlequin Historicals picks the best and brightest new stars in historical romance and brings them to you in one exciting month!

Four exciting books by four promising new authors that are certain to become your favorites. Look for them wherever Harlequin Historicals are sold.

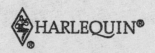

Harlequin invites you to the most
romantic wedding of the season.

Rope the cowboy of your dreams in
Marry Me, Cowboy!

A collection of 4 brand-new stories,
celebrating weddings, written by:

New York Times bestselling author

JANET DAILEY

and favorite authors

Margaret Way
Anne McAllister
Susan Fox

Be sure not to miss Marry Me, Cowboy!
coming this April

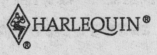 HARLEQUIN®

MMC